The Reunion

By

Adriana Kraft

The Reunion
By
Adriana Kraft

ISBN: 978-0-9894693-2-6

B&B Publishing
1970 N. Leslie St. #560
Pahrump, NV 89060

Cover by
Dawné Dominique
DusktilDawn Designs

Chapter One

Cranking one eye open, Sarah Atkinson confirmed the obvious. There was a man in her bed. She hadn't seen one of them naked in years.

She carefully memorized his rippling muscles rising and falling gently in sleep. The dark-haired hunk wasn't just any man. He was Adam Granger!

Absently, Sarah threaded fingers through her moist pussy curls. Her loins ached from overuse. Recalling the late night and early morning ravishment still sent tingles racing throughout her body.

He'd taken her. Make no mistake about that. They hadn't made love. They'd had wild, abandoned sex. He'd taken her. Not against her will. Hardly!

Sarah flung an arm across her brow. But why now? Why after twenty years?

The reunion...the Bumper High School twenty-year reunion. Bumper, Iowa. How she'd hated that town. She'd wanted more excitement, more challenge, more of everything. She'd never ventured back for a reunion. Apparently, Adam hadn't either. But this time, maybe because it was the twentieth, maybe because of curiosity, maybe because of something ephemeral, she'd come from Chicago and he from Los Angeles.

Twenty years ago they'd seldom acknowledged each other's existence. That didn't mean she wasn't aware of his presence and the pull it had on her—and apparently, on many other girls. She'd dreamed of him—literally—of him caressing her breasts, of his cock filling her mouth, of his fingers working to bring her off. Undoubtedly, he'd never imagined her capable of such carnal thoughts. There was more about her that might've surprised him then—Sarah smirked—and even now.

The chasm between the two of them had to do with small town social class. He simply wasn't part of her crowd. She was the daughter of the owners of the local drugstore and gift shop, which meant she had a favorable social standing. He was the son of short-order cook at a café. No one seemed to know who his father was. He was a loner, preferring his motorcycle and biker chicks to cheerleaders.

He wasn't dumb. As classmates, the two of them had been assigned group papers a few times. She never had to carry his load like she had done for so many others.

He'd never asked her to dance during those high school years. But last night was different. They'd both stood on the sidelines in the hotel ballroom decorated with photos from their senior year. Life had gone on without them in sleepy Bumper, Iowa. Old chums were friendly enough, but they were set in ways that no longer included outsiders as equals. To some, she and Adam were novelties. To others, they were traitors who had turned their backs on their roots when they'd fled small town USA to reshape themselves in the big cities.

Largely ignored by the crowd, the two of them had shared glasses of punch and conversation. Adam was outwardly as aloof and confident as ever. In his youth, there had been a brash cockiness about him. He'd matured into a dangerously arrogant looking man, obviously accustomed to getting what he wanted.

As the reunion celebration wore on, their dancing became more comfortable, more sensuous. Adam's thick arousal searing her crotch through their clothing made it evident he now wanted Sarah Atkinson. For years she'd waited for that moment. She was no longer the head cheerleader and valedictorian—untouchable for the likes of Adam Granger. She was simply a woman he wanted.

And she'd wanted him—last night, and years ago. She used to sneak behind the gymnasium bleachers to watch him wrestle opponents. Wrestling was his one extracurricular high school activity, and he seldom lost. His straining, well-honed muscles had mesmerized her. She'd creamed her panties more than once imagining what his body could do to hers if she'd been the one pinned beneath him.

Maybe she should have been bolder back in

those days. But she wasn't. If they were to cross the line that separated them, he would've had to take that initial step. For whatever reason, he hadn't. So he'd missed out on some of the carnal arts she'd been honing with other boys. She'd believed at the time that was his loss.

Sarah glanced at Adam lying beside her, stretched, and smiled. Now she knew it was *her* loss, too.

They never had finished the fourth dance. He'd pulled her up from her chair and escorted her to the darkest corner of the ballroom. She'd clung to him, swaying to a tune she'd forgotten. One of his hands clutched her butt, grinding her against his hard erection. The other hand covered a breast. His thumb toyed with her nipple. She'd pouted up at him, asking for more. His questioning gaze had locked on her. She'd answered by sliding her hand between them to squeeze his cock.

"Let's get the hell out of here," he said, gruffly. "Before I fuck you right here on the dance floor."

"I may be too old for hardwood floors." She stood on her tiptoes and grazed his lips. "Why don't we go to my room? It's on the first floor."

"That'll work."

He'd grabbed her hand and nearly dragged her out of the ballroom. By the time they hit the exit, she was running to keep up with his lengthening strides. They dashed down the hallway to her room. She'd fumbled with the key card. On the third try the damn light turned green and the door

4

opened.

From there events had become a blur. She soon discovered Adam Granger wasn't into finesse—not that she needed finesse after all those years of waiting. She'd risen to kiss him softly. His lips crashed against her. It was a long, demanding kiss. His tongue soon found hers and their tongues battled, leaving both partners panting.

Their hands weren't idle. She worked on his belt buckle and he had trouble with the tiny buttons of her blouse.

"Shit," he muttered. He leaned away and yanked her blouse open. Buttons flew across the carpet. Her bra suffered a similar fate until his dark eyes feasted on her aching breasts. She hadn't bothered keeping track of the bra. Then he'd swallowed as much of a breast into his hot mouth as he could manage.

She'd taken advantage of that reprieve to unzip her skirt in an effort to save it from the rag pile. She tugged his pants down and dipped into his boxers to free his cock. God, how many times had she imagined doing that?

He'd taken a step backward. Her breath caught at the sight of his frank, foreboding appraisal. "I've wanted you forever," he declared, his voice laced with longing and his eyes filled with adoration.

She didn't want him to place her on a pedestal again, so she'd stepped backwards toward the bed and cupped her breasts as an added enticement.

"Take me now. Why wait any longer?"

Had her provocations unleashed the beast within him? He'd actually growled. He deliberately reached for her panties and ripped them apart while gauging her reaction. She never flinched. He'd driven a finger into her cleft as she stood there trying not to beg. She was so wet and ready he could've done most anything to her.

Impaled on his finger, she'd struggled for breath and focus. She was stark naked and he was still dressed. Turn about had to be fair play. She didn't even try to unbutton his shirt. She grabbed it with both hands and jerked. His buttons joined hers on the floor.

"You like it rough, do you?" His finger probed deep and deeper still. It curled, grazing her G-spot.

She gasped, but did not squeal. "I like it any way."

He'd kicked his pants aside, withdrawn his finger from her channel and tossed her none too gently onto the bed.

Thank God he'd recovered his senses long enough to search the folds of his wallet, where he came up with a condom. He ripped the packet open and put it on.

Quickly, he covered her. His cock had no trouble finding its temporary home. He entered with one solid push. She'd curled her legs to surround his butt. There was no starting or stopping — nothing but old fashioned fucking.

6

Her response was immediate. How long had it been since she'd come? It didn't matter. She was on the verge, and she wouldn't be denied this time—Adam Granger saw to that. "Harder," she'd screamed. "I'm coming. Don't stop."

The orgasm crashed against her inner walls. She'd wanted to lie back and savor it. Adam didn't allow that.

Instead, he easily flipped her so she was on her hands and knees. He rammed into her from behind as if his momentary withdrawal had taken a lifetime.

That time she was determined not to come alone. It was a battle of wills. She chewed on her lower lip, receiving his blows, pacing her next orgasm. When it neared, she reached beneath them and fondled his balls.

"Jesus," he yelped.

Gotcha. She smiled broadly, slamming back against him. She felt him spasm. He slapped her butt with his palm and she shuddered. "Come with me," he growled, reaching for her clit. His fingers were like sandpaper.

"Holy shit," she cried. "Again? Stay with my clit." His hips churned an incessant cadence.

She coiled under his assault. She uncoiled and embraced the largest orgasm she'd experienced in years. She stayed with it, not wanting to miss a single twitch or buzz. It was joyous, delicious, exhilarating. And he was waiting for her when she returned from her climactic journey.

They'd had sex several other ways into the wee hours of the morning. She'd been on top, sideways, just about every way but standing on her head. To think that until last night, she'd begun to believe she was getting too old for sex.

At least that fear had been put to rest. She'd never had better, more mind shattering sex than she'd just enjoyed at the ripe old age of thirty-eight. Would either one of them have believed that was possible twenty years ago?

But now what? The dreaded morning after!

Beyond mutual sexual encouragements, they'd hardly spoken since entering her room last night. Their wanton lust made conversation superfluous. Their joining had simply been flesh on flesh, a lot of heavy breathing, and mutual exhaustion.

Now that it was behind them, would they be afraid to talk to each other?

She was. What did they have in common, other than extremely healthy sexual appetites? She considered combing her fingers through his wavy dark hair.

But before she could decide, Adam's eyes slowly opened and then sprang wide. Had he just remembered where he was and what they'd shared? He glanced at the clock. "Christ, I've got a plane to catch." He scrambled from the bed and lumbered for the bathroom.

"And a howdy, good morning to you, too," Sarah said, to the closing bathroom door. If he heard her, he gave no indication. She pulled the sheet up to her neck.

Adam quickly returned to the bedroom looking slightly worn. Sarah marveled at his long cock dangling between his legs and warmed with pride knowing she'd been able to manage a man his size.

But her lover wasn't coming back to bed. Adam reached for his clothes.

Without embarrassment, Sarah threw back the sheet, exposing her nakedness.

He eyed her with suspicion. His hardening cock thrilled her.

She held his stare, scrambled off the bed and knelt in front of him. Eagerly, she worked his penis with both hands until it was fully aroused. She beamed Adam a smile; he gave her a baleful look but made no move to dislodge her. She rubbed his cock's soft crown under her thumb and smiled when it twitched. Quickly, she popped him into her mouth. Adam's low moans made her smile. She took him all the way in until her lips touched the hairs at the base of his shaft.

It was good having a cock in her mouth again. She bobbed up and down his length, varying her sucking motion according to his reaction. How long had it been—three years? Maybe longer.

She hefted and fondled his balls gently. Giving head was a skill she'd perfected in high school and college. That art form had allowed her to protect her virginity while joyfully pursuing her sexual curiosity.

And she'd wanted to wrap her lips around this particular cock since she was sixteen.

She cupped his butt and encouraged a fucking motion. He complied. She clutched him tight with her hands and with her mouth. His corded thigh muscles tensed, forecasting his approaching climax. He pulled out of her mouth. She grabbed onto his cock. "No," she said, "I want to do you this way." She winked at him before covering him again. "I've fantasized about swallowing you whole for twenty-two years. I won't be denied now."

His features were stony, unreadable really, but he didn't resist when she took him back in her mouth and resumed her work. Instead he clutched her head and began finger fucking her ears.

She tried to ignore the juices pooling behind her pussy. She used her tongue as a funnel and milked Adam's cock until he spread his legs farther apart and began spurting seed. She clung to his ass cheeks and swallowed, keeping pace with him.

At last she leaned back and smacked her lips. She kissed the last drop of come from his cock and looked up into Adam's quizzical face. "Just think. I would've done that for you years ago if you had ever asked me out. I would've done it if you had even given me a ride to school. But I know, to you I never existed back then. Not until last night. You won't forget me now, will you?"

Adam shook his head, his dark hair curled over his collar. "Impossible."

"Good. Give me a minute. I've got to freshen up," she said, rising to her feet and heading for the bathroom.

When she returned to the bedroom, Adam Granger was gone.

- o -

He'd always known he was a bastard. He just never knew how much of a bastard until the last twenty-four hours. Adam Granger leaned his seat back on the jumbo jet headed for LAX and mentally whipped himself.

Sarah Atkinson. She was as stunning—more stunning—than he'd even imagined. And, oh yeah, he knew she existed. She'd always existed. Just out of his reach.

He could still recall trying not to appear too obvious staring at her light blue panties when she did back flips. He'd spent hours obsessing about what lay under those panties and the bulky cheerleader sweater with the large B highlighting her cleavage. How many times had he jerked off imagining her body squirming beneath his?

Jesus. Even in her late thirties, she made his mouth water. And she had passion. He hadn't counted on that. He'd been with many women over the years. Passion was much more important than technique. Truth be known, passion was a rarity.

Thankfully, he hadn't fucked her when they

were in high school. He would've been even worse than last night, if that was possible. Back then it took longer for him to masturbate than to fuck a girl.

Perhaps because of his mother's situation, he'd hoped to marry. But he was getting a little old for that. He'd never found the right girl.

Thank God for older women. It was a couple older women who'd taught him sex wasn't something to be rushed, but rather to be savored, as if sipping an aged claret. He'd never known the first thing about a girl's body, her orgasms, or how to help her have a good experience. He'd rutted girls like any animal in the wild.

Once he'd graduated from high school he'd become fresh meat in his little town — or so it seemed. A thirty-something waitress working with his mom at the café was first to initiate him into the art of lovemaking. Next was the local librarian — he'd always had a voracious appetite for reading. After she took him to the store room he'd developed an equally voracious appetite for librarians. Perhaps it was Mrs. Samuelson who had taught him best to sort the wheat from the chaff. Passion counted more than looks or technique — not that they all couldn't be related.

Mrs. Samuelson was a fair-skinned woman. Her body was well rounded and her passion ran as deep as the ocean. They'd spent many an hour searching for rare books at the small library. She'd met him a couple times at an out-of-the-way

12

motel. She enjoyed riding on the back of his motorcycle down remote gravel roads. She'd taken him home to her bed and continued his education there.

Until Mr. Samuelson came home early from a business trip one afternoon. Two days later, Adam had enlisted in the US Army. Many other women contributed to his learning the ways of love, but none surpassed Mrs. Samuelson. She never had told him her age. She'd certainly have been over forty.

It was in the Army that he'd decided to make something of himself. He'd earned an associate's degree by the time he got out. He passed through Bumper, Iowa on the way to California and never looked back. He'd finished a financial planning degree, but soon discovered he preferred working alone. He hit it big in the stock market during the high tech surge of the nineties. His smartest move was to get out before those high flying stocks plummeted.

He still dabbled in stocks as well as a lot of other adventures. He owned pieces of four race horses and a healthy portion of a stock car. He'd co-produced a few porn flicks as well as being a minority producer of a couple Hollywood films.

Adam's lips thinned. Yes, he'd had plenty of access to women, and Mrs. Samuelson was right — passion was more important than technique. And there wasn't a damn thing wrong with Sarah's technique. Son of a bitch, would she really have blown him back in high school? Or was she teasing him?

He groaned, remembering a group paper assignment in American History. While Sarah had talked easily with him, he'd felt tongue tied. It was easier fantasizing about her from a distance. He'd had no idea how to behave with a classy chick. And she'd always exuded class. She'd been his fantasy girl — seductive, but out of reach.

As they worked together in the library one afternoon, her soft breast grazed his bicep. He'd been flustered and crossed his legs trying to control his erection. She never seemed to notice. Looking back on that experience, he was fairly certain now that her tantalizing touch had been no accident. Where the hell was his brain back then?

Where the hell was his brain now? He'd fucked her like she thrived on explosive sex. Why hadn't he practiced those lovemaking arts he prided himself on possessing? He could be a gentle lover. Passion didn't always have to mean frenzied sex. But he certainly hadn't been gentle with her.

Not that she hadn't played to his unruly side. Whenever he'd begun to slow, she'd yelled harder. Her fiery display had shocked him. She'd certainly climbed off the prudish pedestal he constructed for her years ago. Had he misjudged her that much? Had she actually been the bad good girl? He'd never even heard a rumor about her, but then he rarely associated with anyone in her crowd.

He stifled a chuckle. So even if he was wrong years ago, could she really match the good bad guy? Did he care to know?

She'd looked quite smug licking her lips after bringing him off earlier this morning. Surely, she didn't think she'd tamed him.

He might feel like a bastard because he'd had such unrestrained sex with his teenage vision of the right girl. But he was thirty-eight now—way beyond visions.

Sarah Atkinson hadn't even begun to tap his sexual energy. She was better off not trying. Apparently, he'd fulfilled one of her high school fantasies. That was enough. He smiled. He would treasure the memory.

Damn, she had a body worthy of sacrifice. But did she really have the passion to match his? He sighed. Sometimes visions were best left as visions. There were fewer disappointments that way. That Sarah Atkinson had climbed off her pedestal to spend one night with him hardly made for a relationship.

And he liked his love life the way it was— uncomplicated. Maria, his live-in companion, had a passion that not only fueled his, it could even surpass. At thirty-two, her energy seemed boundless. Her passion, perhaps fed by the island lore of her ancestral homeland, Puerto Rico, had no bounds.

He'd known her for two years and they'd lived together for a year and a half. It wasn't a committed relationship, but then he hadn't had another woman—until last night. Maria had told him she wouldn't take on another man while they were together. Women? Adam smiled. That was another matter. Maria had her share of women lovers. When she found a partner she thought he'd appreciate, she invited him to join them.

Maria never spoke of marriage. They had no future. Yet she never left him, and he stayed by her. They shared much in common, having pulled themselves up beyond most peoples' expectations. Both of them had stayed out of jail.

Basically, Maria helped keep his life uncluttered. He appreciated that a lot.

Sarah Atkinson brought along a lot of baggage, and that meant lots of clutter. He'd done right to leave. He'd been more than rude. But he couldn't afford getting tangled up with a goody-two-shoes.

His eyes popped open. *Damn, she didn't fuck like a goody-two-shoes.* Adam closed his eyes and drifted off to sleep deciding he'd never attend another class reunion.

Later that evening, Adam pumped his cock in and out of Maria's ass. She met him thrust for thrust.

"Give me all you got, lover. Don't leave anything for next time. Claw my back, Adam."

He scraped his fingernails down the length of her back.

"Yes! Pound my ass." Maria lifted her head and

howled. "I'm coming. Come with me."

Perspiration beaded his brow and he accelerated faster, sensing his own storm surge. "Son of a bitch," he moaned. Maria milked him with her ass just as thoroughly as Sarah had with her mouth. Would he ever come again?

Maria's body shuddered beneath him. "Don't pull out," she said, lowering them to the bed. He tongued the back of her neck and rolled them onto their sides and cuddled her body close.

"Very nice, Adam," she purred. After a long pause, she added, "So are you going to tell me about her?"

Adam froze. "About who?"

"The woman you were with at your class reunion."

"But..."

Maria giggled and scrunched her butt against his groin. "It's not a big deal, Adam. We're not in a committed relationship." She canted her head around and grinned at him. "Though I believe this is the first woman since I moved in with you." She looked away, apparently waiting for him to say something.

"You're right on both counts," he said at last. "There hasn't been any other women. And yes, I was with a woman at the reunion."

"Your childhood sweetheart?"

"Something like that. We never dated in high school."

"She was too good for you?"

"Uh, huh."

"So you made up for lost time?"

"Sort of."

"What's her name?"

"Sarah. Sarah Atkinson."

"Was she good?"

Could Maria feel his heart pounding against her back? "Better than I expected."

"I thought so."

"Why? How did you know?"

"Maybe it's women's instinct. You were so determined, so passionate. It was as if you were trying to convince yourself of something. Of what, I don't know. And," she wiggled her butt, "I smelled her scent."

"But I showered."

"But not enough to erase her scent away. Would I like this Sarah Atkinson?"

Adam grinned and pulled on one of Maria's nipples. "Always thinking with your pussy. That's one of the many things I adore about you." He kissed her shoulder.

"So? Would I like her?"

"Probably. But I doubt she's into women or three-ways."

Maria shook her head. Her long black hair brushed his face and he drank in her scent.

"You should've learned by now," she teased, "never to underestimate a woman."

"Doesn't really matter. I don't intend to ever see her again anyway."

"You are a man who loves tempting fate, Adam. It's not exactly like you can prevent her from finding you."

"She won't try."

"How good was it for her?"

"Good, I think."

"You think. You ought to know. Did she boot you out of her bed?"

"No, I left."

"Bastard." She squeezed his semi-hard cock, still encased in her ass.

"Probably."

"I'll lay odds you haven't seen the last of her."

"On what basis are you willing to wager?"

"Call it women's intuition," Maria's voice tingled with laughter. "So lover, are you done for the night?"

Adam blinked. Was he never quite enough to satisfy her? "Yeah, I'm drained."

"Damn, this Sarah Atkinson must be good." Maria pressed his hand against her breast. "I hope I have the chance to meet her."

- o -

Two weeks later, Sarah stood before the floor to ceiling windows of her Chicago high rise condo overlooking Lake Michigan. Sailboats dotted the harbor, and she could make out three large tanker ships against the horizon. She watched a sailboat shifting back and forth, looking as haphazard as she felt.

She'd returned from Bumper, Iowa with an amazingly well fucked body and a badly bruised ego. Couldn't she even hold onto a man for twenty-four hours?

She'd spent at least a half a dozen years safeguarding her virginity before actually giving it to her husband on their wedding night. She'd blown a lot of guys from the time she was sixteen. She'd even learned to love a cock in her ass — anything to save her highly valued virginity — and she'd had a blast making love with a couple sorority sisters.

Wistfully, she recalled those reckless years. Too bad Adam Granger hadn't been more of a risk taker with her, or more aware of her proclivity for giving head. Oh well. It wasn't exactly like she'd gone up to him in the hallway and told him she wanted to suck his cock.

But her flamboyant years came to a silent halt after she was swept off her feet in a whirlwind romance by a law student from a very classy and very wealthy family. She would have gladly given him her virginity before their wedding, but he refused take it. Daniel wanted her fresh and virginal for their wedding night. And she was — at least, that small secluded spot had been.

They'd had a good marriage. The sex was pedestrian, with the primary purpose of procreation. She hadn't realized how traditional Daniel and his family were. They were conservative Republicans and fundamentalist Christians. After the fact, she learned she'd been quite the sinner in her earlier years. She did feel guilty about her past, but she wasn't about to confess her sins to Daniel or to his mother.

She'd figured out how to fit into a conservative lifestyle and how to dress to conform to the image her husband desired. She gave up her aspirations for a career in the art world and channeled her energies into being an advertising exec and the best wife she could be. She'd stood by Daniel when he campaigned and won a seat in the statehouse. She'd been instrumental in his advertising campaign.

And then her life imploded. Doctors informed her she would never conceive. Daniel became distant. His family wanted him to run for the US Senate. They concluded that he needed a family to have a successful go at the senate seat. She became dispensable. She and Daniel quietly and amicably divorced after ten years of marriage. It was amicable, in part, because she left the marriage a very wealthy woman.

So she was cast adrift at thirty-two only to make a second huge mistake. Russell caught her on the rebound. Vice-president of a Chicago bank, Russell had made a couple passes at her when she was still married. Once she was divorced, he was relentless in romancing her. He flew her to Paris and Vienna, where he proposed. How could she possibly have said no?

For him, it was all about the chase. Once married, he turned cold and ignored her almost as if she was a thought he'd forgotten. She was a piece of arm candy he'd wanted for years but couldn't taste. Once he had her, the fun was over. She'd thought she found a compatible lover. He didn't ring her chimes, but he wanted sex often, which had held some promise.

When their marriage started to crumble she thought refueling their sexual fire might be what was needed. She suggested that he take her in the ass. Russell turned putrid, dashed to the bathroom and threw up. He never joined her in bed again. Three years with Russell was like three lifetimes used up. Their divorce was also friendly enough, in large part because she became even wealthier.

Since Russell she'd given up on men and sex. She'd never seriously thought of striking up a relationship with a woman. Both of her former college female lovers were happily married, at least as of the previous Christmas.

Even her vibrators must've been in danger of deteriorating from lack of use. That was hardly a danger since she'd returned from her class reunion, though. Sarah smiled and padded across the living room. She flopped down on the couch and untied the sash of her robe.

She loved teasing her pussy while remembering how Adam had satisfied her the night of the reunion. Was she regressing? She'd played with herself incessantly as a teenager, often imagining the bad boy of Bumper High. Now she was doing it again, even as a woman too close to forty.

She threw her head back against the couch and pushed a finger past her moist slit into her warm channel. She licked her lips. Damn, he was good. Even better than she'd expected.

She pulled on her nipple before lowering her other hand to strum her clitoris. She brought her feet to rest on the couch cushion.

What would he think if he could see her now?

She held her breath, arching against her finger. Would he want her?

She didn't think he'd walk away. She slowed and caught her breath. Was Adam Granger capable of slow? He certainly hadn't demonstrated any desire for slow the night of the reunion, and she hadn't complained at all.

Since returning to Chicago, she'd done some research on the ubiquitous Granger. He lived in Pacific Palisades, no doubt in one of those large California houses with red-tiled roofs overlooking the ocean. He probably had a gardener and a maid. Somewhere along the line, Adam Granger had hit it big. Apparently, he now had a number of ventures to keep him busy. He certainly didn't have to work to make a living. Not bad for the son of short-order cook.

Sarah widened her pussy with a second finger, maintaining her edge. She clamped down on her lip. She could orgasm whenever she wanted. Would Adam want her to finish? Or would he try making her hang on that delicious precipice as long as possible before letting her freefall into orgasmic bliss?

She blew air through compressed lips as she probed her interior. She was going to have to do something about Adam Granger. She didn't want to spend the rest of her life bringing herself off pretending it was his fingers, his lips, his cock.

Her fingers moved faster. He hadn't bothered to call her, but then she hadn't called him, either.

She rotated her head from side to side, driving her fingers deeper. Furiously, she massaged her clit. She wouldn't call the bastard. Rejection would be too easy.

"Holy shit," she gasped, lurching forward, riding her fingers. "I'm coming. Adam, I'm coming for you."

Chapter Two

Boldly, Sarah rang the doorbell. She cleared her throat. The house was as large as she'd expected and it did indeed have a red-tiled roof, as well as a spectacular view of the Pacific.

The door opened and an attractive copper-skinned woman dressed in a yellow smock greeted her with a friendly smile. "Can I help you?"

"Yes, please. I'm Sarah Atkinson. I've come to see Adam. Is he home?"

"Ah," the woman said, assessing her more thoroughly than she thought appropriate for a maid.

"You are his maid, right?" Sarah asked, brushing back her hair that was being whipped by the wind.

The woman's face lit up with a smile and her eyes snapped. "Do come in. I'm sure Mr. Granger will be pleased to see you. He does know who you are?"

"Of course," Sarah stammered, entering a grand entryway. "We're old high school classmates."

"So you know him well," the woman said, ushering her to a sitting room. "Wait here, and I'll tell Mr. Granger he has a very beautiful visitor."

Sarah blushed and watched the provocative maid sashay out of the room to inform her employer.

- o -

Maria entered Adam's office without knocking. "Do I have a surprise for you," she announced, sweeping into the room.

Would Adam be pleased with his visitor? She beamed a smile as he gave her a distracted look from behind his desk. He should be. Sarah Atkinson appeared to be a woman of much promise. Maria's loins tingled with anticipation. The classy dark-haired woman she'd just ushered into the house was stunning. The Atkinson woman's slight air of vulnerability only added to her allure. It took balls to track down a man like Adam Granger.

In time, she might throw the interloper out, but she would have this Chicago woman before showing her the door. Adam had had Sarah Atkinson. It was only fair that *she* have her, too.

"What is it?" Adam groused, frowning at her. "I'm really quite busy, Maria. Can't you wait until tonight? Maybe later this afternoon we can fuck."

"Oh, it's not just me you have to worry about satisfying, Adam." She stepped behind his desk, wrapped her arms around his shoulders and kissed his neck. "I expect Sarah Atkinson wants a share of your cock, too."

26

"What?" He swung around to face her.

His startled look elated her. Adam wasn't as unflappable as he liked to believe. She nodded. "She's in the sitting room off the foyer. She's come to see Adam. As your dutiful maid, I've come to get you."

Adam bolted from his chair. "You're kidding! Aren't you?"

Maria shook her head.

"Jesus. What's she doing here?"

Maria patted Adam's hardening cock. "I believe you have something she wants."

He ignored her hand. "And you told her you were my maid?"

Maria shrugged. "That's what she wanted to believe. I didn't try to change her mind. Besides, that little deception might be useful for awhile. As you said, she's probably not going to be into threesomes right away."

"Right away? I'll send her packing." He started for the door.

"Why would you do that?" Maria asked sweetly. "Are you afraid of her?" She smiled when Adam came to an abrupt stop and spun around to confront her.

"She's only a woman," Maria said, easily returning to Adam's arms. "She's not the vision of your youth, Adam. But she looks damn delicious." Maria pouted. "Don't send her away. Not right away. Give me a chance with her. Please. If she'd showed up with a shorter skirt than she's wearing,

I might've taken her in the foyer." She raised an eyebrow. "I've shared a lot of women with you, Adam. You owe me."

Adam smiled and lowered his lips to her puckered mouth. "Maybe I do. She'll run like hell when she figures out what you're after."

"That's more like it," she moaned. "And that's a chance we'll have to take. Give me a little something before I escort you to your other woman, Adam." She pulled his hand up under her smock.

"Of course," he murmured, finding his way through her folds until he had a finger seated deeply inside her. There were many advantages to going commando.

He fingered her roughly until she grabbed his shoulders and came in a massive shudder. She smiled and backed out of his embrace. "Thanks, that'll tide me over for a while." She lifted his finger to her mouth and sucked it clean.

"We better get you to Ms. Atkinson before she has a fit." She winked at Adam. "When you're done with her tonight, don't forget about me."

"Where will you be? I guess we'll have to change our sleeping arrangements until she leaves — which probably won't be long."

"I'll stay in the second guest room, for now. I'll move my things from the master bedroom while you're showing Sarah around." She smiled broadly. "I won't be far away. You can count on that."

28

"I'm sure you won't." He gave her a thoughtful grin. "Go slow with her, Maria. That's all I ask."

"I'll be like a little bird peeking over your shoulder. This is going to be so much fun, Adam." She resisted the urge to twirl around like a little girl. "Why are we so lucky?"

Adam shook his head. "I don't know." He headed out the door, not waiting for his maid to escort him.

She grinned. That was okay. He and his visitor could probably find a thing or two to talk about without her presence, and she had much to do. She needed to sanitize the master bedroom and prepare the anteroom.

She hurried down the hall toward the room she and Adam shared. So was a maid expected to cook? She'd give it her best.

And did the hired help eat with the master? She skipped lightly in front of the large bed. She didn't much care as long as she got to eat the master and his guest.

Hardly able to contain herself, she scurried about. She had so much to do before the show. She chuckled. Should she make popcorn?

- o -

"So what inspired you to fly all the way out here, Sarah?" Adam plopped down in a seat across from her, his facial features tightly controlled.

Sarah couldn't decide if he was pleased to see her or angry she'd shown up uninvited. If she'd waited for an invitation, they never would've seen each other again.

She crossed one knee over the other. Her temperature rose at the sight of him staring at her crotch. Her miniskirt didn't leave much to the imagination. Her bikini panty should provide exactly the sort of view she'd planned. She didn't have to glance down at her nipples to know they were hardening under his assessment. She hadn't bothered with a bra. That had seemed rather futile, given her objective.

She tried to stay focused on her objective as she studied the outline of his enlarging penis. She had no long term goal in mind. All she wanted was more of that shattering hot sex only he seemed capable of giving her. She'd come for his body. It was as simple as that, and she wasn't about to be denied. She had no idea how long it would take to get her fill, but she'd hadn't taken a vacation in a long time.

She wet her lips before responding, gathering her courage. "I haven't been to California in years. It seemed like a good time to come." She toyed with strands of her hair and gave him a sorrowful look. "Are you unhappy I came?"

He never batted an eye. "Depends on what you want, I suppose."

She uncrossed her legs and watched his nostrils flare. "Did you really think you were going to ravage my body after twenty years and walk away without saying goodbye?"

"You don't know the first thing about being ravaged." He nearly spit the words out. "And I didn't ravage you. If I remember correctly, you were just as intent on pillaging my body as I was yours."

Her lips turned up in a smile. "Of course. Why do you suppose I'm here? We hardly got started before you ran off."

"You're playing with fire, woman. You were smart enough in high school to stay away from me."

"I count that as the colossal mistake of my lifetime. I'm not about to make that mistake again—" she smoothed out her skirt, drawing his attention to her fingers lingering over her crotch, "unless you send me packing."

"I'd be a fool to send you packing." He rose to his feet with more grace than she could manage, reached for her and drew her into his arms. "My cock would never forgive me," he growled into her ear.

She chuckled against his firm chest. "Well, I've missed your cock, too." She tipped her head back and he covered her mouth with his. Before she could blink, he had the top of her blouse undone and lowered his mouth to a breast. His warm tongue worked its magic until her nipple fully extended. She ground her loins against his hip, seeking relief.

31

He let her ride his hip but never gave up his perch on her breast. She'd worked herself to the cusp of a small orgasm.

"Just set the drinks down there, Maria."

His words jack-hammered her brain. Sarah's eyes popped wide open to see the maid smiling her approval. She grabbed for her blouse. Intentionally or unintentionally, Adam's hands prevented her from concealing her breasts from the maid's sparkling gaze.

Apparently at ease with her partial nudity, Adam gave her a slight grin. "I believe you've met Maria, but you probably weren't properly introduced."

He wheeled her around so her back was against his broad chest. His hands clutched her breasts. Her nipples peeked through his fingers at the maid. "Sarah, this is Maria Ramirez. Maria, this is Sarah Atkinson. She'll be staying with us for a while."

"That's great, Sarah," the woman squealed delightedly. "I'll do everything I can to make your stay a pleasant one."

"Thank you," Sarah mumbled, trying not to blush.

Maria set down two glasses of lemonade. "If you don't mind my saying so, Sarah, you have the most beautiful round breasts. And your nipples flare out so bewitchingly." The maid paused as if expecting a response.

"Thank you," Sarah whispered. If anything, her

nipples had extended farther than she'd thought they could.

"They look so hot." Maria reached out a hand as if she was going to touch them. Perhaps she saw something in Adam's eyes. She jerked back her arm and grinned. "I'd best be going and let you two get back to what you were doing. I have much work to do."

Once the door to the sitting room closed, Sarah spun to face Adam. "What the hell was that about?" She began buttoning her blouse.

"So the little tease from Bumper, Iowa is running scared already." Adam smirked at her. "And she isn't even unpacked."

"I'm from Chicago. And I'm not a tease. You should know that by now. But I'm not accustomed to showing off my boobs to the help."

"Ah," Adam tweaked a covered nipple. "Still a little snobbish, are we?" He leveled his gaze at hers. Her body chilled. "Let's get things straight. You came to my turf uninvited. You can leave at any time. Got that?" He cupped her chin.

Sarah nodded.

"Good. That's a start, and maybe an ending. As long as you're here, you'll do what I say. If I want to show off your tits to Maria, you'll do that with a smile. No condescending airs. Understood?"

Sarah wet her lips and nodded. This was a dangerous man. She should probably leave while she could, but damn if she was going to let him scare her away so easily, as if they were still teenagers.

It *was* poor form of her to point out a class difference with the maid. That had been an open wound for Adam Granger ever since he came to understand his social standing in life. She studied the antique furniture in the room with a practiced eye. Clearly, his social standing had risen since Bumper, Iowa.

"So what will it be?" Adam demanded, glaring at her. "Are you staying or leaving?"

How could she explain her reaction to him? But then he wasn't looking for an explanation. She wasn't a brazen woman, but her panties were soaked. Was it the hint of danger, or the scent of the sexiest male she'd ever known that had her unglued? If she stood there much longer, her juices would drip down her thighs.

Her belly clenched. "What else will you want me to do?"

"I haven't decided yet." He pulled her roughly into his arms. "No need to tremble, Sarah."

A large hand massaged her back. "You're right on the edge, aren't you?"

Sarah cast her gaze downward and nodded.

Adam reached under her skirt, slipped fingers inside her panties and fondled her clit. She clung to him for support and he brought her quickly to a heavenly orgasm. She half expected the maid to reappear. She mentally whipped herself for sobbing against his chest.

He caressed her back, shoulders and neck. "It'll

34

be okay, babe. I won't let anything hurt you. You know that."

"Yes," she squeaked. She managed to push herself away from his chest. "Do you want me to do you?"

"No, I'm fine. I do love it that you come so easily." He gave her a half-smile. "So was that because of me, or because Maria stumbled in on us?"

She remembered Maria's gluttonous brown eyes and knew she couldn't lie. She'd hadn't completely forgotten how turned on she could get by another woman's lust. "Both," she admitted, softly.

"Good. Maria will be pleased to hear that. Why don't we get you settled in, and then I'll take you out for dinner."

"That sounds fine," she said, not convinced Maria's intrusion had surprised Adam. He hadn't flinched at all when the maid appeared. Was she accustomed to having her boss expose his women to her? Did Adam require the maid's assessment as a second opinion?

If so, Maria seemed quite enamored with her breasts. Sarah shook her head trying to clear her mind and ignore her tightening nipples as she remembered copper fingers reaching for them.

What the hell had she gotten herself into? One moment Adam could be considerate and the next incredibly demanding. What was his game? She squared her shoulders. Whatever it was, she'd play with him. That's what she'd come to California to do. If he demanded more than she could give, she knew where the exit was. And she wouldn't be afraid to use it.

She smiled as Adam led her upstairs. She still had one advantage. He thought she was much more innocent than she actually was. He might yet trip over his dilemma of keeping her on a pedestal while wanting her for his sex slave. The two didn't fit, at least for him. She hadn't made up her own mind about that yet. But if nothing else, she planned on treating herself to some lively sex for however long she stayed.

- o -

To say Sarah was fetching was the understatement of the year. Adam tried not to gawk at the dark-haired enchantress sitting across from him at a table tucked away in the corner of one of his favorite seafood restaurants overlooking the ocean. She'd dressed casual but classy. It was a halter dress that plunged nicely, showing ample cleavage.

Maria was definitely right. Sarah did have outstanding round breasts, and they were still quite firm. The dress was tied behind her neck and fell to just above her knees. A gold chain graced her neck. Her dark hair nestled on her shoulders. He so wanted to reach around her and untie the knot that held it all together.

At least they'd got one necessary conversation out of the way—she'd had herself tested before leaving Chicago, and he'd told her he was also clean. As was Maria, but he hadn't told her that, yet.

Now, he was horny. She knew it and seemed quite pleased with herself. He'd deal with that consideration later. "How's your Mahi Mahi?"

"Delicious. I don't think I've had it before."

"It's a west coast delicacy. I'm glad you like it. Are you warm enough?"

Her mouth cracked a smile. "If I get any hotter, I'll burn up."

He groaned.

"I'm fine, Adam." She shrugged. "I'll put the sweater on if I need it."

"The oceanfront can get quite chilly in the evening."

"So I've heard."

"About your other overheated condition." He lifted his glass in a toast. "I have a partial solution.

Sarah lowered her eyelashes. "Oh, I think you have a full enough solution."

"Probably so. But I won't be around all the time." He shot her a penetrating look. "So let me tell you one of the ground rules of staying at my place, and it'll also help you stay cool."

He was pleased to see her frown and a trace of fear flickering in her eyes. "You will from now on go commando."

"What?" Sarah grabbed her napkin and dabbed

at the corner of her mouth.

"You know what commando means?"

"I'm familiar with the term — no underwear."

Adam watched the color rise in her cheeks. "That's right. As long as you are staying with me, you will dispense with underwear. Unless you need it for your monthlies."

"Monthlies." Recognition crept across her face. "Oh, that. Not to worry, I've had a partial hysterectomy. And by the way..."

He was beginning to enjoy when she thought she'd taken the offensive away from him.

"No need to worry about babies. I can't have any. Never could. That lost me my first husband."

"Sorry."

"That's life. He wasn't a big loss anyhow."

"Must not have been, if he voluntarily left you."

She grinned at him. "I like your way with words."

"Speaking of words. Have you forgotten what I said, or are you going back to Chicago?" He kept his voice even, devoid of emotion.

Sarah's eyes blazed. "Commando. You mean right now?"

"Isn't that what I said? From now on."

She nodded faintly. "Okay. I'm not wearing a bra. I'll go to the restroom. I'll be right back." She started to push her chair away from the table.

He grabbed her arm. "No. I don't want you out of my sight. Take'em off right here."

"But..."

"You can do it, Sarah." Her eyebrows arched in shock. His heart rate increased. He'd finally gotten to her vulnerability. Now maybe she'd go back to Chicago before subjecting herself to more shocks. He wasn't about to let up. "It's dark enough in here you could give me one of your favorite blow jobs and no one would see." He watched her hesitate. "Do it, Sarah. Or do you need help?"

He laid a hand on her knee beneath the table. "No," she said, slapping his hand away. She glanced around at the nearby vacant tables. "I'll manage."

Her hands disappeared under the table. He wet his lips.

"Don't you want me to tell you what I'm doing?" Her voice became sultry. She didn't wait for him to respond.

"I'm inching my dress up over my thighs. There. You look so fierce when your jaw is set like that. In case you wondered, I'm wearing bikini panties."

She leaned back fractionally. "I have both thumbs hooked over their waistband. I'm raising my butt. To throw off anyone who may be watching I'll lean over and kiss you."

Her soft lips burned his. She sat back down and grinned broadly. "I'm sliding them down my legs. First one foot, and then the second."

She paused and scowled at him. "I won't crawl under the table and blow you. But here is a memento of this little kinky display you

39

concocted. Enjoy."

She laid her hand on his crotch. He grabbed for it, but she jerked away and smiled triumphantly. His fingers curled around her bikini panty.

"Maybe you'll find a use for them. I hope you like red." She arched an eyebrow. "My, commando is freeing. Should I tell you what I'm doing to my pussy?"

He glowered and raised his hand. "Waiter, check, please. Hurry!"

"But Adam, we haven't had dessert." She pouted like a disgruntled teenager.

"I'm looking at dessert," he huffed. "And unless you want to be eaten right here—which I am quite capable of doing—you will keep your mouth shut until we reach my house."

"Yes..."

He squeezed her hand. "Now!"

Her soft nod did nothing to erase the gleam in her eyes. She knew she'd bested him at his own game.

Damn, she was turning out to be a lot more than he'd expected. Passion? She had it in bushels.

- o -

How badly had she infuriated Adam? She'd turned the tables on him and he didn't like it one bit. Neither of them had said a word until they'd arrived at his bedroom, and then he'd been cryptic. "Stand right there," he'd commanded.

And there she stood, facing a floor length mirror with Adam standing behind her looking darkly at their reflections in the mirror. She locked her gaze on his and reached behind her for the tie of her dress.

"No," he said, hoarsely. "I've wanted to do that all night."

She leaned her back against his chest and arched her neck forward. He lifted her hair and unknotted the tie. His lips grazed her bare neck. Shivers coursed throughout her upper torso.

"Lean your head back against me." She rested her head on his shoulder. Each of his hands fondled the underside of a breast. He avoided touching her nipples, which if they could speak, would have begged for attention. She remained silent.

He slid her dress down over her hips. He drew an earlobe into his mouth and chewed on it. He rimmed her navel with a finger. She moaned her applause for his efforts. He was playing her like she was a finely tuned instrument. She was his bass viol propped against his chest. At last, one nipple found relief between his thumb and finger. His other hand traced the thin line of hairs leading to her pussy. She wet her lips. Adam Granger could definitely do slow.

She nestled her butt against his crotch. He pinched her nipple until she squealed. "No," he said, "stay still. This is my game."

His game! She'd show him. She tried to

41

concentrate on anything but what his fingers were doing to her labia, or his breath on her ear. She marveled at the king-sized bed. He hadn't invited her to his bed yet. The bedroom was huge, with a couch, three soft chairs and several doors. One door led to a bathroom and the other to a walk-in closet. Mirrors hung strategically at both ends of the bed and along one side. It was a room constructed for lovers and voyeurs. She relished being both.

She caught his eye in the mirror and watched his fingers move across her glistening pussy folds. He slid down her back until he knelt on the floor. His teeth nipped first at one butt cheek and then the other. He peeked around her to see if she was paying attention to their reflection.

Apparently satisfied, he plunged a finger into her throbbing channel. Her gasp was involuntary. His tongue moved back and forth from one butt cheek to another. A second finger entered her pussy. He bent her over slightly.

His tongue pressed against her anus. She strained forward on her toes. It had been years since she'd felt a tongue there. His muffled laugh reached her ears. He clutched her buttocks tight, pushing his tongue inward.

"Son of a bitch," she sighed. This wasn't what she'd expected when he said she'd be his dessert. This surpassed her expectations.

He gave her no slack to gather herself. His fingers assaulted her from the front and his tongue from the backside. She gritted her teeth. Her head threatened to explode. Her brain couldn't keep up with his movements. Had his fingers met his tongue somewhere deep inside her? Was she a vessel of liquid nitro? If so, he was more than jostling the vessel.

"Stop," she screamed. "No! Don't stop. Adam. Adam. I can't take any more."

He didn't heed her plea. It was his game. She wasn't even a player. She didn't care. She was beyond caring. Her body quaked. His fingers drove harder — if anything, deeper. His tongue reamed her over and over. Her thighs quivered. Her legs gave way. Boneless, she collapsed against his frame. She had no choice. He'd turned her into quivering jelly.

"It's okay, babe," he soothed. He petted her pussy with an open palm. "It's okay. You shatter like a fine piece of crystal. You have such a beautiful pussy and such a gorgeous ass. I've never had a better desert."

He lifted her in his arms and carried her to the bed. He tucked her under the covers. His fingers brushed against her forehead. As if from a distant, foreign place, she heard him softly say, "Sleep soundly. When will you learn that you can't tame me? I'm beyond you. Way beyond."

- o -

Behind the one-way mirror, Maria pulled the

still humming vibrator from her pussy. Adam had put on quite a show for her. What had gotten him so pissed that he hadn't loved Sarah? He'd only brought her off—thoroughly, but rather abruptly. Here she'd been prepared for a long evening. Good thing she hadn't made the popcorn. Maybe he'd purposely saved more of himself for her.

She shook her head. She knew from experience that Adam was easily capable of satisfying more than one woman on any night.

Maria pulled down her skirt and wiped the vibrator clean. Patience. She'd have to have a lot of it. She could just about taste Sarah this evening. Adam had placed the dark-haired visitor standing so she had a perfect frontal view. Sarah's round tits were as splendid as she remembered from earlier in the day.

She couldn't wait to sink her teeth into those fleshy nipples—and her pussy? Wow! Not quite hairless. A trim line of soft curls marked it. Her clit had been a sight when it peeked out from beneath its folds. She hugged herself. She hadn't been able see what he was doing to her ass, but it wasn't hard to imagine what the naughty boy had been up too. He was her man, after all.

"Jesus, Adam, fuck me!" Maria screamed. With her legs stretched over his shoulders, she dug her heels into his back. Her head pivoted from side to side. Adam's face was a mask of contortion. The smaller guestroom bed, although more constraining than they were accustomed, proved adequate.

He emitted a hoarse groan. She smiled as his release splashed deep in her body and she gave herself permission to ride the crest of her own waves. She closed her eyes. Could this get any better? Yes, perhaps if she had her tongue buried in the pussy sleeping in the bedroom she usually shared with Adam. Adam's cock in her cleft and her tongue in Sarah's, that might be as close to perfection as Maria Ramirez would ever get.

Gasping for breath, Adam pulled out and collapsed beside her. She pouted at him. "You didn't have to leave me so soon."

"I'm not going anywhere," he said, pulling her close. She cradled his head against her breasts.

"That was spectacular, Adam. Even for us. Maybe we should keep Sarah around for an aphrodisiac."

"Maybe. She's at least good for that." He idly played with her belly button. "So did you have a good view?"

"Perfect. You had her positioned just right. She looked better than crème brûlée. Didn't you give her short shrift?"

"She got more than she deserved," he snapped. "The bitch."

Maria combed his hair with her fingers. "Poor boy. So she's not taking orders too well?"

"Hardly."

Maria shuddered when his palm covered her

pussy. He wasn't trying to turn her on. It was his way of showing he cared. She knew Adam Granger very well—certainly better than Sarah did, maybe even better than Adam did. He might have a tiger by the tail in his new woman—in *their* new woman.

"So what did she do to piss you off so?"

He hesitated before replying. "She gave me a blow by blow description of stripping off her panties under the restaurant table."

"Neat! So she's going commando."

"Oh, yeah. All the way."

Maria giggled. "But you hadn't planned on the play by play analysis?"

His palm patted her pussy.

"What else did she do?" There was no response. "What else would I have done if some macho guy I admired wanted me to take my panties off in public?" Awareness dawned. "She didn't." She grabbed Adam by the hair and jerked his head back so she could see his face. "She brought herself off, didn't she? She gave you a heads up description of stoking her pussy."

Adam scowled. "I didn't let her. We left."

"And that's why the quickie in our bedroom. No hot loving. Yet, you brought her off expertly. My vibrator matched your fingers. How was her ass? You must've been rimming her. Sarah's eyes grew to silver dollars when she first felt your tongue penetrating her anus."

"She was good."

"I knew it. Adam, we are truly blessed. She came with such abandon. I wish I had a picture of the ecstasy that woman displayed. Too bad there's no sound in our little alcove."

"Too bad you missed that, Maria." Adam gave her a half-smile. "She is a hellcat. Meows like a kitten and screeches like a lioness."

"But you didn't fuck her."

Adam scowled. "She didn't deserve that."

"So do you think she'll stay?"

"She'll stay, for now. So how long before you seduce her?"

Maria pulled herself to a sitting position and brushed long strands of dark hair from her eyes. "I won't seduce her. She'll seduce me."

"Right." Adam made no attempt to contain his sarcasm. "Hell will freeze over before Ms. Goody-Two-Shoes tries to seduce you. You ought to know that."

"We'll see. So are you going to go back to our bed and join her?"

"No, I think I'll spend the night in my office. There's less temptation there." He planted a kiss on Maria's mouth. She sucked his tongue in as much as possible and then let him go.

After he put on his robe and prepared to go downstairs, he asked, "So what is my maid serving for breakfast?"

She stuck her tongue out at him. "I may be able to manage scrambled eggs, bacon and coffee. If you're lucky. "

47

"And pussy on the side?" He arched an eyebrow.

"Don't I wish."

He laughed and headed out the door.

Maria fluffed up her pillows. Would Adam be laughing if he'd seen the pure sexual delight on Sarah's face when she came all over his fingers? He'd thought he was punishing her. Adam might have met his match. Hell, both of them might have met their match. Sarah Atkinson didn't strike her as an innocent cheerleader who could easily be led astray.

If anyone was to dominate their relationship, it might very well be the Midwestern princess who looked like she'd just won the sexual *I gotcha* contest when Adam drove his tongue into her ass. Maria crossed her arms over her breasts. No one could convince her this was the first time that woman had her ass violated.

And she'd lay money on the table that Sarah Atkinson would seduce Maria Ramirez, and not the other way around. Maria pulled on her nose. Not that she couldn't provide a helping hand now and then.

- o -

Slumped in his office chair, Adam sniffed the brandy before swallowing deeply. The resulting fire burned his throat, but did nothing to quench his thirst. The woman upstairs sleeping in his bed

48

had his gut churning. He wasn't easily confused by any woman. But he'd have to keep his guard up around Sarah. She'd have to conform to his desires—not the other way around. That was the way it was. That's how it was with Maria—wasn't it?

He scowled and swore. How had Maria become his partner in all of this? But she was. She definitely was. He knew she'd watched him bringing Sarah to a boil from the other side of the mirror. He'd played to her as his audience more than once.

Sarah didn't seem to mind, but then she hadn't known they were being observed. What would she have done if she had known? Would she enjoy being watched?

He drained the brandy. He'd surely find out before this charade was finished. The damn woman was too used to controlling things. No wonder she'd been divorced twice.

- o -

Hugging Adam's pillow tight to her chest, Sarah tried not to think where Adam might be. She'd fallen asleep immediately after her luscious orgasm. He must've taken advantage of her condition and left. If nothing else, Adam Granger was an expert at leaving.

Sarah brought the pillow to her lips. He was also quite expert at loving. She'd nearly fainted when he rimmed her ass with his tongue. This was getting better and better.

But he was a bit too much into making demands. What was this thing about commando? Maybe it was a California thing. So was Maria commando? Had she been naked under the smock she'd worn earlier?

Was Adam fucking the maid's brains out right now? Maybe she should get up and make a room to room search. She settled deeper into the mattress. No, if Adam was banging his maid, so be it. He clearly had enough cock to go around.

Sarah caressed her breasts. That was a woman who bore watching. She giggled. Particularly if she was commando. Now how was she going to find out about that? Curiosity might kill a cat, but she was no cat.

She let her fingers find their way to her damp pussy and patted it. "Take a rest, girl," she whispered. "Looks to me like you're going to see plenty of action without having to take things into your own hands. Sweet dreams."

Chapter Three

Humming to herself in the shower, Sarah considered what to wear for her first full day as a guest in the Pacific Palisades mansion. It hadn't surprised her that Adam didn't bother coming back to her bed. She'd clearly cramped his style by showing up unannounced, but he hadn't kicked her out, and she wasn't about to voluntarily leave. At least not yet.

She was having too much fun enjoying playing the naïve good girl. It was a long time since she'd given herself permission to explore her sexuality, and even then that experimentation had been limited by a desire to protect her virginity.

Nothing held her back now, and she was definitely in an exploring mood. She'd allowed herself to grow stale sexually. She'd been in danger of becoming a thirty-eight year old celibate. According to some researchers, she was supposed to be at her sexual peak. Adam Granger, and possibly even his maid, could greatly help her attain that peak. Of the two, he might require more convincing. Sarah's nipples strained as she recalled the admiring gleam in Maria Ramirez's eyes when she gazed unabashedly at her exposed boobs. The maid wouldn't need much coaxing at all.

But Adam was as edgy and unpredictable as she'd remembered. They'd only been acquaintances in high school, but he'd always seemed so mysterious racing off on his motorcycle. She'd wondered who he was meeting and what they were doing. She'd even fantasized about riding with him with her arms tightly wrapped around his waist. Would she be bold enough to brush a hand against his arousal? And would he be aroused if she rode behind him? But he'd been like a simmering pot on a stove, inviting but dangerous. She'd learned at a young age not to touch a simmering pot. To get involved with him then would've only led to scandal, if not worse. But that hadn't stopped her from dreaming about the dark haired hunk who often seemed angry with the world.

Sarah lathered her breasts and loins. She'd been reluctant to take a risk with him then. But that was then and this was now. Was she less afraid to risk? Or did she merely have less to lose?

She massaged her soapy scalp. Would he want to do that for her? Or maybe Maria would. Sarah shivered. Did washing female guest's locks fall under the maid's job description?

Sarah rinsed her hair, slid the shower door open and reached for a towel to dry herself. She'd decided to remain modest in her choice of attire for this initial morning. It might take a day or two to become accustomed to the absence of underwear.

She pulled a flowered print dress over her head and tied it at the back of her neck. The dress barely reached her knees. She hadn't packed anything longer. She might have to go shopping if she stayed for any length of time. She could've worn shorts, but that seemed like a cop out. Adam Granger wasn't going to think she was afraid to show off her body. Plus there was also the maid, who might be craning her neck to take a peek. She'd have to assess the maid a little more carefully this morning. Of course, she'd be more circumspect than the Ramirez woman had been the day before.

Walking down the stairway to the first floor, Sarah surveyed her reflection in the hallway mirror for a final time before seeking out Adam. She saw no need to tease her nipples — their alert state was quite visibly evident.

The smell of brewing coffee led her to a large kitchen. A mug sat by the partially emptied coffee carafe. Muffled voices reached her through a doorway leading to a deck. After filling the mug and taking her first swallow of coffee, she followed the hushed sounds of conversation.

Ah. There they were. Adam and Maria sat on the deck overlooking the ocean. Sarah ignored the fog enshrouded view of the Pacific to focus on her host and his maid.

They sat side by side on a Rangoon bench. Maria's hand rested casually on Adam's thigh. Cozy. Sarah smiled to herself. She'd been rather certain not everything was as it first appeared. The two of them were much more comfortable together than any maid and employer she'd known. So was Maria really his maid? She had little doubt she was his lover.

And where did that leave her? Was she an unwelcome competitor? Or something else entirely? Maria had been quite friendly, almost seductive.

Stepping out onto the deck, she cheerfully said, "Good morning. What a lovely view."

"Good morning, Sarah," Adam said, without getting up. "I never tire of watching the morning fog burn off the ocean. Each day it's a little different. Have a seat."

She sat in a chair next to the couch. She listened to the calls of birds she could not see. This was a good way to begin a day. At least her dress wasn't too revealing—and she was less on display there than if she'd sat across from Adam and Maria. Where had her desire gone to flaunt her wares before them?

"You look quite refreshed, Sarah. I trust you had a good night's sleep." Maria smiled broadly. She had one leg tucked under her and she wore a long red dress with buttons down the front. If she was commando, there was no telling, though it was obvious she wore no bra. Her nipples stood at attention.

"Very. I often get overtired when I travel." Sarah tried not to stare at those pointed nipples.

How could they possibly be growing larger? There were so many questions she wanted to ask. "So how long have you lived here?"

"Two years," Adam answered. "I'd wanted a place up here for a long time, and when this place came on the market I picked it up right away."

Maria rose from the bench. "You two probably still have a lot of catching up to do. I'll go and start the omelets. Does that sound okay for you, Sarah? We also have a variety of juices and fresh fruit."

"That sounds fine. But please don't bother on my account."

"It's no bother." Maria's smile brightened. "We all want to eat."

Sarah watched Maria glide through the door, her dress swishing at her ankles. Was the maid eager to eat only breakfast? "You have a gorgeous maid, Adam."

"Yes, she is."

Adam's sparkling eyes did nothing to dissuade her from her hypothesis. Maria was much more than his maid. But why would they bother disguising her role? Sarah grimaced. Of course, *she'd* been the one who'd made that assumption. But still, there was no need for subterfuge.

What was Adam's game? What was *their* game? Where did she fit in it? There'd be time to sort those questions out. Adam probably wouldn't be forthcoming with answers, but Maria might be more willing to talk.

"I was sorry to hear about your mother's death,

Adam," she said, altering the direction of their conversation.

Adam's face went blank, but not before she witnessed a wave of sadness. "Thanks. It's been a couple years. But I do miss her. How about your folks? Are they still living?"

"Oh yes, very much so. They sold the business about ten years ago and moved to Florida. Other than the hurricanes, they seem to enjoy Fort Lauderdale very much. I usually see them a couple times a year."

"Good. They always seemed like fair people. Most store owners either wouldn't allow me and my friends on the premises or would watch us like hawks. Your folks were different. They didn't seem to prejudge."

Lacing her fingers at her waist, Sarah flushed. It pleased her immensely to know her folks had been fair with Adam. He probably hadn't found her nearly as evenhanded as her parents. As captain of the cheerleaders, she'd had status to protect. She could fantasize about the mysterious dark-haired boy, but she'd never allowed herself to reach out and touch him. Fair or not, that was the way things were in her social group.

Adam's mouth crinkled into a smile. "You look very good, Sarah. Commando is a style that fits you. You look ready, eager and willing."

She shrugged, dragging herself back to the present. "It'll take some getting used to." Here she was again talking to him about sexual matters as if they were discussing baking cookies. "But I suppose you're right. I am more alert and on edge. You wouldn't think the absence of a slim piece of fabric would make that much difference."

"Maybe it's the changes in the mind more than in the fabric. You're going to have to be patient." Adam stood and stretched a hand out to her. She grabbed it and he helped her to her feet. He kissed her lightly on the lips. "I have things to do this morning in the city. We weren't expecting your visit, you know."

She grinned broadly, glancing toward the doorway leading to the kitchen where she could hear the maid clattering dishes. "That's obvious."

"So, I've asked Maria to show you around the house and grounds this morning. She can take you shopping if you like, or sightseeing if you want. I probably won't be back until late afternoon. I think Maria's planning a picnic for us this evening in the gazebo. It's in that clump of pines to your right."

"That's fine," Sarah said, glancing in the direction he pointed. "But I don't want to be trouble for Maria. She must have a lot do to keep up with a place this large."

"Nonsense," Adam said, lifting her chin and giving her a winsome look. "You are our guest. I'm confident you are at the very top of Maria's to do list."

Was it her wild imagination, or was everything Adam and Maria said laced with sexual innuendo? It was probably just her. She squeezed his hand as he escorted her toward the kitchen to put her in Maria's care. Sarah tried her best to ignore the pooling of juices between her thighs, hoping it wasn't the result of an overwrought imagination.

By mid-morning any chill that might have existed between Sarah and Maria had evaporated. Sarah loved the woman's humor and wit. Maria took most everything in stride and didn't seem a bit annoyed that the task of showing their visitor around had fallen to her.

After breakfast, they'd toured the grounds first. The manicured lawns had the feel of a small private park. Eucalyptus trees and pines along with a privacy fence provided seclusion. Flowers of countless shapes and colors flooded the yard as if it were a painter's palate. Small stone walkways led to the gazebo, the gardener's shed, and to a heart-shaped in-ground pool.

Maria had suggested they might like a swim after lunch. Sarah looked forward to being in the pool. It was inviting, and she did enjoy time in the water. One of the problems with living in Chicago was the limited amount of opportunity for swimming. She'd never found a private pool in the city that met her expectations.

Maria had made lemonade when they returned to the house mid-morning. Sarah sipped the frothy drink as Maria guided her from one room of the house to the next. There were eight bedrooms in all—plus a living room, sitting room, den and a few rooms they hadn't visited. The bedrooms were sizeable. One had been turned into a dance studio with mirrors lining all four walls. Maria seemed vague about its current use.

But it was another room where they now stood that had sharpened Sarah's interest. She and Maria stood at the center of a darkroom. Photo equipment of great variety filled the shelves. Maria demonstrated the safelight and the entire room turned to a very familiar red glow.

"This is precious," Sarah breathed. "This has to be as large as the darkroom we used at college."

"So you're a photographer," Maria said. "What was your medium?"

"Calling me a photographer is a stretch." Sarah couldn't keep the longing out of her voice. "But it was my passion in college. I was an art major. I couldn't paint my way out of a paint can, but I was fairly good at photography. I specialized in black and white. I liked playing with contrasts, with light and shadows."

"You make it sound like past history," Maria said, turning the red light off and returning the room to its natural light.

"Ancient history. My first husband thought it was a frivolous hobby. It was out of the question for a career." Sarah shrugged. "I got involved in advertising instead."

"A more honorable profession?"

"Something like that. So who uses all of this equipment?"

Maria hesitated before responding. "Adam used to use it some, but hardly any more. If he takes any photos now, they're all digital. I'm sure if you'd like to use this room while you're here, he'd be delighted. Would you like that?"

"I'm not sure." She crossed her arms. "Sometimes maybe it's best to let past passions fade away."

"I see." Maria paused and took a step forward.

Sarah tensed but didn't back away as copper hands fluffed her hair off her shoulders. Maria smiled warmly and ran the back of her hand across her cheek. Trying to breathe evenly, Sarah kept her hands at her sides. It was too soon. They had to clear the air about Adam before exploring each other. Did that make her methodical and Maria spontaneous?

Maria gave her an impish smile and took a step back. "I think you may be talking about your passion for Adam as much as your passion for photography."

"Maybe." Sarah took the opportunity to take a seat on an old stuffed couch. She knew she was buying time. She wanted to reach out and run her fingers through Maria's long curly hair. She wanted to unbutton Maria's dress slowly, to ogle her breasts as Maria had ogled hers. But she needed more time. She needed some answers. "Maria, can we be honest with each other?"

The younger, cinnamon-skinned woman looked only slightly wary before nodding. "Sure, why not? What's on your mind?" Maria curled up on the floor in front of her.

Sarah took a deep breath and locked her gaze on Maria's. "Are you a maid as well as Adam's lover?"

Maria didn't blink. "I wouldn't know the first thing about keeping a house this large clean. No. You're right. I'm not a maid."

"But..."

"I never said I was Adam's maid." Maria shook her head. Her long black hair swished around, hiding first one side of her face and then the other. "You assumed I was. You wanted to believe that I was. There was no need to disabuse you of that belief. Not then."

"But—Adam and me." Sarah frowned. "I'll pack my things and be gone before he gets back." She stood.

"No." Maria clambered to her feet. "Please, Sarah—sit down and I'll try to explain."

Sarah retook her seat and watched closely as Maria stood before her with feet planted wide apart, as if to block her exit.

"It's okay," Maria said quickly. "You and Adam, I mean. You and he go way back. He returned from the reunion troubled, on edge and," Maria smiled, "thankfully horny as hell. You got to him. Maybe you're only a vestige from his past. Maybe you're his vision of what a woman should be. I don't know. I doubt if he knows. But believe me, Sarah, you are under his skin—and until the two of you work that out, he's going to be trouble to be around, even for me."

"How long have you two been together?"

"Two years. I moved in a year and a half ago."

"Two years. And you want to just throw two years over?"

Again, Maria shook her head. "Not at all. This isn't a contest between you and me. Adam and I do not have a committed relationship—at least not in the way most couples talk about it."

"I don't understand." Goosebumps began clambering up and down her arms.

"You're the first woman Adam has been with since he and I got together."

"And you're not jealous?" she squeaked.

Maria shrugged her shoulders. "Why should I be? I've not been with another man since I started up with Adam." Maria knelt on the floor. Sarah didn't flinch away from Maria's hand resting on her bare knee. "But I do take other women to my bed from time to time. And occasionally Adam joins us."

The air in Sara's lungs whooshed out. "Oh." She covered her mouth. "Oh."

"But you must be something very special," Maria said, squeezing her knee and removing her hand.

"Why do you say that?" Sarah managed to whisper.

"Because Adam is letting you stay here in the house."

"Those other women?"

Maria shook her head.

"Oh my God. But I just showed up on his—on your doorstep. I wasn't invited."

"Maybe not. But don't you think there was a hotel room available somewhere in Pacific Palisades, Santa Monica, or L.A.?"

Sarah nodded. So what was the woman saying? Was Adam pimping for his lover?

"I know what you're thinking, Sarah. You're thinking Adam let you stay so I could play with you."

Smoothing out her dress, Sarah couldn't help wondering if Maria was commando.

"That's not the reason." Maria's lips formed a sly smile and her eyes snapped. "But I wouldn't mind playing, if you'd like to. You're the first woman Adam—in a round-about way—brought to me." She held her palm up. "But no rush. I'm a very patient woman. If it's meant to be, then it will happen."

"So," Sarah huffed, "I'm supposed to stay here and fuck Adam."

"Isn't that why you came out here?"

"Yes, but...I didn't know he was attached."

"And I'm telling you that doesn't matter." Maria arched an eyebrow. "I don't mind sharing, at least for a time. I don't know where all of this goes. I do know if you leave, both you and Adam

63

will have lots of unfinished baggage. At some point, too much baggage functions like a large anchor, pulling you down."

"You don't have to explain that to me. I've gone through two husbands. Or maybe two husbands went through me."

Maria gave her a puzzled look. "Were you planning on marrying Adam?"

Sarah blinked. "Not hardly. Twice burned, I'm not too eager for that."

"So you traveled out here to fuck and be fucked until maybe your body was too sore to carry on."

"Yeah." Sarah giggled softly. "Something like that, I guess. I haven't had much sex in years. The reunion was an eye-opener. It seemed like a good thing to pursue."

Maria flashed a broad smile and plopped down on the couch beside Sarah. "Good sex is always something worthy of pursuing."

Sarah tensed but did not shrink away.

Maria took her hand and turned the palm up as if she were a palm reader. "So you must be wondering about me. How hard will I pursue you? Do you owe Maria a good time because she's willing for you to fuck her man?"

It was Sarah's turn to shrug. Both questions had flashed through her mind.

"Let me take them in reverse order," Maria said, tracing the lifeline of Sarah's palm. "You owe me nothing. Adam is his own man. I can see if my future with him is to continue, he—and maybe we — must work through what it is you desire. As far as my pursuit is concerned, I won't seduce you."

Sarah couldn't hide her bewilderment. The woman was tying her into knots. "But I thought..."

"You," Maria said with a measured degree of haughtiness, "will seduce me."

Sarah's lips parted but no words came.

"That doesn't mean I won't take steps now and then to assure you of my willingness and my desire. But you will initiate our lovemaking, not me. Do you understand what I'm saying?"

Sarah nodded, not entirely sure she had a brain anymore.

"Good." Maria squeezed her hand, but did not yield it. "So tell me about your photography passion. I too have dabbled in it. More than Adam, really."

Exhaling softly, Sarah welcomed the sudden shift in conversation. She'd have to sort out the implications of what Maria had said later. Apparently, Maria and Adam operated from the same premise, that Sarah had the ultimate veto in matters of sex. That was good enough for now. She avoided looking at their interlaced fingers, but couldn't ignore the amazing warmth radiating from them. "As I said, I loved to play with light and shadows, so I focused most of my energy on black and white photography. There's something more primal, more stark about the medium that appeals to me."

"Yes, I understand. So are you most interested in landscape, animals, people or what?"

"I never was much into landscape. I did enjoy working with animals. But mostly I did studies of people. Faces. Some laughed. Some cried. Some were angry. Emotions."

Maria squeezed her fingers.

Sarah hesitated, and then squeezed back. "Black and white photos are a wonderful way of depicting emotions."

"What else? Tell me more." Maria's thigh pressed against hers. "You really should pick your passion up again, Sarah. You can't be whole if you don't honor your passions."

"You may be right. So how old are you, Maria? You sound like such a voice of wisdom."

Maria sobered. "Some people say I'm thirty-two going on sixty. But we were talking about you and your passion for photography. What else?"

"Oh. I did people at work. Farmers. Factory workers. Teachers in the classroom. Cops. Welfare mothers." She felt herself blush but suddenly she couldn't stop chattering. Maria was an excellent listener. "I always wanted to paint, so I did several series lifting up the nude body."

"Really!"

"Yes, it was supposed to be an initial step toward painting, but I never was able to follow up well."

"But the photos—how were they?"

"Some of my best work. You'd be surprised

how light and shadows can be used to celebrate the human body."

"Beautiful. I think I know what you mean." Maria gave her a genuinely shy grin. "Maybe you can do me?"

"What?" Sarah gasped. "I don't have the equipment." She glanced around the room, suddenly aware equipment was hardly an issue.

Maria rose from the couch, pulling Sarah with her. "I really like the idea of you doing a pictorial study of me. I think Adam would appreciate that, too." She closed her fingers around Sarah's. "And this isn't seduction, Sarah. You must know from experience that nudity can actually be desensitizing."

"That's true." It was increasingly difficult, though, to imagine Maria's nude body having a desensitizing effect.

"Let's go have lunch," Maria said with a soft laugh. "Later, we'll let you try out the pool."

Had their conversation been that stimulating? Sarah couldn't take her gaze off the shapely rear end swaying back and forth in front of her, leading the way downstairs toward the kitchen.

- o -

Draining his beer at the oyster bar, Adam wondered if the women were getting along or if they were fighting like two cats in heat. He'd have to figure out what to do with Sarah soon. The

67

quicker the better.

Had she really traveled across the county just to get fucked? That should be an ego booster, but it also served as a warning sign. Weren't there guys capable of satisfying her closer to home?

She shouldn't have to find a husband. From the research he'd done on her, he knew she was at least as wealthy as he was. So what the hell was she after?

Had she come to chase a teenage fantasy? Or maybe to tame the wild boy she could never quite confront in her youth?

No matter, he wasn't about to be tamed. If that was her scheme, she was going to be greatly disappointed.

And what about Maria? She'd taken to Sarah even before she'd met her. Her intuition bothered him more than it should. But she had an uncanny sense, particularly regarding women.

Sarah was at least a little frightened of him. That was good. Maybe he could use that leverage to send her packing. But she wasn't a slut. She was Sarah Atkinson. Thankfully, she'd taken back her maiden name after her second divorce. She was Sarah—she wasn't supposed to be his sex slave.

That was supposed to be Maria. Not that she'd ever been particularly adept at submission. She could dish out as much as she took. He doubted Sarah could come close to matching her.

At least Sarah hadn't balked at going commando. That should keep her uneasy a little, thinking about why he'd want her available at all times. Maybe she was having second thoughts already.

He glanced at his image in the mirror behind the bar and scowled. He'd wanted to show her the kind and considerate lover he could be. She deserved that. She would welcome that. Wasn't it her praise and warmth he'd wanted back in Bumper so many years ago? But she'd denied him then.

He should deny her now. He shook his head. How could he deny a vision?

- o -

Standing at the pool's edge, Maria breathed deeply, watching her guest cautiously. It was time—beyond time—to take another one of those steps toward the inevitable. Sarah would make the final decision, but a little help along the way might help. "I so enjoy a daily swim. I don't know if I could live in a place where that's not possible."

"It's tough," Sarah acknowledged. "I'm in the water a lot in the summer, but I've yet to find an indoor pool I really like for the colder months."

"Not a problem here." Maria reached for the buttons of her dress and began unfastening them as if it were the most natural thing to do. Sarah's inquisitive look caused her to pause. "I only swim in the nude," she explained. "I love the freedom of it. Is that okay with you?"

"You do what you want." Sarah swallowed, but didn't glance away. "I'm not sure I'm ready for that."

Maria showed her white teeth and continued undoing buttons. She shrugged out of the dress and pulled on her aching nipples.

"You *are* commando," Sarah gasped, her eyes rounding.

"Of course." Maria responded, fluffing up the curls guarding her pussy. "What did you expect?"

"You're...you're beautiful. So exotic. Your nipples look cold."

"Warm them," Maria teased, "if you like."

Maria stilled as Sarah tentatively raised her arms and then clamped them to her sides. She shook her head.

"Too bad. Later, maybe." Maria whirled and dove into the water, which did little to cool her growing heat.

She paddled to the middle of the pool and turned in time to see Sarah reach behind her neck to untie her dress. It pooled gracefully at her feet. Maria wet her lips, elated that Sarah hadn't requested a swimsuit — at least not yet.

Sarah stretched and cupped her breasts as if unaware of her audience of one. Maria smiled to herself, recalling Sarah's sexual delight when she'd climaxed the night before. Yes, this woman knew how to tease. Maria's toes curled in the waters as she conjured up more patience than she thought she possessed.

Sarah stood and stared at Maria for the longest time, as if waging an internal debate, before knifing into the water. She swam underwater like a fish and popped up right beside her hostess.

"You're stunning, Maria," she intoned, treading water. "I've never seen such dark nipples. You must taste like cinnamon."

"I'm not telling," Maria bantered. "You'll have to find that out for yourself, if you really want to know."

Sarah gave her a curious look. "Maybe I will." Then she arched her body and backstroked across the pool, giving Maria a most erotic view before turning and swimming back to her.

Maria climbed onto a floating cushion and held another out for Sarah.

"Spicy." Sarah's eyes glittered. "That's an apt description for you—you do make me think of cinnamon." Sarah's cheeks turned red and then she closed her eyelids, as if to hide her desire.

Maria nodded. She could wait. It was just a matter of time before Sarah's sexual curiosity or hunger would induce her to act.

They floated lazily for a while. Smoothing her belly, wishing it was Sarah's fingers caressing her skin and dipping lower, Maria watched Sarah's breasts rising and falling gently. She licked her lips and rubbed her mound. It was tempting to bring herself off with the sun warming her skin and Sarah warming her blood. But she pulled back from the edge. "Hey, you."

Sarah cocked an eye open and gave her a small smile. "Yes."

"You're not used to the California sun. Unless you want to rival a red lobster, we'd better get back under the shade." She pointed toward the lounge chairs beside the pool.

"I do burn easy." Sarah rolled off the cushion and angled toward the chairs.

Both women climbed out of the pool at the same time. "Damn," Maria said, "I forgot to bring out towels. Guess we'll just have to dry off out here." Maria stretched out on the nearest chaise and pointed to the one beside her.

"How convenient. You are so forgetful." Sarah shook her head and flashed a smile as she stretched out on the lounge. "Of course, any seducing will be up to me."

"Of course." Maria frowned. "You're not going to hold it against me for wanting to flaunt the possibilities?"

Sarah leaned back and sighed. "You're a delight to look at."

"Our skin tones will do nice together, don't you think?" Maria tried not to purr. "Cinnamon and ivory."

Sarah closed her eyes. "I'm trying not to think about it too much."

"Too bad," Maria sighed. "I can hardly imagine anything else. We're going to be damn good together, you know?"

"So do we tell Adam I know you're not his

72

maid, but rather his lover?"

Maria grinned wickedly at Sarah peeking through lowered eyelashes. "Why should we? It might be more fun to let him think you're buying into the charade."

"That might give me the advantage I need."

"What is it with you two?" Maria turned on her side. "It sounds like each of you thinks you're engaged in some sort of life and death battle."

"Maybe we are."

"I doubt that. You looked like you'd found a sexual heaven when you came for him last night." Maria smiled as Sarah' eyes suddenly went wide.

"You?" Sarah jerked upright. "You didn't!"

"Uh huh." Maria didn't attempt to hide her smugness. "There's a full length one-way mirror in our bedroom. Adam had you standing right in front of it. I could've reached out and touched you."

"Oh my God." Sarah crossed her arms below her breasts. "You saw him fingering me and licking me."

Maria nodded. "Your pussy looked scrumptious. Your clit craved attention. And when Adam tongued your ass, I thought you were going to implode. But Adam was too quick with you. Way too quick. Rest assured, I'll never be that quick with you. You have a body worth adoration and very, very slow sex."

"You better shut up," Sarah said hoarsely. "Or you're going to talk me into an orgasm—and I'm the one who's supposed to be the seducer. Right?"

"Right." Maria giggled. "Though I've never heard of anyone not wanting an orgasm."

"Well, you have now. Me." A shadow crossed Sarah's face. "I'm glad you enjoyed watching. If I'd known, I might've been able to put on a better show. So did you come with me?"

"Absolutely." Maria blew her guest a kiss. "You don't think I was going to be left out entirely, do you? You were so hot. Pepper—I called you Pepper when I came."

Sarah blinked.

"Your hair is so black against your creamy skin. You were hot when I first greeted you at the door. I wanted to stroke your nipples when Adam displayed them for me in the library. They were so rosy they looked like they were blazing hot." Maria paused to wet her lips. "I can hardly wait to dip my tongue in your pussy. I know you must be hotter than hot. Is it okay if I call you Pepper?"

Sarah chuckled and made a show of fanning herself. "You have a vivid imagination, I'll give you that. Call me whatever you want. I've been called worse." Sarah arched an eyebrow. "So is the master bedroom the only room that has an ante room for watching?"

"Ah. You are a clever lady. No. So does the room where I'm staying."

"I thought it might." A corner of Sarah's mouth turned up. "So you're going to show me this room off your bedroom so I can watch you and Adam."

"Of course. That sounds only fair." Maria grinned and padded toward the house tugging Sarah by the hand. "I was wondering how long it would take you to ask. Knowing you're watching will be so exciting."

Chapter Four

Adam bit down on a hamburger trying to make sense of what was happening around him. He sat at one end of the picnic table and Maria and Sarah sat on either side of him. They'd been frolicking like two young fillies. Both of them had said they enjoyed spending time getting to know each other.

How well did they know each other?

They'd both changed clothes since he'd left in the morning. Had the maid helped their guest with that task? Maria had on a lace halter that did absolutely nothing to conceal her dark nipples. She also wore a short black skirt that revealed everything she had to offer when she bent over to take beer out of the cooler.

He glanced at Sarah, grinning at Maria as if they shared a secret. With satisfaction, he noted their visitor had also dressed for the picnic. She wore a man's style denim shirt knotted below her breasts, exposing a bare midriff and an appealing navel. She hadn't bothered fastening any shirt buttons, so her breasts threatened to pop out whenever she twisted from side to side. She also wore a short denim skirt. He hadn't seen her retrieve a beer but he was keenly aware if she did she would be exposed completely to him and Maria—and that possibility didn't seem to bother

her at all.

So what had happened while he was gone? A lot, apparently. Had Maria already turned Sarah into her sex slave? He had no doubt that she could and she would. Sweet Sarah Atkinson didn't stand a chance.

Why did that thought gnaw at him? They were two adult women. He had no sole claim on either one. He reached for a beer trying not to stare at the by-play going on between the two of them. If Maria hadn't enticed Sarah into her bed yet, it wouldn't take much longer. And Sarah had no idea what that could entail. She wasn't accustomed to living on the sexual edge. Maria thrived on it.

Who should he be pissed at? Maria for her wily ways, or Sarah for her innocence?

"You seem very pensive, Adam," Sarah said, touching his arm. "Are you feeling okay?"

"Fine." He swallowed at the sight of a nipple peeking out around her shirt and watched Sarah absently tuck it back behind the blue fabric. "So what did you two manage to do all day?"

"How many times do you have to ask?" Sarah looked perplexed. "Maria gave me a guided tour of the grounds and the house. We did some shopping. Chicago styles are a little different from those here in California. And we went for a swim." She batted her eyelashes. "Too bad you couldn't join us."

"How did you like the pool?"

"It's great."

"Sarah's an expert swimmer," Maria chimed in. She laughed, her breasts bobbing freely. "I almost had to drag her out of the pool before she got burned."

"I bet you did." Why did Maria look so amused at his response? Was he being petulant? He blinked. Was he jealous? No way. But if so, which woman was he jealous about—his lover for the past two years, or the interloper?

"I've always been envious of California tans," Sarah said, "probably ever since my mom played the Beach Boys singing *California Girls*."

Maria reached for another ear of corn. "You'll have to spend a long time out here to get that kind of tan."

Adam watched Maria gnaw on the corn cob. She started at the small end and worked around it with deliberate care. She winked at Sarah and placed her lips over the end of the cob. Maria closed her eyes and worked the cob in and out, chewing and sucking.

Adam's cock cramped in his tight shorts. He peeked at Sarah, who appeared mesmerized by Maria's actions, almost drooling. Maria didn't stop. Sarah flushed. She ran a hand across her neck. And down her cleavage.

"Ahem."

Startled, Sarah looked blankly at him. He grabbed her hand and got up from the table. "It looks like you're ready for bed." He glared at

Maria, who had stopped long enough to gawk at him. "The maid can clean up and play with as many cobs as she can manage."

"But," Sarah protested, "I'm not done eating."

"I understand that," Adam growled, patting her rear. "Believe me. You definitely are not done eating."

"Isn't that better than any old corn cob?" Adam said, looking down at the back of Sarah's head bobbing up and down.

"Absolutely," she said, quickly catching a breath before returning to his cock.

"You are an expert," he muttered, pulling her up into his arms. "But not yet. Come. Lie down on the bed. I never really had the opportunity to finish desert—last night or tonight."

"You could have stayed the night," Sarah huffed. "I wasn't anywhere near finished."

"That wasn't an option."

"Will you stay tonight?"

"Maybe," he said, covering her mouth with his. She opened, inviting his tongue. Instead, he slowly licked her lips and pecked at the corner of her mouth. He traced her jaw line with his lips. Her little mews of desire pleased him. He knew she wanted him to be quicker, but she was going to learn about slow love. *Correct that. About slow sex.* He inched down the cord of her neck, leaving wet evidence of his presence. He worked his tongue down her cleavage. She arched her back.

He chuckled.

"Not yet, baby. Not nearly yet." He slid past her breast, tracing the crease of her abs. He rimmed her belly button with his tongue. Was she remembering him doing the same thing to her ass the night before? She hoisted her hips off the bed. She was greedy. He'd never thought of Sarah Atkinson as greedy, particularly when it came to sex.

Ignoring the invitation of her hips, he worked back up to the underside of her breasts.

"Oh my," she whimpered. Her fingers wove through his hair.

He licked each breast thoroughly before teasing a nipple with his tongue. He stopped just short of touching it. He smiled watching it extend, seeking his mouth. He settled his mouth around the nipple and as much breast as he could manage and suckled.

His steady sucking taunted the woman beneath him. She waggled her bottom from side to side, offering her ultimate treasure. He refused to touch her there. She lowered her hand in search of pleasure; he slapped it away. She groaned and lay back, apparently resigned to the slow torture he had planned for her.

Nothing he could do, however, could keep her from coming. He wasn't going to try. When he moved to suckle the second nipple, Sarah raised and lowered her chest rapidly and moaned hoarsely.

"You son of a bitch. You made me come without even touching me."

He raised his head. "I beg to differ, my lady. I am most certainly touching you." He stuck out his tongue at her and smiled.

"That's not what I meant. Why do you want to torture me this way?"

"But isn't it a sweet torture?"

"Yes," she whimpered. "But enough. Fuck me."

"I'll fuck you when I'm ready and not before." He flashed a broad smile at her. "But don't hold back waiting for me. Come as often as you need to." With that said, Adam worked his mouth back down to her navel. As before, he knelt by her side and kept his hands to himself, relying only on tongue and lips to tease and caress.

His lips moved along the hairline guiding him to her pussy. Sarah's body stilled in apparent anticipation. But he didn't follow that hair line to its conclusion. He traced a path to her thigh and kissed his way to her knee. There he paused long enough to discover that it, too, was an erotic zone for her. He couldn't help but wonder if she already knew that. He licked a path along her calf and ankle. She had the creamiest skin he'd ever seen, right down to her toes.

When he shifted his position to work up her other side, Sarah thrashed as if undergoing great pain. "Hasn't anyone ever taken the time to love you slowly and thoroughly," he said lightly when he reached her knee. She didn't answer.

He advanced up her inner thigh. Again, Sarah's body quieted. Was she uncertain what he might do next? She should be. He stopped.

"No," she cried. "Touch me, please. My pussy." She lowered both hands across her belly.

Adam grabbed her wrists and held them tight. His mouth hovered over her mound. "No," he countered. "I don't need your help." Her pelvis bucked, demanding.

He laughed against the outline of her moist lips. "You can be quite single minded, can't you?" He blew at her pussy, starting at its bottom and moving toward its apex. He smiled at the hard nubbin peeking out at him. Adam tapped the clit with the end of his tongue and Sarah muttered, "Damn," and was off again.

He waited. Maybe she would learn he could be a very patient man when he wanted to be.

"Enough," she said.

"Hardly," he responded, lowering his tongue to her widening pussy. He slid it up and down her folds and then easily slithered into her portal.

She gasped. She lay still and did not resist his hold on her wrists. She must be agonizing over what he would do next. Would he tongue her roughly to orgasm? Or would he continue taking her bit by bit to a monster climax?

He proceeded to take her bit by bit.

This time she seemed to acquiesce to his wants. She spread her hips wide. He curled her fingers in his hands, giving her something to hold onto in the face of the forces building within. He worked his tongue languidly around her heated interior. Her hips quivered. Her fingernails dug into his palms, then her pussy clamped around his tongue. He maintained a steady pace traversing in and out.

"Jesus!" Sarah exclaimed, starting to scrunch away from him, then giving herself up to his erotic torment. "It's starting. Again!" Her hips sank into the bed.

Adam pressed his tongue deeper, waiting. Then she detonated. Her hips drove up, grinding against his mouth, bruising his lips.

"Oh," she gasped. "Huge...never before."

Disquieting emotion swept through Adam as he gulped at her flow. With each lunge of her hips she gushed anew, until she collapsed.

He clutched her tight, not letting her roll away into her private world. Instead, he continued kissing her pussy lightly until she relaxed and breathed evenly.

At last, he looked into her eyes. They were pools of moisture. Her plaintive plea tore at his innards, but he knew what he had to do. He climbed off the bed, pulled on his trousers and tossed on his shirt. He leaned over and kissed her forehead. "Now you know. I can do slow, too." He quickly turned and walked out of the bedroom before he could change his mind.

Sarah lay alone in his large bed, trying not to take his departure personally. After all, Maria had needs, too.

Hugging a pillow to her bosom, she looked at the mirror. Had Maria been watching? She waved at the mirror and felt foolish. If she had, she wouldn't be there any longer. She'd be getting ready for Adam.

Sarah struggled to a sitting position. Damn, could she still stand — let alone walk?

Yes, Adam Granger could do slow. Had she ever known sex was akin to torture? Had she ever been loved more thoroughly?

She stumbled toward the door. But Adam hadn't come. Sarah managed a small grin. That wasn't her worry. Maria was probably taking care of that.

Sarah closed the bedroom door behind her and padded softly down the hallway until she came to the entrance to the anteroom next to Maria's bedroom.

She stepped in to find a small room set up with two small soft chairs. One had a note pinned to it.

> *Hi Sarah,*
> *You looked delectable tonight! I'm glad Adam took you slowly. I can hardly wait for my turn. I have to run and get ready for Adam. He should have buckets tonight. Enjoy the show.*

Feel free to use any of the toys.
Love,
M

Sarah sat down and raised the curtain covering the one-way mirror. She hadn't arrived soon enough to catch the preliminaries, but Adam was no doubt in a big hurry by now.

She watched with fascination as Maria rode his pole. Adam was on his back. Maria was on top facing away from him and squarely facing the mirror. Clearly Maria had chosen the position for the delight of the voyeur as well as the participants.

There was no sound. That was a huge drawback. But she'd never before watched a man and woman make love. Not that she could see much of Adam. Well, she could certainly see his most important parts.

She wet her lips and parted her robe to pull on her own nipples just as Maria was pulling on hers. The woman's mouth was moving. She was crying out even though Sarah couldn't hear what she was saying.

Even while climaxing, Maria kept her gaze focused on where Sarah sat. Adam's hips began pumping — his climax must be approaching.

At the last second, Maria backed off of him and used her hands to pump his seed all over her belly and pussy. She'd been right. Adam came in buckets. Maria was laughing. She dipped her fingers in the come pooling at her waist and held a finger up for Sarah to see and then slowly sucked it clean.

Sarah clawed at her clit and came quickly without taking her gaze off of Maria cleaning herself and Adam. Once she was able to breathe again, Sarah stood on shaky legs and exited the small room, leaving her host and hostess to themselves.

In a few short minutes, Sarah threw off her robe and crawled under the sheets of Adam and Maria's bed. Would she ever fall asleep? She couldn't shake the image of the triumphant Maria beckoning and inviting.

How long could she hold out before seducing the woman with cinnamon skin? It was no longer a matter of *if*; it was only a matter of when. She was probably the last one in the house to acknowledge that.

- o -

"I'm not seducing her, Adam," Maria insisted. Trying to remain cool, she sat next to Adam on the Rangoon bench as they typically did, watching the early morning fog roll out. It seemed later than usual this morning. "You weren't too concerned about what Sarah and I were up to when you came to my bed last night. Why the sudden grilling?"

"I had other needs then and you know it,"

Adam growled. "And what the hell were you doing with that corn cob last night, if not seduction."

Maria tipped her head back and laughed. "Turning you and her on. It worked, didn't it? You couldn't get her away from the table fast enough. And I didn't see Sarah resisting."

"No, I suppose not. Still, you said you wouldn't seduce her, that she'd seduce you."

"She will. You can take that to the bank." She scowled at him. "That's still okay with you, isn't it?"

He glared out at the bay.

"She's not your private property." Maria tried to calm herself. *Breathe deep. Remember your yoga teachings. Don't let your man buffalo you.* "Well?"

"She's not my property. You're right." Adam exhaled. "I can't explain it. She has my guts twisted up."

"Ah." Maria stroked his bare arm. "I wonder which of the two of you is the best rendition of Jekyll and Hyde."

"What?"

"You jerk her off roughly one night as if she is nothing more than a sex toy. The next night you love her as if you're worshiping her pussy. She's not the teenage fantasy of your youth, Adam. She's neither sex slave nor the girl on that high out-of-reach pedestal."

Adam cleared his throat. "What is she, then?"

"One moment she's demure—waiting, wanting

to be pursued — and the next she's the pursuer, as if she's played this game all her life."

"That's where you are dead wrong. Sarah Atkinson doesn't know the first thing about the kinds of games you and I play."

Maria shook her head. "Maybe you're right." She didn't believe her words for a split second.

"Good morning," Sarah said, stepping onto the porch with a mug of coffee. "I can't seem to get ahead of you two. I must still be adjusting to the time change."

"No problem. Something must be agreeing with you. You look rested and ready to take on the world this morning." Maria smiled and took in the dark-haired woman dressed in a thin pink tank top and a short black mini skirt. Sarah took a seat across from the bench and crossed and uncrossed her legs. Adam choked on his drink and Maria suppressed another smile. Their visitor's vulva had opened and closed as if issuing a private invitation — but to whom?

"I am. I am at that." Sarah sipped her coffee seemingly unaware of what she was displaying. "Adam, I have a favor to ask."

"What's that?" he responded hoarsely.

"Maria showed me your darkroom yesterday. I used to love doing black and white photography in college."

"She gave up her passion for her first husband," Maria added.

"Would it be okay with you if I use the

darkroom and equipment? I'm going to go bonkers here if I don't find something to do," she lowered her eyelashes, "other than waiting for you."

"That's not a problem. Of course, I don't know how good the stuff is anymore; I haven't done much with it lately. You'd probably have to pick up fresh film."

"I'm not sure I would know how to use the hi-tech gadgets on the market today. I may be more comfortable with the old ways."

Adam gave Maria a knowing look and then looked back at Sarah. "I'm sure you are. So what are you going to shoot?"

"Maria."

"Maria!" Adam cast a quelling look at her.

Maria smiled demurely in return.

"Yes, Maria. I used to specialize in black and white photos of people. Maria has agreed to help me get in touch with my lost passion. Don't you think that's sweet of her?"

Sarah tugged at her mini-skirt, which only drew attention to her bare necessities. Maria swallowed a giggle. Their guest played Adam like a marionette. He glowered at the ocean. Maria covered her mouth. Did Sarah have any idea how much she was driving Adam over the edge with her feigned innocence?

"Whatever you decide is fine with me," Adam finally said. He rose to his feet and grimaced at Maria. "I have to get going."

"You're not doing breakfast?" Maria asked.

"I'll leave that to the two of you. I told Johnny I wouldn't be late for his court appearance."

Sarah frowned. "What was that all about?" She asked after Adam left.

"I'm not completely sure." Maria dipped her chin. "He's searching for something. Maybe he'll know what it is when he finds it."

"What about Johnny?"

"Oh, Johnny. Johnny is a sixteen year old kid going on forty. Adam is his mentor." Sarah shook her head in confusion. "You know, sort of like a big brother."

"Oh. Adam? Really?"

Maria laughed, stood and headed toward the kitchen with Sarah tagging along behind. "You don't really know Adam. He's a great guy. You may only think he has a big cock, but he also has a big heart."

"I didn't know."

"Don't chastise yourself too much. It's not as if he wants people to know. Maybe you, especially."

"Why not me?"

"Then you might not think he's the big bad wolf and he won't be able to scare you away."

"What else does Adam do that makes him such a great guy?" Sarah said, refilling their coffee cups.

Maria shrugged. "He'll probably be pissed if I tell you, but he's a major contributor to women's shelters and programs for abused kids in the area."

"Really? He never said."

"Did you ever ask?"

Sarah shook her head.

"Of course not. You only tracked him down out here so he could fuck you into the next year. You're not interested in his heart or his brain."

Sarah blanched and her eyes misted.

"I'm sorry, Sarah." Maria grabbed Sarah's hands. "That was too harsh. I shouldn't have said anything."

"But it's true. I don't know anything about him — or you."

"And that's okay. We can both show you a good time, and we'll have a blast too. But you might be surprised if you actually tried to get to know us. It's not only sex games we play. But enough of this serious stuff. How long will it take for you to get the camera equipment ready?"

"At least the morning. I'll probably have to run out and pick up fresh film and materials. Don't feel that you have to nurse me, Maria. I have the rental car and can find my way around."

"Good. That'll free me up to run some errands I have to do down the hill. Like they say, life does go on. Maybe we can reconnect after lunch. Where do you want to set up the photo shoot?"

"I was thinking maybe the room you have fixed up for a dance studio. We can play with reflection as well as light and we can easily put up and take down wall coverings."

"That sounds great. Maybe later you might want to try the gazebo as a photo setting."

"Excellent. Then I can play with natural light. This is going to be so much fun, Maria." Sarah hesitated. "And don't feel too badly about what you said earlier. I expect there is a lot of truth to what you said. I do want to learn more about you as well as Adam — and not only the curves of your body." Sarah leaned over and brushed her lips across Maria's.

Maria responded in kind to the soft kiss. She did nothing to press her visitor farther than she wanted to go.

Sarah broke away. "That was nice."

"Very nice. Will you be back for more?"

"Probably." Sarah's smile split her lips. "But I am the seducer, remember?"

Maria nodded and watched Sarah saunter down the hallway toward the darkroom. Leaning against the counter, Maria drained her coffee. It looked like Sarah Atkinson was as skilled at the art of seduction as she was. Maria smacked her lips. She could hardly wait for the next foray Sarah would make as she led them down the road toward sharing their bodies completely.

- o -

"Turn your chin a little to the right. Good. Down a bit. Perfect. Hold that pose." Sarah clicked several rapid shots of Maria posing on a wooden stool clad in a blue velvet bikini.

"You want to take a break?" Sarah asked, setting aside her camera.

"I'm fine." Maria arched her eyebrows. "I'm ready for more if you are."

"Okay." Sarah breathed deeply. The implications of what Maria wanted were hardly lost on her. Her nipples tightened. She could handle this. She could be professional. Though she fully intended to have sex with Maria, she wasn't going to mix pleasure with her photography. "Take off your top." She stepped around a pole of lights and changed them slightly. She caught her breath studying Maria through the view finder. "You might want to play with your nipples a little so they stand out."

"No problem." Maria's lips turned into a huge smile and she twisted her nipples. "I thought it was okay for the artist to help her model show herself off as best as possible."

Sarah held her ground and started snapping pictures. "Great. Stretch them. Fantastic! Drop your hands. Good. You're a natural at this, Maria."

Maria smiled. "I should be. I've spent many years doing exotic dancing."

"Really?" Sarah peeked around her camera. "You mean stripping in front of people?"

"Uh huh. Swinging on poles and all that stuff."

"My goodness." She tried to blot out that alluring image. "I wish I could be so comfortable in my body. Not that I'd want to be an exotic dancer."

"Of course not."

"So you probably have a portfolio of glamour shots for marketing."

"Precisely. Are you ready for me to shuck the bottoms?"

"Sure. Why not?" Sarah struggled to breathe. "Damn, Maria, you do have a stunning body."

"A little turned on, huh? I'm glad you like it." Maria cast her gaze downward and Sarah clicked her camera. "But I'm still not telling you whether I taste like cinnamon. That's for you to find out on your own."

Sarah stuck her tongue out. "I didn't expect you would. I'm going to change the lighting again. I want more shadows falling across your belly. There."

"Turn a little to your right. Spread your legs wide. Make the woman admiring the pic want to nibble on you. No. Not that way. Don't play with yourself." Sarah moved around the camera and picked up the bikini bottom that had fallen to the floor. "Here. Hold onto these. Play with them. Bring them to your mouth and bat your eyes like you're not quite sure what will happen next. Pretend you're teasing your lover." She stepped behind the camera and chewed on her lower lip as she refocused the lens. "That'll work." Her froggy voice surprised her.

"This getting to you a little, Pepper?" Maria

turned her head and gave her a grin. "And you know I'm not pretending."

Sarah snapped the shutter button. "That should be great." Sarah giggled. "If a pussy can smile, yours is. Can you get down on the throw rug? Give me a good angle. Leave one leg on the floor and prop the other knee up, like this." She placed Maria in position and stepped back. "Pull on your nipples a little. Perfect. Now stretch an arm out so you're resting on your elbow. Splay the fingers of your other hand across your belly. That's right— they're pointing toward your treasure. Spread those lips just a little bit. Give me some pink and then back off. Suggestive, but not raunchy. Oh, yeah. Scrumptious. Hold that pose."

Sarah took several shots. "That should be enough for now. Is there anything you can think of that we forgot?"

"Maybe some tease shots." Maria's eyes sparkled with challenge. "If I'm actually going to use them in my portfolio, then I will need some of those."

"Okay. I thought these were some tease shots." Sarah checked to see how much film she had left. "Why don't you do what you think are tease shots and I'll keep up with you."

"Good idea." Maria turned, faced the wall, and bent over to touch the floor. Sarah clicked the camera. Maria reached back, clasped each butt cheek, and spread them. Sarah bit her tongue at the sight of two orifices opening for her and clicked the camera. Thank goodness it was on a tripod.

She watched Maria's fingers slide slowly from beneath her body to palm her pussy. She held her breath and clicked the shutter button. "I'm almost out of film," she squeaked.

Maria turned. "Just a couple more." She sat back down on the stool and spread her legs into a splits. Sarah snapped the camera. Maria played with her pussy just enough for her clit to peek out from its covering. Sarah ignored her increasing pulse rate and clicked the camera.

"I'm out of film," she said, setting the camera on the floor. She picked the velvet bikini off the floor and handed it to Maria. "Maybe you'd better put this on."

Maria stood and tied the bikini bottom in place. "Got you horny, did I?" Maria gave her a full smile. "That's what tease shots are supposed to do, you know. Hope you have some good pics."

Sarah reached out and traced a dark nipple with her index finger. "There will be. You were quite effective. You're a fabulous model."

"Ah," Maria moaned.

Sarah dipped her head and sucked the nipple into her mouth. She bit it gently and backed away. She giggled at the surprise in Maria's eyes. "That's for teasing me." She palmed Maria's pussy through the velvet. "And for forgetting that I'm the seducer."

She turned on wobbly legs to retrieve her

equipment. How much longer could she put off discovering whether Maria tasted of cinnamon?

For her part, Maria didn't bother putting on the bikini top. "You're something else, Pepper. Are you ready for another swim?"

Sarah turned around. "Sure. Maybe that'll help."

Maria smiled coquettishly. "You're fighting a losing battle, girl. The only way you'll calm down is to allow yourself to let go."

Maria's dark eyes locked on hers, questioning. Sarah's breath caught in her windpipe. Wasn't she supposed to be the seducer? She blinked. What difference did that make at this point?

Perhaps reading her thought, Maria nodded and lifted Sarah's tank top enough to bare her breasts. She ducked her head. Sarah gasped as the heat of Maria's mouth covered her nipple. She closed her eyelids and rose on her toes, wanting more. Her fingers sifted through Maria's long curly tresses. A tongue slid around her nipple. A sense of being savored swept through her body.

The cool draft assaulting her wet nipple brought Sarah back to her senses. Maria brushed a dark nipple against her rosy one. "There," Maria said, backing away. "You're the seducer. I just matched your play, but I could've taken you right here on the floor, on the couch, or standing like this. Isn't that so?"

"Yes," Sarah sighed. Finding her voice, she added, "Why didn't you? I wanted you to."

"I know. But you might do too much second guessing afterwards. You'll taste me only when there's nothing else in the entire world that can tempt you not to." Maria darted her tongue out to tap Sarah's nose and lowered a hand to Sarah's crotch. "As I thought, you're sopping. It won't be much longer now, don't you think?

Sarah tasted blood as she chewed on her lower lip. She shook her head at Maria who waved her bikini top as she exited the room. Sarah didn't follow. Going for a swim with Maria at the moment would lead to only one thing. But she still was not ready, even though the dampness between her legs argued strongly against that conclusion. She shook her head and headed for the master bedroom. An ice cold shower might help.

Chapter Five

Smiling with satisfaction, Sarah hung the last photo of Maria to dry on the line stretched across the dark room. She might burst if she stared at her handiwork longer. The pics had turned out quite fine. Super, actually. After all those years, she hadn't lost her touch. Some were better than others, but that was to be expected.

Somehow she'd caught the wide range of emotion Maria could so easily project. The woman should've been an actress. Sarah pursed her lips and studied one of the pictures of Maria stretched out on the floor, turned toward the camera. Fingers spread across her abdomen pointed suggestively to an aroused clit. The photograph was in soft focus. Some observers might not even notice the protruding flesh caught up in the shadows, but to any who did notice, that picture would be a complete turn on.

A soft rap on the door interrupted Sarah's perusal. She lifted hair from her shoulders and sighed, trying to set aside the pleasant erotic mental journey that photo had prompted. "Come in."

Maria poked her head around the partially open door. "Is it okay to come in?"

"Sure." Smiling at Maria's feigned nonchalance,

Sarah waved her newest model into the room. "You must be dying of curiosity. Come on in. I want you to see these. What do you think?"

Maria stood by Sarah and ran her gaze across the string of photos. Hugging herself, she exclaimed, "My! You are an artist with a camera, girl." Maria shook her head. "I know I'm good at seductive posing, but I'm not that good."

"You're better," Sarah proclaimed.

"No way. You accentuate the innocence and refine the bawdy. Even those tease photos are filled with mystery and allure. You've made them so tasteful." She turned to face Sarah directly, grinning broadly. "The girls are going to love you."

"What?" Sarah scowled at Maria. "What girls?"

"Didn't I tell you?" Maria asked, pretending surprise.

Sarah began shaking her head. "What are you getting me into now? I've only known you for a short time and you are already my personal quicksand."

"Complain. Complain." Maria hugged Sarah around the waist. "I'm a city girl. Brooklyn. LA. San Francisco. But doesn't quicksand have tremendous sucking power?" Maria asked, mimicking a sucking motion with her lips.

Sarah couldn't help but laugh at the quizzical look on Maria's face. "Yes, it does. You've made your point. We'll get around to that. I'm positive. Now tell me about these girls."

Maria's smile was as bright as sunshine. "So you've finally decided to discover for yourself whether or not I taste like cinnamon."

Sarah nodded, not trusting herself to utter a sound.

"And I bet you're creamy, like your ivory skin." Maria pouted. "So, how can you be so cool about it?"

"What girls?" Sarah insisted. She wasn't about to be sidetracked into comparing tastes. Maria had more on her mind than sex. Sex no longer was a hurdle, but she'd already learned how determined and devious Maria could be when she wanted something.

"Oh." Maria's expression was suddenly nonchalant. "One of the many things I do is connect girls up with the exotic dance world and erotic film industry."

"Porn?" Sarah failed to censor her shock or tone.

Maria's face contorted and she took a quick step back. "Don't look down your nose at those women. They're hard working, many are God fearing, and some are damn good actresses."

"But—exotic dancing, I sort of understand," Sarah stammered. "But..."

Maria's eyes snapped a warning. "You traveled across the country of your own free will to get your brains fucked out and now you're questioning the morality of women who are willing to fuck—to legally fuck for pay."

"I wasn't aware it paid that much," Sarah said weakly. "I'm not trying to cast dispersions."

"You could've fooled me. It doesn't pay, with the exception of the occasional meteoric young star, for beginners—like most any other industry. Top pay goes to those with seniority and the best skills."

"How do you know so much about all of that?" Sarah wanted to retract the words as soon as they'd escaped her lips.

Maria folded her arms and glared. "Because I've been there. I was only active in the industry for two years. I discovered having sex for my job screwed up my personal sex life. Many women can adjust to that. I couldn't, so I got out. As I said, I still help girls make the right connections and try to do my best to see that they only work with producers and actors who believe in health testing and practice what they believe."

Sarah frowned trying rapidly to process this new information about the woman she wanted to taste. She didn't know what to say. How many women had Maria been with? Did it matter? Maria was right. She'd traveled half way across the country for one purpose only—to get fucked. How had her world become suddenly so complex, suddenly so simple? She bit her tongue, wishing for an easier way out.

"So," Maria sneered. "Maybe Adam is right. Maybe you are a Ms. Goody-Two-Shoes."

Sarah stiffened. That was one way to get her off

square one. Was she going to let that old good-girl image get in the way? "No, don't say that, Maria." She reached out and grazed Maria's cheek with the back of her hand. Thankfully, Maria didn't flinch from her touch. "Your working with the porn industry shocks me, I admit that, but it doesn't diminish how I see you—not at all. If anything, it makes me feel like a naïve idiot. I probably haven't spent five minutes in my lifetime thinking about porn stars. But I'm sure you're right. One industry is basically like any other, in some respects. The rewards go to people with longevity and skill, or to people who know people."

Maria scowled and then her mouth turned up in a small smile. "That last part is too true."

Sarah drew in a deep breath. "So tell me about these girls."

"They're women, typically eighteen to forty, who are trying to keep their portfolios updated for booking agents, directors and producers. You can't simply send around the same photos year after year. Some are dancers. Some strippers. Some erotic actresses. None are hookers."

"And you want me to shoot them."

Maria nodded. "You're an exceptional photographer, Sarah. You could make a difference in some of these women's lives. It's not that they don't have the skill it takes, they just don't fathom how to best package and market themselves."

"That's my forte—at least for other people. I've

never been great at marketing myself."

"Then you'll do it?"

"They'll come here?" Sarah said, quickly beginning to take to the idea. "I don't have to go somewhere else?"

"They'll come here." Maria grinned. "We'll use the dance studio like we did this afternoon. Will you at least try?"

"You beg well, Maria." She shrugged. "Yes, I'll try. I can't believe how exciting it was taking these pics of you. Some of them really are super. But I did have a super model," she whispered softly, again dragging her fingers across Maria's cheek.

Maria licked her lips provocatively.

Was it pent up sexual energy, or the recognition that during the last several minutes their conversation had drawn them across a chasm? Sarah had no fear of falling. She wrapped her arms around Maria's neck and drew her close. Their mouths joined as if it were the most natural thing to do. Their tongues played leisurely. Sarah tingled with anticipation. Without breaking their kiss, she cradled Maria's butt and ground their crotches together. Maria reciprocated slowly and then more fervently.

Abruptly, Sarah stepped away from Maria. She knew she must look like a wild-eyed tease, but she didn't want their first shared orgasm to occur while fully clothed. There was, after all, that important matter of tasting. "I'm sorry," she mumbled. "I don't want it this way." She saw

Maria's look of dismay and felt a catch in her throat. "Soon," she whispered, slanting a finger across Maria's lips.

"Oh, I forgot to tell you." Maria shot her a wary look. "Adam called. He won't be home till very late tonight. We're supposed to go ahead and eat without him. It's something about the kid he saw at court, the one he mentors. Trying to get him set up in an apartment of his own — or something like that."

"Too bad," Sarah said, studying the pictures of Maria hanging on the line. "How convenient. It'll just be us tonight." She heard Maria's catch of breath. She was amazed she could detect that over the pounding of her own heart. She paused a moment to listen to her soul. She found no internal debate.

Sarah angled her face toward Maria and smiled. She pressed her smile against Maria's lips. She chewed on Maria's lower lip, then kissed the corners of her mouth and slipped her tongue into Maria's open mouth.

"Ah," Maria moaned.

Sarah stepped back and met Maria's gaze, suddenly aware the wild passion in Maria's eyes reflected her own. She interlaced her fingers with Maria's. "Let's do it. Let's pour some wine and put together a platter of cheeses and crackers and then retire to the master bedroom."

"You're on. You select the wine and I'll join you shortly." Maria slanted her warm lips across

Sarah's and backed quickly away. "You won't regret this."

Sarah didn't know if that was a question or a statement. "I know I won't. I hope you won't."

Maria laughed. "No way. I'm getting the feeling you and I have been preparing for this moment all our lives."

With a trace of sadness, Sarah watched Maria nearly skip out of the darkroom. Why the sadness? They should've made love right there on the couch or on the rug. Now she might have too much time to think. What had Maria meant about preparing for this moment all their lives? Sighing, Sarah tidied up the room with trembling fingers. She couldn't shake or explain the feeling Maria was right. Now that she'd made her decision, she knew making love with Maria was not only right—it was inevitable.

Sarah whirled around the small room feeling as free as she'd felt after she'd gotten accustomed to going commando. Steeling herself not to look beyond tonight, not to look beyond Maria, she closed the darkroom door and headed for the kitchen.

She smiled to herself. She had little doubt where Maria had disappeared to. She was probably summoning their audience of one. Air escaped from Sarah's compressed lips. If she knew how to contact Adam, she would've invited him herself. But she didn't know where he was, and she trusted Maria to issue the invitation on their behalf.

Sarah set the serving platters down in the master bedroom and turned to meet Maria's gaze. The next move was up to her. She took the lead, embracing her hostess and sliding her lips across her soon-to-be lover's mouth, dropping several butterfly kisses. Maria stroked her neck and back. Reluctantly, Sarah moved out of their embrace. "Hope that will tide you over for a few minutes. I'm not changing my mind. No way," she insisted, catching her breath. "but I have to check something first. I think I forgot to turn off a machine in the darkroom."

"That's okay," Maria replied. "I want to freshen up a bit anyway."

"Good. I'll be right back. Don't start without me."

Maria lifted her breasts and wiggled. "I wouldn't think of it. Just don't take too long."

After stopping in another bathroom down the hall to make final preparations, Sarah rejoined Maria in the master bedroom and grinned broadly at her. Maria sat fully clothed absent only her shoes on an overstuffed chair across from the bed. She set the wineglass she held on an end table and interlaced her fingers, waiting for Sarah to take the lead.

"Don't be so pensive. I'm here now," Sarah cooed, pulling Maria to her feet. "Thanks for waiting for me."

"I may have waited for you my entire life." Sarah watched Maria's tongue dart out to trace her lower lip. "A few extra minutes were nothing."

Knowing it was up to her to take the lead, Sarah pressed her lips against Maria's. It was a tender kiss, a kiss filled with longing and promise. Sarah took a step back and unfastened the top button of Maria's sundress with surprisingly steady fingers.

Maria smiled her encouragement.

"Do you think he's watching?" Sarah whispered as she worked on a second button.

"What?" Maria blinked, her brow furrowed.

"Adam. Do you think he's watching us?"

Maria chuckled softly. "You're not only an artistic woman, you're clever. Probably. I did let him know you were about to succeed in seducing me." Sarah giggled. "I wanted him to at least have the opportunity to share this first time with us, even from a distance." Maria swept Sarah's hair off her shoulder. "I hope that's okay with you?"

Sarah had three more buttons undone and freed a dark breast before she answered. "I'm thrilled. I hope he's there. I do hope he sees it is I who am seducing you." She lowered her mouth to cover the pebbling nipple.

Emitting a sharp gasp, Maria entwined her fingers in Sarah's hair and clasped her tight to her bosom. "He should be able to figure that out. But let's forget about Adam for a while. Okay?"

Sarah tapped the dark nipple with her tongue

110

and worked on more of Maria's buttons. "Absolutely," she murmured. "There's only you and me in this bedroom, and I intend on sampling you in a variety of ways." Sarah tugged on the sundress and it dropped to Maria's feet. "You are so striking. I've seen you nude many times in the last two days and each time it's like seeing the sunrise for the first time."

Maria reached for the buttons on Sarah's blouse.

Sarah shook her head. "No, let me," she said. She slowly undid her blouse, freeing her breasts. The look of adoration in Maria's dark eyes warmed her blood. Sarah unzipped her skirt and let it fall to the floor, stepped out of it and held out her arms, welcoming Maria.

Again she covered Maria's mouth with her own. This time their tongues collided, stoking banked fires of passion. Sarah rubbed her breasts against her lover's, and Maria reciprocated. Reluctantly, Sarah slid her mouth off of Maria's and lowered her head until she was licking first one brown breast and then the other. Maria fondled her neck and uttered soft moans. It pleased Sarah that the more experienced Maria let her continue being the seducer.

She trailed fingers down across Maria's taut belly until they came to rest atop her neatly trimmed dark pussy. Her folds were already wet. Without hesitation, Sarah pushed a finger into Maria's inner chamber. "You're so hot," she whispered, going to her knees.

Maria widened her stance. "Hot for you, Pepper. Caliente," Maria groaned, "for you."

Sarah studied the tiny black ringlets and smiled as Maria's clit emerged from its protective folds. She slipped a second finger into Maria and lapped at the glistening pussy opening wider before her.

Maria's breathing quickened. A familiar pounding started in Sarah's head. She brought her free hand to bear on Maria's clit. Willingly, Maria stood before Sarah's probing quest, succumbing to fingers and tongue. She clutched Sarah's head between her hands, offering guidance. She wailed in Spanish and English praising the gods for this gift. She bore down on Sarah's fingers and tongue. Sarah held nothing back and neither did Maria.

"Now!" Maria cried. "Taste me now."

Sarah flicked out her tongue and grinned at the first taste of Maria's nectar—exquisite. Leisurely, Sarah covered Maria's flow with her mouth. Cupping Maria's buttocks, Sarah helped her rock back and forth on her heels as Maria's flow tumbled over her lips and tongue. Sarah swallowed over and over, going beyond tasting, trying to quench her thirst. At last, the flow stopped. Sarah leaned away, giving Maria's pussy one last kiss. As for her thirst—it would certainly take more than once to quench that particular thirst.

Pulling playfully on Sarah's ears, Maria moaned, "That was adorable. But I want to do you, too." She fell back on the bed, bringing Sarah with her.

Sarah placed her love stained lips across Maria's. She smiled. "You do taste sort of like cinnamon. Maybe a little nutmeg, too."

"Thank you." Maria tweaked Sarah's nipple and it was her turn to gasp. "But I can't wait any longer. I want to taste you, too. Why don't you turn around and cover my mouth with your pussy?"

Sarah quickly turned to comply with Maria's request. She slid over Maria, straddling her until her chin brushed against what was quickly becoming her favorite pussy. It already felt like a dear old friend. She teased it with her tongue, but soon lost her ability to concentrate.

Apparently intent on catching up, Maria's tongue and fingers were quite busily engaged in their own exploration. Sarah tensed as the tongue snaked in and out of her tingling channel. Tears formed in her eyes. She'd nearly forgotten how powerful it was to be loved by a woman. Maria squeezed her butt with one hand while fondling her clit with the other. Maria's nose slid along that most sensitive ridge between pussy and anus. Sarah squealed at the sudden pleasure shocks strobing across her clit.

Lifting her head, which felt incredibly heavy, Sarah moaned, "Whatever you're doing, don't stop." She used one hand to tug on her own nipple. She let it go and returned to massaging

Maria's pussy.

Maria never let up her assault and both women knew Sarah neared her edge. But Maria lagged behind. Sarah took her lover's clit between her teeth and suckled. She slid a hand lower and drew small, tight concentric circles teasing Maria's anus.

"Oh my!" Maria exclaimed. "You do know a woman's body. This is certainly not your first time with a woman."

"Don't abandon my pussy," Sarah ordered, excited by Maria's quivering thighs. She was about to crash again. "I want to come too. I need to give you my juices."

As if remembering what she'd set out to accomplish, Maria's tongue quickened and her fingers continued to strum Sarah's throbbing clit.

Sarah smiled against Maria's mound. She felt her climax work its way from the back of her skull down her back. Her butt quivered. Her hips ground her pussy against Maria's face, driving Maria's tongue as deep as it could possibly go. She sawed at Maria's ass which had opened to accept her finger. Simultaneously she nibbled on Maria's clit. Both women groaned as flesh buried into flesh until each was drinking the fluids of the other.

Sarah heard Maria gasping for air. She rose to her hands and knees to give her lover more room to breathe. Catching her own breath, she licked her lips and peered at the one way mirror. She doubted her smile came close to reflecting the glow warming her body. Maybe Adam could tell that.

Forgetting him, she turned around and cuddled Maria. Her hostess pecked at her lips and gave her a delighted smile. "That was something, girl. You were worth the wait."

"I know." Sarah grazed Maria's smile with her lips. "*We* were worth the wait."

- o -

Sitting behind the one-way mirror, Adam watched the women lying on his bed idly caressing and murmuring to each other as new found lovers tended to do. He wiped his cock clean with a handkerchief. They certainly had put on a show. Now what?

Was he supposed to go storming into the bedroom angry they'd made love without him? He had no question the two women had made love. They hadn't just had sex. How could they be so emotionally bonded so quickly? Scowling, he tucked his cock back in his pants. He never would understand women.

Did they have any idea how elegant they looked together? How balanced? Brown on ivory. Ivory on brown. They were finely matched, like a set of rare crystal.

Even without sound, he could tell each woman listened well to the other's body. There had been no competition between them. They had sought and found mutual satisfaction.

115

He was quite experienced with the look of satisfaction on Maria's face when she'd come, standing before the kneeling Sarah. But it was the look of pure pleasure on Sarah's when she'd come that had surprised him. He'd seen her come many times. But this was different. Her face hadn't been contorted. She hadn't fought it or spurred her orgasm on. She'd simply let it happen and he'd seen it spread across her body like a bubbling spring. As long as he lived, he'd never forget that image. If bliss could be tangible, then he'd seen it. And he had enjoyed it.

He pulled the slip of paper from his pocket and reread the note he'd found on the chair upon entering the anteroom.

> *Dear Adam,*
>
> *I hope you find this note because that will mean you were here when Maria and I first made love. She is such a gift. I'm positive you know that. And I'm sure neither one of us wanted to do this without including you, if only as an observer.*
>
> *So if you are watching, enjoy. Maybe you'll want to join us one of these times. I'd like that a lot. Maybe this will help you realize I am not the girl you thought I was. I never was.*
>
> *Love,*
> *S*

Adam folded the note carefully and shoved it in

his shirt pocket. No girl or woman had ever written him a note. Why had that touched him so? He was becoming an emotional basket case.

And what was he to do with Sarah? With Maria, for that matter? Things were changing around him and he didn't see any way of forestalling more change.

Clearly, he'd misjudged Sarah. She was no longer his teen angel. He shook his head grimly, remembering her comment about giving head in high school to a select number of basketball players. Maybe she'd never been an angel. The corner of his mouth turned up. But then, had he really been the devil incarnate? Things seldom were as they appeared.

Intimidating Sarah into leaving wasn't going to be an easy task. He wasn't even sure he wanted to. Now that she seemed aligned with Maria, it might be nearly impossible, no matter what he wanted.

Obviously, Sarah was the seducer in the drama he'd just witnessed. She hadn't hesitated at all about having sex with a woman. That was not her first time. How could he have been so wrong about her?

Could she really play their sex games? He shrugged. He wasn't about to bet against her at this point. She might offer up many more surprises.

But the women were playing a much higher stakes game than he was prepared to play. Did Maria know it was Sarah dictating the rules?

Maria never showed that kind of passion — that kind of love — with another woman. It had always been fun and games. Heads up, no entanglements, no-holds-barred sex — the way he liked it. The way he thought Maria liked it.

Sarah brought along another layer, more insidious, more threatening. And Maria was smitten. His worldly sexy companion of two years was being drawn into a web he doubted Sarah even knew she was weaving. She spun it with her natural air of innocence, vulnerability, and willing passion. It was a web that might threaten all of them if he allowed her to stay much longer.

Would Sarah Atkinson steal Maria from him?

Adam walked quietly down the hall to the foyer and let himself out into the night. He wasn't sure where he was going, but he had to get away from the house. He had to get away from the two women sharing his bed. Before he stumbled and fell.

He'd never allowed himself to stumble and fall because of a woman. He wasn't going to begin now.

- o -

The following morning Sarah snuggled in the circle of Maria's arms, pressing her back against Maria's chest, overwhelmingly pleased with herself and her new lover. Maria surpassed anything she had ever imagined. She grinned at the empty trays near the bed. While there had been little sleep, they had managed to refuel — sometimes in rather creative ways. She'd never tried pussy a-la-Chablis before. She regretted have missed out on such a treat for so long — especially, missing out on Maria. They'd consumed each other as if making up for lost time. Now time had finally overtaken them. "Guess neither one of us is in a hurry to get up today."

"Why would I want to leave this cocoon?" Maria wiggled a finger down Sarah's back. "You are a pleasure to snooze with."

"Umm. You, too."

"You're sure the note you left for Adam is missing?"

"Yes, I looked quite thoroughly to see if it had dropped to the floor. It's gone. So, apparently, is Adam. Did you expect him to join us?"

"Not last night." Maria dropped a kiss on Sarah's shoulder blade. "Maybe this morning."

"So why didn't he?"

"Adam is a very complex man. He can be quite moody. Seeing you with me may have sparked one of his moods."

"But why? I thought he'd relish having both of us at the same time." Sarah turned over to face Maria, parting her lips to greet Maria's. When Maria eased back, Sarah said, "You don't suppose he's jealous."

"Wouldn't surprise me," Maria grunted. "Bet that'll shock him."

"But he should know we want him to join us."

"It might not be that simple."

"But..."

"Why don't we leave it at that? Let's wait and see what Adam has to say for himself when he shows up."

"Okay. So how did the two of you meet?" Sarah covered Maria's breast with a palm.

"The first time I met him was on the set of a porn shoot."

"Oh my," Sarah gasped.

"Yeah, it was some crazy film a friend had talked Adam into co-producing. That means he put up the bucks."

"Adam?"

"Sure. He's co-produced several films. Though I must say his more recent efforts have been much more tasteful. I hooked him up with a few female directors."

"Female directors?"

"Don't look so surprised. You don't know much about the adult industry, do you?"

Sarah shook her head.

"Anyway, some of these women directors specialize in films for women and for couples. Adam liked their work and supported their efforts. He believes it's a way to help people who are having difficulty in the bedroom or are in danger of shriveling up due to boredom."

"Another grand cause," Sarah teased.

"To a certain extent, yes. Anyway, that's how

120

we met. We were introduced and he hung around and watched me work. I didn't start seeing him for another year or so after that."

"How did you wind up in the adult entertainment industry?" Sarah swallowed, hoping she didn't sound judgmental.

Maria snickered. "I'll want to know more about how you settled for advertising over your art." She paused. "One thing sort of led to another. I majored in dance at NYU, attending part-time."

"You did. College."

Laughing, Maria ticked Sarah's belly. "Don't be so surprised. I got good grades, too. But I never had enough money to go full time. I started dancing at clubs because the money was better than I was making clerking in a department store. I've always been easy with my body, so stripping came naturally, and I learned I really enjoyed turning on guys and women. Turning on an audience that couldn't touch. It was a form of play for me and for them, and it was always dance."

"One of these days will you show me in the dance room downstairs?"

"Of course I will. As for the porn, it started as much out of curiosity and a dare as anything. I made pretty good money. It didn't hurt that I was a Latina. I was moving up the ladder and the pay scale, but my personal love life sucked."

Sarah snickered. "Adam came along."

"Something like that. So I stay involved in other ways. I may yet want to try my hand at directing.

Adam will bankroll me, but I haven't tried that yet."

"I think you'll be good at whatever you set out to do. You've crammed a lot into your life. In some ways I'm jealous." Grimacing, Sarah added, "I've done the same old same old for so long I nearly failed take the opportunity to fly out here."

Maria flashed an eyebrow. "But you did, and you're not disappointed."

"Not at all." Sarah squirmed closer. "You were worth the trip. And we may get Adam to come around. Imagine! I didn't even know you existed until you met me at the door. If I hadn't gotten up the nerve to come out here, we never would've met."

"I like that word *we*." Maria pecked at Sarah's neck and hugged her tight. "You're a pretty damn spunky lady. Adam Granger doesn't stand a chance facing the two of us."

"I'm not so sure," Sarah said, fighting the feeling that all was not well in nirvana. "So, Maria, does Adam love you?"

Maria withdrew and scowled. "That's not a word in his vocabulary. He cares for me more than he has for anyone, unless for the image of you."

"Do you love him?"

Maria didn't flinch. "Yes."

"Yet you still take other women to your bed."

"Yes. Loving a woman is quite different. I haven't found a woman I could be true to." She offered a quirky smile. "Yet."

"Oh." Sarah worked at staying calm while considering the import of Maria's words. "But you wouldn't give up Adam for the right woman."

"No, the right woman would have to love him as much as me. All sides would have to have equal strength."

"Like an equilateral triangle."

"Exactly."

"I wonder if that's possible."

Maria sighed. "Maybe it isn't."

- o -

While nursing his morning coffee on the deck, Adam heard the women rummaging in the kitchen. They were late. He didn't have to spend much time pondering why.

He was still uncertain what to do with them, though he didn't want anyone to think he was running from them, either. So he'd come back to the house in the wee hours of the morning. He'd checked to make sure they were sleeping before going to his couch in the office. He'd thought about joining them this morning, but decided not to.

His gut remained in knots. His brain was as clear as the sky over the ocean, which was not visible at all because of low hanging fog.

The women came onto the deck and he sat up straighter. As usual, Maria sat next to him and Sarah sat across from them. Both were attired in light tank tops and mini-skirts. Sarah crossed and uncrossed her legs seeming completely unaware of what she was showcasing for him. Or was she flashing her pussy for Maria?

"You both look quite pleased this morning," he said, trying to keep his voice devoid of emotion.

"Shouldn't we be?" Sarah declared. In any other context, he might describe her smile as bashful. "I trust you found my note."

"I found it." He patted the pocket over his heart.

"Did I disappoint you?" Sarah asked in a hushed voice.

Maria squeezed his thigh, sending him a cautionary signal. Maybe Sarah was more vulnerable about all this than he thought. He wasn't about to blow everything to hell, at least until he wanted to. "No. You surprised me. I didn't know you were into women." He pursed his lips. "Clearly you are into Maria. How could I be disappointed in what I witnessed last night? You were magnificent." He glanced at Maria. "You were both magnificent."

"I am so pleased you watched us, Adam."

If a woman could purr, then Sarah was purring.

"There's a lot you don't know about me. I don't want you confusing me with the idealized image you may still hold of me from our high school days. I'm not that young innocent girl—I probably never was. But now I'm a grown woman with multiple wants and needs. I don't bruise easily.

124

Not anymore."

"I could see that."

"When you make love with me next, Adam, I don't want you making love with a fantasy." Sarah crossed her arms and narrowed her eyes. "I want you making love with me—flesh and blood, Sarah Atkinson."

"I know." Why had his heart stopped beating?

"And I don't want you thinking Maria somehow snared me in a trap. I seduced her willingly." Sarah beamed brilliantly at Maria. "And thank God, I did."

Adam caught Maria's flushed look of happiness. "I know you seduced her. That was evident. Apparently, you are quite adept at the art of seduction."

"So when will you join us, Adam?" Sarah looked at him frankly. She wasn't begging. She wasn't commanding. She was simply naming her expectation.

"I don't know if I will." Adam wasn't sure he believed his own words. He wanted nothing more than to bed the two eager women awaiting his response. But could he risk himself in their arms? If nothing else, he'd buy time to sort out his own reactions. "Maybe it's time you tried seducing me."

Sarah sat across from him and stared for the longest time. A tiny smile crept across her lips and he knew she was about to call his bluff. Then she nodded, accepting his challenge. "Maybe I will.

That might be fun."

He watched Sarah wet her lips and run a palm over a breast. She tweaked a nipple through her top and gave him a come hither look of expectancy.

Adam rose to his feet. "I'm not that easy, Sarah." He turned to Maria. "I've already had a bagel. I'll be in my office if I'm needed." Without glancing again at Sarah, Adam ambled toward the kitchen.

- o -

Maria giggled, clapped a hand over her mouth and giggled some more as she watched abject disbelief cloud Sarah's features.

"What's so damn funny?" A rosy blush crept up Sarah's cheeks.

"No need to be embarrassed," Maria said lightly. "You looked quite appealing, but Adam's changed the rules of the game. Now it's our turn to seduce him. Mainly yours, I suppose. But I don't intend to be left out—nor do I imagine he intends that, either."

"So it's still a game," Sarah murmured. She folded her hands in her lap. "I've always been good at games. We'll have to cook up something special for our friend Adam."

With satisfaction, Maria admired the spunk of her new lover. Sarah wouldn't wilt under Adam's surliness. "Knowing him, it may take more than one assault. Adam can be quite tenacious when he makes up his mind, and right now it appears he's decided to play hard to get."

"That's the game he honed back in Bumper, Iowa. At least it's a game I'm familiar with." Sarah's smile spread ear to ear.

"You're cooking up something good, Pepper." Maria hugged herself. "I can hardly wait. And until Adam gets off his high horse, I don't have to share you."

"There is something to be said for that," Sarah said, with a gleam in her eye. "Yes, I believe we ought to have a photo shoot in the gazebo this afternoon. When do you think we can get some of your women friends to show up for picture shots?"

"Whenever you're ready."

"I'm ready." Sarah rose and marched into the kitchen.

Maria opened Adam's office door quietly and entered, bringing him a second cup of coffee. She placed it on his desk. "Are you okay?"

Heaving his shoulders and avoiding direct eye contact, he nodded. "Sure, why not?"

"I could think of a few reasons."

His gaze settled on hers. She witnessed pain before he was able to hide it.

"How was she?"

"Succulent." Maria wasn't going to lie. "You know, like when you take the first bite of lobster soaked in butter. It is so scrumptious you're not sure you dare take a second bite for fear it will disappoint. That's Sarah."

A flash of emotion flickered across Adam's face before he muttered, "I know. But you took a chance and went back for more. So will you take her from me?"

Startled, Maria chose her words carefully. "You've done little to hold onto her, if that's what you want."

"I took her slow," he said, defensively.

"Right. Even then you threw it back in her face by leaving her bed." Maria didn't quite know how to respond to this Adam who was slumped before her. He'd always seemed so strong—defiant, when necessary, but always resilient.

"I don't know what I want from her."

"If you want to use her up and send her back to Chicago, you're making good progress. If you want to hold onto her as more than a whimsical sex toy, then you're doing a damn poor job. Maybe *you* should be practicing the art of seduction—romantic seduction, that is."

He raked his fingers through his hair. "Maybe I should throw both of you out."

Maria glared at him put her hands on her hips. "That's your choice."

Adam stared stoically back at her.

"You're fighting a myth, Adam. Sarah was right when she said she's not your teen angel or youthful fantasy. She's capable of bleeding. And thank God, she's capable of loving."

Without waiting for a response, she spun on her heel, leaving Adam to brood alone.

- o -

Two weeks later, Adam fumed while trying to concentrate on contracts spread across his desk. Sarah Atkinson wasn't as adept at seduction as he'd supposed. Either that, or she was damn slow. Oh, she'd made suggestive remarks and made sure he hadn't forgotten what her body looked like.

Her nipples often loomed large behind silk and her pussy frequently played peek-a-boo from behind short skirts. Once in a while, she'd bend over to pick up a stray piece of something from the floor he hadn't noticed. It was those times when her entire gorgeous ass came into view. That view was intoxicating. There were so many things he wanted to do to her ass, but he'd stayed in control of his lust thus far. Barely.

While he'd been trying to appear unaffected, Sarah and Maria had found an endless number of ways to enjoy themselves. Maybe he wasn't needed. He'd watched his women a few times from the anteroom, but that amounted to self-flagellation, which he wasn't into, so he stopped watching. The gazebo was another of their favorite love nests. And he hadn't been able to pull himself away from the scene of Maria eating Sarah poolside. Sarah had sat spread-eagled on the pool's edge while Maria remained in the water.

They made time to swim each afternoon. They always swam in the nude. It had only been a matter of time before the pool became another venue for sex. He'd never been invited to join them for a swim. He should just go out there some afternoon and dive into the water. It was *his* damn pool.

Sarah had rolled her big round eyes at him when he caught them going at it in the kitchen. She was propped on the kitchen counter with her thighs wrapped around Maria's head. She'd blown him a kiss and given him a small wave before he could turn and exit. Her squeals followed him down the hallway to his office. He should've at least pulled out his cock and plowed into Maria's bare ass. But that thought hadn't even occurred to him until he was slouched at his desk.

They'd taken over his bedroom. He never attempted to kick them out. Life seemed simpler that way. He'd moved his stuff to another of the guest rooms. That was temporary. The day of reckoning was approaching. He'd allowed the women to get away with far too much already. They derived some perverse satisfaction in taunting him. That was not seduction. Pretty soon he'd have to reestablish his claim on them or move out.

Picking up a pen, Adam checked off several boxes on a contract and wrote a note to question the content of another. He checked the time on the grandfather clock in the corner. It was half past ten. The women had gone to bed a half hour earlier — to his bed.

He scowled at the clock. Enough was enough. He pushed his swivel chair back from the desk and stalked toward the door.

- o -

Reluctantly lifting her mouth from Maria's pussy, Sarah glanced up to see Adam entering the bedroom. If there had been a rap on the door, she hadn't heard it. Her heartbeat skipped. Had he come for her? She knew immediately when Maria realized they were not alone. Her pussy chilled as soon as Maria's warm mouth left it. They'd been on their sides, leisurely nibbling each other, in no hurry to get anywhere. They'd been quite satisfied prolonging their journey — until Adam barged in.

He stalked defiantly to the edge of the bed. Sarah did everything she could not to cower or giggle. She couldn't decide if the red-faced intruder looked enraged or comic.

Maria rolled onto her back and broke the silence. "What does your presence mean, Adam?"

Adam's cock poked through the fold of the green robe he wore. "What do you think," he spat out, surrounding his cock with a fist. "I've been celibate for two whole weeks. Enough is enough!"

His gaze bore into Sarah. "I've come to fuck

131

Maria—that is if you don't mind too much."

Sarah's flesh chilled. He was furious with her. He would deny her again. So much for trying to make him jealous. She and Maria had thought that might be enough to bring Adam around to their way of thinking. Apparently not.

Holding her chin high, Sarah clambered off the bed and reached for her clothes, preparing to leave the two of them alone.

"No," Adam commanded. "You stay." He pointed to one of the chairs. "You might as well watch in here. It's a better view than from behind the mirror." He sneered. "Don't you want to hear your lover's screams of delight?"

"But..."

Her protest was drowned out. "Stay!"

"It'll be okay," Maria assured her. "We can't expect Adam to go without a woman forever. His virility might shrivel." Maria winked at Sarah. "In the long run, that wouldn't be good for either of us."

Sarah quickly stifled a giggle when she saw the dark glower Adam cast her way.

"Don't say a word," he snapped. "Try not to make a sound. Though I'm sure that will become more and more difficult." He shrugged out of his robe and nodded at Maria. "On your hands and knees, woman. It's time. Past time."

"Yes, Master," Maria chided. "Anything for the Master. I love it when you take me from behind."

Hoping the longing on her face wasn't as

obvious as that on Maria's, Sarah settled on the settee trying not to be overcome with jealousy. Why wasn't it *her* he wanted on hands and knees? Why couldn't she at least help?

Adam slapped Maria's butt cheek and palmed her pussy before catching Sarah's eye. "You have her nicely primed. But I'm taking over now." He held his cock in one hand and gathered Maria to him.

Sarah felt her eyes strain at the sight of Adam's cock disappearing into Maria.

Maria arched her neck, licked her lips and pushed back against him. "Jesus, it's good to have you in me again. I've missed you."

"Me too, Maria. Me too." He leaned over Maria's back and trailed his lips down her spine.

That small gesture spoke more of love to Sarah than she'd imagined the man was capable of. She squeezed both of her breasts while watching him take Maria slowly. The two of them fit together like gloves. Her darker skin only accentuated his masculinity. They worked together like a team — each partner ably reading the subtle cues of the other, cues Sarah hadn't even begun to learn.

Maria shifted her position so her head and shoulders carried her weight, freeing a hand to fondle their point of mating. Adam groaned but showed no signs of wanting to pick up their pace.

He peeked at Sarah and gave her an undecipherable grin. "You do like to watch, don't you? I've never seen your nipples so extended."

"Yes," she admitted. "I didn't know I did until recently."

"Tell us what it does for you, Sarah," Maria said. "You're looking hotter by the moment."

Emboldened by Maria's smile and grateful she was being included, Sarah tried to answer honestly. "The two of you are a visual turn on. I'm not sure a different couple would do the same for me."

"I hope not," Maria said.

"Aren't you jealous?" Adam huffed, making a show of pulling nearly out of Maria before refilling her.

Sarah stared at Adam. "At first, maybe. Not really. You two look perfect together. You are so synchronized. Envious, maybe, but not jealous." She lowered her hands to her pussy. "And you haven't put your cock in me since I arrived, Adam."

She parted her labia and was pleased to see the tension mount across Adam's face. "Maybe I should be angry with you, but how can I be jealous of Maria?"

"That's sweet, Pepper." Maria beamed. "His cock is delicious. It's nearly splitting me. Too bad he can't be inside both of us at the same time. Play with yourself, girl. Don't be left out. Bring yourself off. I love to watch you when you come."

Maria flexed her butt, grinding against Adam. He couldn't hold out much longer and they all knew it.

Why shouldn't she enjoy herself, too? This wasn't Sarah's idea of a three-way. But it'd work. "Why not?" She worked two fingers into her moist channel. "I can put on a show, too. How long will you deny yourself my pussy, Adam?" He glowered at her and she stretched her opening. "You fit quite nicely. Remember?"

"Doesn't she have a saucy looking pussy, Adam?" Maria said. "So delicious and so hot."

Spurred on perhaps by both women, Adam started churning in and out of Maria.

Sarah rose part way out of her chair and began riding four fingers.

Adam pummeled Maria until he howled as if to a full moon. His pent up sexual energy uncorked in a savage fury. His fingernails scraped Maria's back and the force of his hips moved them both up the bed. Maria squealed beneath him, riding his fury. She laughed and screamed her ecstasy in Spanish.

Sarah laughed aloud as her orgasm swept across her. She couldn't stop laughing. Why was she laughing? He'd rebuffed her. But there he knelt still buried in Maria, fully spent, gulping in air, looking like he'd been caught with his hand in the cookie jar.

Gasping, Maria settled on the bed and then began to giggle with Adam still covering her. Adam wasn't laughing. To her chagrin, Sarah saw him turning beet red. He might have released sexual energy, but clearly not pent up anger.

Trying not to laugh, she slowly pulled her fingers from her pussy and awaited the fire of his temper.

To her surprise, he abruptly pulled out of Maria, backed off the bed, grabbed his robe, and without bothering to put it on, stalked toward the door. After hearing the soft thud of the door, Sarah glanced quickly at Maria.

Grinning broadly, Maria waved her hand, beckoning Sarah. Sarah fell into Maria's outstretched arms. Neither woman could contain her giggles.

At last, Maria said, "I do believe we've cracked the Master's exterior."

Sarah nodded. "You and he are magnificent."

"So are you and I," Maria replied, stroking Sarah's hair. "So are you and he. So will the three of us be. Trust me. You'll see."

"I am trying." Sarah cuddled against Maria's bosom. "I just wish it was easier."

"If it was easy, it wouldn't be half the fun."

Sarah snickered again. "He did look outrageous kneeling behind you with his cock going limp, trying to look casual while the two of us laughed our heads off."

Chapter Six

The next morning Sarah stood in front of Adam's desk waiting for him to acknowledge her. Conversation at breakfast had been light. Adam smiled to himself, ignoring her shifting from foot to foot. She could wait a little longer. He congratulated himself on doing quite well, given the embarrassing situation of the evening before.

Actually, that wasn't so bad. He'd been able to screw the woman who'd become important to him and watch the woman he'd dreamed about so often masturbating. He and Maria might have turned Sarah on, but Sarah's brazenness had turned him on, too. He narrowed his eyes, remembering the sight of her fingers disappearing deep in her body only to reappear to tantalize her and her audience. More than once he'd almost lost track of what he was doing. If Maria's back and hips quivering beneath him had been any indicator, she'd also been quite excited watching the woman from Chicago ride her own hand.

He sighed before looking up at Sarah. He still had no idea what he was going to do with this woman in the long run. She stuck like epoxy. And she was right. It had been a mistake not to screw her since she'd arrived in his house. He'd have to rectify that untenable situation sooner than later.

But he had face to save.

He set a letter aside. Her cute ass would look quite fine draped over his desk. He shook his head, ridding himself of that image. She hadn't earned his cock. Not yet.

He glanced up and held her gaze steady. "What can I do for you, Sarah? You seem a little uncomfortable." He saw a pink blush start to creep up her throat and smiled. "I trust I'm not the cause of any discomfort."

Sarah folded her hands primly at her waist. "First, I do apologize for laughing at you last night. I don't know what got into me."

He waved her apology off. "It's good you have a sense of humor. I'm sure you'll need it again before you fly back to Chicago." That sobered her nicely. "Are you buttering me up for something?"

She ignored his jibe. "You know I've been doing photo shoots for a number of the women Maria helps find jobs. They need updated portfolios."

"How could I miss that fact?" Adam leaned back in his chair. "Most weekdays there are three women in the morning. They stay from a half an hour to an hour. You work in the dark room most afternoons—that is, until you and Maria go for your swim in the nude, which is often followed by an afternoon snack. I'm sure a little taste now and then is needed to tide the two of you over until evening."

"I didn't know you paid such close attention to

my activities, Adam." She jutted out her chin. "And you could join us in the pool."

"I wouldn't want to interfere with your afternoon snack."

"We don't do that every time." Her lips curled up in a smile, taunting him. "Here I thought you were a hungry man. But then maybe your appetite is waning with the years. Too bad men are slowing down just when women are peaking."

"I'm sure Maria is giving you a peak experience," he huffed. "And you seem to be holding your own with her. So did you just barge into my office to trade barbs with me, or do you have some other scheme clogging that pretty little head of yours?"

"I wanted to talk with you about the women." She pushed hair back off her brow. "Adam, I want you to help some of those women."

"What?" Adam shifted back in his chair. He had enough headaches already without getting involved in Sarah's charity cases. "I already subsidize much of their work."

"I know you do—and that did surprise me." Sarah frowned. "But no matter. Many of these women are completely naïve when it comes to financial planning. I've talked to several who are experienced enough to be making some pretty good money, but it goes through their fingers like water."

He crossed his arms. "And I'm supposed to help them manage their money?"

"How are they ever going to get ahead if they can't even balance a checkbook, see no value in saving, and haven't a clue about investing?"

"True." He arched an eyebrow. "But why should you care?"

"Why not?" Sarah stretched to her full height. She was still quite short, but she did look especially cute when piqued. She was definitely on a roll. Nothing seemed to inspire his women more than a cause — unless it was sex.

"They are decent women," Sarah rattled on. "Some have kids to feed. Many have keen senses of humor. They love to tell their stories and I love to listen. They deserve to know how to preserve the money they work hard to earn."

"And they're not bad to look at either." He studied her closely. How involved was she with these women?

"Many are quite pleasing, actually." She ignored his unasked question. "I'm doing my best to show off their best assets — whatever they may be. The women seem quite pleased with their portfolios."

Adam grimaced. "I imagine they are. So what did you have in mind for me to do?"

"You could begin by meeting them in small groups."

"I've never been much into the group thing, into orgies."

"Adam!"

"Okay, sorry. I imagine I could put together

140

some resources for them and walk them through the basics. What else? It didn't sound like that's all you expected from me."

"Often we need a second and third shooting. You could meet with the girls one-on-one after I'm done with them."

"Now that does strike a fascinating picture," he chided. "So I get seconds. I do know how super you are at preparing a woman for me."

"Adam," she snapped. "Please, this is important for them. It's important to me."

Adam stood. "Okay, Sarah. I can do that. But I have only a limited amount of time."

"Of course. Whatever you can manage will be appreciated."

She took a step back as he rounded his desk, then she stood her ground. He gave her credit when he reached for her. He untied the knot holding her shirt together. Her breasts sprang free. Her eyebrows arched.

"Would you resist me, if I laid you over my desk and fucked you from behind?"

Sarah's tongue slid across parted lips. "No," she whimpered.

"Maria isn't here to protect you, is she?"

"No."

He guided her to his desk and bent her over. He flipped her mini-skirt onto her back. "What a gorgeous ass."

He squeezed each butt cheek. He ran his finger tips down the crevice. Her breathing had nearly stopped. She thought she finally had him, but he was not about to satisfy her yet. Not in that way.

He lifted his open palm and smacked her butt.

She jerked forward. "Ow."

"You've been a naughty girl teasing me so. Haven't you? Say it, Sarah." He waited.

She shook her head in defiance.

He slapped her butt again a bit harder.

"Yes," she whimpered, "I've been a naughty girl."

"Good. That's more like it." He raised his other hand and slapped her other cheek. Her ass quivered. Her pussy glistened and her asshole puckered. But Sarah uttered not a sound. She was temptation personified.

Adam shook his head, trying to ignore his rigid cock wanting to be freed from its confinement. It took all of his will power to stop. He stood her back up and turned her around to face him. He ignored the tears welling in her eyes. Adam held her chin between two fingers. "Don't push me too far, Sarah. Do you understand?"

She nodded.

"You better find some more compelling ways to seduce me than having Maria deprive me of sex. I like the way your nipples enlarge when you're excited." He twisted both nipples until she gasped. "And you are excited right now, aren't you?"

She nodded.

"Say it." He tapped a bruised nipple.

142

"Yes. I'm excited." Her words were hardly audible. Her eyes rounded — was that fear, or lust?

"What do you want?"

"You. Your cock." Her voice turned bold.

"Where do you want it?"

"Anywhere." She lowered a hand toward his waist.

He caught it and squeezed hard. She flinched. "No. You've been too naughty to deserve my cock." With all the self-control he could muster, he knotted her blouse, covering her breasts back up. "Get out of here before I remember how many other ways you've been a bad girl."

Sarah moved quickly toward the door. Before she exited she turned and said, "I'll have the girls stop by to check in with you. At least those who are willing."

He shrugged his shoulders. "Willingness isn't always a prerequisite."

"I noticed." She gave him a coy smile bent over, flipped up her skirt and slapped her bare butt harder than he had. "Until next time — bye."

Adam didn't know whether to laugh or spit nails. She always seemed to have a trump card ready to play no matter what he did. So she wasn't appalled at being spanked.

- o -

Maria sipped lemonade in the gazebo later that afternoon eagerly listening to Sarah's description of her encounter with Adam in his office. "So our macho man has you under his skin and can't shake you." She twirled a finger around the rim of her glass.

"He's still trying to shock me." A flash of humor skittered across Sarah's face. "A little spanking is hardly going to do that."

"Don't I know?" Maria closed her eyes and imagined Adam spanking their guest. Too bad she'd missed what must been a looked of amazement on his face when Sarah slapped her butt for him. "You do have a shapely ass that begs for attention."

"I'm glad you noticed. At least Adam agreed to meet with some of the girls about managing their finances."

"That'll be good for them and him. Adam sometimes chastises himself for not doing more for people who have to struggle to make it like he did."

"Meeting with the girls will keep him around the house more." Sarah set aside her empty glass. "So what kind of show should we put on for him next?"

Maria shook her head. "This entire game is getting a little tiring. You and I've made love almost under his nose in nearly all the ways I can imagine. He watches. You know he wants to join us. But he doesn't. Last night doesn't count. That was a desperate man seeking relief."

"Maybe he doesn't actually want to join us.

Clearly, he still wants to screw you."

Maria watched Sarah gulp and hold a tight rein on her composure.

"Maybe it was a huge mistake coming out here." Sarah's eyebrows flew up. "No. I don't mean that. Finding you, Maria—being with you has been a breath of clean fresh air I haven't experienced in so long."

Maria cradled Sarah's hand. "For me, too."

"But maybe being with Adam is simply not in the cards. Do I go back to Chicago? What else can I do?"

"We're not giving up." Maria squeezed Sarah's fingers. "There's too much at stake. It's not only about Adam—it's also about you and me."

Sarah closed her eyes and breathed sharply. "I know."

"And I'm not ready to give you up," Maria insisted, grazing Sarah's chin. "I don't know that I ever will be."

"And I don't want to lose you." Sarah opened her eyes. They were filled with determination and longing. "Not after just finding you. I feel like we've known each other existed forever and we only now found each other. But I don't want to hurt Adam."

"Come here, girl." Maria pushed her chair back. "Come let me hold you."

Sarah settled on Maria's lap and hugged her. Warm tears spilled down Maria's neck.

"It's okay, Pepper. We'll find a way out of this

maze. Together we'll get through to that dunderhead."

Sarah pushed away to smile at Maria and then she leaned forward. Her lips tasted of lemonade. Maria moaned. Lemonade had never tasted so good.

Maria slid a hand between Sarah's parted legs until her fingers covered Sarah's mound. "Do you want a little climax?"

"No. But don't move. Just hold me." Sarah rested her head on Maria's shoulder. "You are so loving, Maria. I'll never get enough of you." Her chuckle reverberated against Maria's skin. "Adam's idea of no underwear has turned out be quite a boon."

"You think it was his idea?" Maria pressed her fingers more firmly against Sarah's dampening folds.

Sarah giggled softly. "Of course it would've been your idea!"

"Damn, you are so open." Maria's index finger slipped into Sarah. "You sure you don't want to come?"

"This is fine. Stay where you are, but I'm feeling quite mellow. I don't want to alter the mood."

"Fine. So when is Rachel coming back in for her follow-up shoot?" she asked softly.

Sarah frowned and paused a minute. "This Thursday at ten, I think. Why?"

Maria winked. "If our dear friend Adam hasn't

come around by then we may have to up the ante."

Sarah hesitated. A smile crept across her lips. "You don't mean?"

Wiggling her finger and enjoying Sarah's gasps, Maria nodded. "Do you think you can handle two women at once?"

"Handle it? You've got to be kidding. I'm almost hoping Adam doesn't get his act together until after Thursday. So will you talk with Rachel before then? How do you know she'd be willing to help us out?"

"I'll call her. I can guarantee she'll be willing. She was singing your praises when she left the other day. She couldn't understand why a photographer who photographs nude women shouldn't also be nude." Maria smiled broadly. "She'll be primed and ready by Thursday."

"I can hardly wait." Sarah kissed Maria warmly. "I've changed my mind. I'm primed and ready right now. If you'd wiggle just a little, I'll come all over your finger."

"I was hoping you might say that." She probed Sarah's pussy slowly, twisting side to side and moving deeper. Sarah's teeth bit into her shoulder. Maria cuddled her shuddering lover close. Her hand moistened with Sarah's juices. "You are so unstoppable, woman. This has got to all work out. Somehow."

- o -

Thursday morning Sarah took extra time preparing for a special day. She'd taken a longer shower than usual. Rather than donning one of the ankle length dresses she usually wore when working behind the camera, she'd put on a wrap-around skirt that fell only half way down her thighs. It wasn't exactly a mini-skirt, but it was close enough. She'd also picked out a ruffled blouse and had only buttoned enough buttons to prevent her boobs from popping out prematurely.

She ran a brush through her hair and rechecked her appearance. Comely. Available. Sexy. Edgy. Willing. Nice curves. Fairly tight body— particularly for a thirty-eight year old. She smiled. She looked good enough to eat. The corner of her mouth curved up. At least she hoped she did.

So why hadn't Adam succumbed to her wiles— to the combined craftiness of herself and Maria? Even Maria was baffled by the man she'd known intimately for so long.

Time. Didn't they say time took care of everything? She didn't want to waste any more years without Adam or without Maria. She knew that now. Maria had to have a permanent role in her future. There was no saying what that might mean. Maria might be an occasional lover. They might travel back and forth from the coast to Chicago. Or meet in Denver or Vegas. She didn't allow herself to imagine beyond that.

Adam? Adam might simply remain the sphinx that couldn't be cracked. She hoped he was enjoying himself—not that *she* wasn't. Still, it would be so much better if he were a willing participant.

But enough wasted thoughts on Adam. Sarah wanted her complete attention focused on her next appointment. Rachel Bailey, part-time exotic dancer, part-time porn star, and apparently a woman who was quite taken with imagining her photographer stark naked, writhing beneath her. Sarah tried to calm her nerves. How true that was going to be. Who would be first to acknowledge what this appointment was really about?

Rachel Bailey breezed into Sarah's makeshift studio ten minutes late. Sarah started breathing again. She thought maybe she'd been stood up. That hadn't happened since high school days and seldom then—since Adam Granger failed to show up for a work project. Not that he'd regarded it as some sort of date. She had, but then she'd had a vivid imagination as a teenager.

"Sorry I'm late," Rachel apologized, doffing her tank top. "The traffic on the interstate was rugged for this time of day."

Sarah smiled. She didn't have to be a connoisseur of women to appreciate those huge breasts. Maybe she'd get up the nerve to ask if they were natural.

The buxom blonde slid off shorts and panties to

pirouette comfortably in the buff, obviously accustomed to being naked in front of others.

Sarah blinked—she'd stared overly long, even for a photographer.

"Like what you see?" Rachel palmed her breasts and pinched her nipples.

"You're a beautiful woman, Rachel," Sarah said, buying time. She didn't want to appear too easy, and she did have a job to do. "Of course, you know that. So tell me what you want to achieve in this photo shoot."

Rachel's broad smile made it clear she wasn't thinking about photos.

"Let me ask that question again," Sarah said, picking up a camera. "What do you want the person who looks at your pictures to see?"

"I know what you mean," Rachel said, her eyes twinkling. She sat on the stool and became all business. "We have to have some come-hither shots, but I'm most interested in something more subtle. Some of the pics you took the other day were close to what I'm thinking about. Mystery. Even an air of innocence, if that's possible at this age. I don't mean that teenage innocence crap. No one in the industry has that anymore. That's so fake!"

The woman's vehemence surprised Sarah.

"Maybe that's it." Rachael's face lit up. "I want to be seen as real—as a real person. With certain gifts, of course," she added, hefting her boobs as if Sarah might have forgotten them. "But capable of laughing, crying and loving. I'm one of those women in film who doesn't fake orgasms. Fortunately, I come easily, but I truly believe the viewer shouldn't be conned."

"That's good," Sarah murmured, looking through the view finder, "I suppose."

"Yes, well it wasn't always that way. I had to work my way up in status to be able to call some of my own shots — taking time to show my partner what I needed to orgasm. I hated faking it." Rachel gave her a crooked smile. "Maybe that's my sense of integrity. That must shock you. A porn star with integrity."

"Not at all," Sarah protested, poking her head around the camera. "I'm beginning to understand from you and others that you have your rules and expectations. They may not be the same as the average person on the street, but they are just as important to you." She ducked behind her camera for safety as much as anything else. "But let's take a few shots and see how we do. Why don't you put on that silk robe lying over on the chair and play with it? Use it to seduce your lover. Be genuine about it."

Sarah clicked pictures as Rachel lifted her long blond hair off her shoulders and the robe parted. She played at seduction, covering one breast with silk and then the other. She lifted a foot to the stool and let the robe slide across her thigh. She twisted from side to side. She bent over and flipped the gown over her back. She waggled her butt.

Trying to breathe evenly, Sarah snapped one shot after another. There were full shots and zoom shots of Rachel's ass, her breasts, a pouting nipple, and her trimmed, blond pussy with moisture already quite evident. There was no question Rachel was aroused. She wasn't faking her desire. Sarah didn't have to glance down to know her own nipples stood tall, filled with want.

"Sarah, does this look genuine enough for you?" Rachel parted her pussy lips.

The glistening pink opening drew Sarah like a flesh-covered magnet. She took a step forward and stopped."Yes, very genuine."

"The true test is whether these photos will turn anyone on." Rachel smirked and stepped close enough to reach out and graze one of Sarah's nipples. Sarah didn't flinch. "Did I do this?" Rachel teased, "Your tight nipples suggest these pics might be working after all."

"I'd be surprised if they didn't," Sarah said, hoarsely.

"Are you as wet as I am?"

Sarah gave a half smile and widened her stance, letting Rachel answer her own question. "Check for yourself."

Rachel's eyes rounded as she dipped a hand under Sarah's skirt. "Christ, you're wetter than me."

Sarah grinned as Rachel lowered her head to smother Sarah's mouth. Sarah parted her lips and stepped into the embrace without dropping her camera. Their tongues clashed briefly. Sarah pulled away from Rachel's insistent fingers fondling her pussy folds.

"I knew it. You are a hot little thing," Rachel said, holding Sarah by the hand. "So are we done taking pictures?"

"I think so." Sarah nodded. "I doubt I could push the shutter button down at the moment. Maria's waiting for us. She's going to be pissed if we get too far ahead of her. Why don't we hurry and join her?"

"Super." Rachel slipped into the gown. "I have a different button I'll bet you'll be able to do just fine with."

- o -

Adam scowled at the office clock. Rachel Bailey, the blond bombshell he'd once hired for some damn movie called "Destiny Rides Forever," had shown up nearly two hours ago. What was taking them so long? Women had been streaming in and out of the house each morning for a couple weeks or more. Some stayed for a half hour; some for an hour.

The photos of the women Sarah had shown him were damn good. He'd never realized how talented she was with a camera. Clearly it was an endeavor of passion for her.

Passion. He swore at the clock. Slamming down the pen, Adam dashed out of his office at a near jog and took the stairs two at a time.

Flinging open the anteroom door off his master bedroom, he chilled at the sight of the three naked women frolicking on his bed. Sarah was at the bottom of the pile with her mouth covering Rachel's muff. Rachel was reciprocating, driving her tongue rapidly in and out of Sarah. Maria knelt behind Rachel with her strap-on in hand.

Maria mouthed something and the blonde rose to her knees. Maria placed the head of the false cock at the blonde's pussy and eased forward. The woman arched her back and pushed backward, impaling herself on the cock. He could make out Sarah's fingers teasing Rachel's clitoris.

Not able to stop himself, Adam whipped out his cock and kept time with Maria fucking the blonde. He swore both women came at the same time. Both collapsed on either side of Sarah, leaving her fully exposed to his view. She reached for the slippery cock and said something to Maria.

Nodding, Maria rolled onto her back. Sarah rose to her knees, straddled Maria and positioned herself over the false cock. While she faced away from him, Adam clearly saw his fantasy girl slowly take the false cock in her ass. "Jesus H. Christ." His hand skimmed the length of his cock.

Initially, Sarah was cautious. Then she began to ride with increasing abandon. Her arms flailed above her head. With each rise and fall, the cock emerged and disappeared in her ass. His hand kept pace with the movement of her rear. It was *his* cock that should be in her, not some fake piece of hardened plastic.

Not to be left out, Rachel knelt beside the women and began kneading Sarah's pussy. Maria pulled on Sarah's nipples. There was no doubt when Sarah passed from one reality to the next. He thought he could even make out her screams. She gyrated like a puppet with no strings.

"Sarah," he whispered, exploding with her. One moment she was climbing higher and higher vertically and the next she fell forward, squashing Maria's breasts, trying to catch her breath.

Then she was laughing again. What was it with the woman? When had sex become so funny? She was like a giddy high school girl on a first date.

But Sarah wasn't a high school girl, and this wasn't a first date.

Adam cleaned himself up. He should bust into his bedroom and kick the blonde out. He heaved his shoulders. Neither Maria nor Sarah would forgive him if he did. Surprisingly, that mattered.

He opened the door to the hallway. He'd deal with his women later—but he would deal with them. They'd gone too far this time. They'd toyed with him and taunted him for too long. He'd allowed them to get away with their antics. But no more. This was his house—his home, damn it. And they were his women.

Adam stood behind the office window curtain and watched Rachel Bailey climb into a powder blue sports car. The woman wore a smile that would charm a priest. He could personally attest to her erotic skill. Maria had chosen well. It was no accident she'd selected a girl they'd shared several times in the past. Now Sarah had shared her too, but without him.

Adam waited until he heard the clatter of plates and silverware as the women prepared for a late lunch. They'd missed regular lunch by over an hour and a half. Rachel must not have any tricks left in her bag.

By the time he reached the kitchen Adam was in danger of exploding, yet he tried to calm himself. He studied the women. Glowing. Tired. Sexy as hell. They each turned and gave him a good-boy smile when they heard him enter.

He grabbed a beer from the fridge and opened it with his fingers. He brought the bottle to his lips and swallowed deeply. Maria and Sarah sat to eat their chicken salad sandwiches. Did they think they could simply ignore him? Did they expect him to evaporate?

"So how was your morning?" he asked, pulling out a chair and plopping down.

"Splendid," Maria said.

"Absolutely heavenly," Sarah added, with a smile splitting her face.

His fist hitting the table rattled dishes and silverware. Both women looked at him with hesitancy and fear. "No more women. Do you hear me?"

"Why?" Maria piped.

"Because I said so! This is still my house. No other women — or men, for that matter."

"Adam, we wouldn't do that." Maria looked appropriately hurt.

"I wouldn't put anything past the two of you anymore."

Sarah sat rigid. She'd caught a second wind. Adam knew she would challenge his authority. Somehow.

"But Adam," she began sweetly, "sometimes we want a third. We need a third."

Adam grabbed her chin and leaned over so his nose nearly touched hers. "No more women or men. You have a third."

Sarah's eyes rounded.

Adam rose and glared down at the two of them. "*I'm* your third."

"Oh, Adam." Sarah's smile was bright. "I'm so pleased you've decided to join us."

"We'll see how pleased you are after you play our games." He turned and glowered at Maria. "And what do you have to say for yourself, Ms. Ramirez? Your fingerprints are all over this charade you and your lover are trying to pull off. You know Sarah is in over her head. Why do you persist?"

"Maybe I don't agree with you."

"Humph."

"Why don't we let Sarah decide when she's had enough?" Maria's tone carried a laugh and a challenge. "Or if she ever can have enough."

Adam scowled at her. "Why aren't you complaining about not having access to other women? Won't that cramp your style?"

"Sarcasm doesn't affect me. You should know that by now." Maria sipped from her glass and set it on the table before answering. "If you must know, Sarah satisfies that part of me that craves a woman. I don't need others." Maria arched her eyebrows. "As you know, Rachel can be lots of fun in bed, but I don't need her. Not like I need Sarah. Think about that, Adam. Think about the implications of that when you can think rationally again."

Stunned, Adam grabbed a second beer and headed toward the safety of his office.

Not able to sit, Adam paced the length of his office. What the hell had Maria meant — *Sarah satisfies that part of me that craves a woman.*

Was Maria preparing to leave him for Sarah? How did he feel about that? Like shit. Empty. How had things fallen apart so quickly? It was the work of his minx. Sarah Atkinson had turned his world upside down and seemed to be enjoying herself immensely.

What were his options? She didn't seem in a rush to leave. When she did go, would Maria follow her back to Chicago?

But if Sarah only satisfied that part of Maria that craved a woman, did she mean she still craved a man—him, in particular? She'd damn well better. He wasn't ready to find a replacement for her. Not yet.

Maybe he'd simply gotten too accustomed to sharing his bed with the same woman. Had he fallen in that ancient trap of needing a particular woman? It was probably a passing need—like being on a sugar high.

He'd have to get to the bottom of his conundrum before it undermined his way of life. He'd begin tonight by reclaiming his bed. If its occupants wanted to move on, so be it. It was still his bed.

- o -

"What the hell was that about?" Sarah's voice was filled with rage.

Maria smiled. "Don't bust your buns, girl. I only said what I feel. You're more than enough for me. Should I lie about that?"

She knew she'd put her finger on one of Sarah's sore points: integrity.

"No, of course not." Sarah brushed her cheek with the back of a hand. "It felt like you were using me to threaten Adam. I don't want him feeling warm fuzzies for me because you made him do it."

"Whoa. This is the guy who had you on such a high pedestal he couldn't find a ladder tall enough to reach you. And you don't know Adam very well if you think either one of us could make him do anything."

"But he wants to be our third. Didn't we make that happen?"

Maria shook her head. "We encouraged him to own his own feelings, his own desires. There's a difference. A huge difference."

"Sometimes that's difficult to figure." Sarah pushed her largely uneaten lunch away. "I hope he doesn't feel like he has no choice."

"We all have choices. Remember, that's the fundamental ground rule to the game we're playing. Each of us can opt out at any moment. Adam has to be pushed a bit to commit himself to play the game on our terms. For me, that means he has to remain open to options that may never have occurred to him."

Maria watched pain and fright compete for Sarah's attention.

Sarah wadded her napkin. "Maybe you know some options I'm not even aware of."

"That wouldn't surprise me at all." Maria rose and began clearing dishes. "But let's not get ahead of ourselves. Do you have film to develop this afternoon?"

Sarah nodded, chewing on her lower lip.

"Will you have time for our late afternoon swim?"

"I don't think so." Sarah ran a hand up and down her arm as if fending off a chill and then the corner of her mouth turned up. "Our late morning escapade with Rachel has set me behind schedule."

"But that was worth it?"

"Oh, yes." Sarah's mouth turned up into a brilliant smile. "That was memorable. Maybe we finally got Adam's attention. Do you think Adam will join us this evening?"

"Oh, you've had his attention since that night at the reunion. I'd bet my house we won't be without male companionship tonight," Maria grinned, "if I owned a house."

Sarah shook her head and laughed and held her arms out to Maria.

Maria didn't hesitate to accept the invitation. She tried not to wince at the pressure of Sarah's fingernails digging into her back.

"You are so good for me, Maria. But I don't know what to do with you. The ride is a fun ride, but like all carnival rides this one will come to an end, too. Won't it? It has to."

Maria slid her lips along Sarah's exposed neck. "Maybe. Let's not try to write the ending of our story until we know its entire beginning and middle." She leaned back and slid her lips across Sarah's. "Believe me, Pepper, we've just begun."

Chapter Seven

Sarah frowned at the closed bedroom door. She peeked over at Maria stretched out on the bed beside her. "Are you sure he'll come to us tonight?" She couldn't help asking again. She felt like a teenager waiting for a first date.

It wasn't exactly like Adam had set a time and place for being their third, but she'd assumed he'd want to stake out his territory sooner than later.

That was exactly how she'd experienced his pronouncement. Territory. She was his. Maybe not his property, but at least his territory. He might not own her, but he had a claim to her. Maria could tread on that territory, but no one else could.

She'd been astounded how easily Maria accepted Adam's pronouncement forbidding them to take other women to their bed. It was one thing for him to place restrictions on his guest, but to extend those restrictions to Maria, who was accustomed to inviting other women to her love nest whenever she wanted, seemed entirely unreasonable. Was Maria being chastised for getting involved with her? What gave Adam the right to set new restrictions on his long time lover?

But Maria never flinched. She'd stood up to Adam and stuffed his admonition back in his face.

Adam's questions and demands had only prompted Maria to stake out her own exclusive relationship with Sarah.

More importantly, how did she, Sarah Atkinson, conservative business woman—make that *formerly* conservative—feel about being in an exclusive relationship with a woman, with Maria? She watched goose bumps pebble on her arms and hugged herself. That was her answer. Sarah scrunched her shoulders as warmth crept throughout her body.

Of course their relationship wasn't exactly exclusive, because there was Adam. At least she hoped there was Adam. Good old reluctant Adam. Would he show? Or would he hop on his motorcycle and speed away, scattering pebbles every which way as he'd done so many times before?

"He'll be here." Maria turned a page in the novel she was reading. "Are you a wee bit nervous?"

Sarah nodded, clutching her book to her lap. "Maybe I don't wait so good."

"You've waited a long time for this. Actually, you're much more patient than me. And you do look stunning in that green demi top." Maria reached over to cradle a breast through the soft green silk. "Silk heightens a woman's sexiness, don't you think?"

Sarah covered Maria's hand and squeezed it. Her breast tingled with anticipation. "Doesn't leave much to the imagination, particularly when I'm not wearing the matching tap pants."

"We're not going to be big on imagination tonight. You want to cuddle while we wait?" Maria chuckled softly. "That might keep you tethered to the bed, anyway."

"Sounds nice." Sarah fluffed the pillows. Within seconds she was snuggled against Maria's breasts, whose nipples were barely hidden under a light blue silk gown.

There was no knock announcing Adam's entrance. Sarah hadn't expected one. He marched directly to the foot of the bed and parted his robe. His hard cocked jutted forward. Lust filled his eyes.

A surge of matching desire sapped Sarah's strength. His raw sexual passion pleased her immensely. At least anger wasn't the only emotion they had to contend with.

She and Maria lay before him. She knew their readiness was more than evident. Although their breasts were partially covered, no fabric hid the nether regions Adam closely examined. Sarah smacked her lips. Her juices already pooled in anticipation. His approving smile expressed his appreciation.

"Is there something special you'd like, Adam?" Maria bantered.

Adam shook his head. "No. Why don't you surprise me? You can be the conductor. That's a role you seem to have taken to lately."

That he so readily gave Maria control in the bedroom surprised Sarah. She'd half expected him to storm the bed in a rage and take them roughly, as if he were a barbarian. So which Adam was this? Not one she was very familiar with.

"Stand right there, Adam. I have to check to see if our partner is prepared for you." Maria leaned over and ran her tongue across Sarah's lips. Sarah darted her tongue out to say *hi*. Maria smiled, rolled onto her back and spread her thighs. "Watch while Sarah and I prepare ourselves for your hefty cock."

Following Maria's lead, Sarah pulled her green top over her breasts and lifted them for Adam's inspection. She twisted a raised nipple and was rewarded to see his cock weaving to and fro. "Hefty, hefty," she teased. Taunting Adam sharpened her senses. Her skin itched for him. His aftershave filled her nostrils. She wanted to touch him. She wanted to taste him.

Hearing Maria giggle, Sarah saw her skitter a hand across her brown abs to play with her labia. Sarah watched Adam lick his lips, then watched his gaze follow Maria's hand as she moved it to cover her mound. She worked one finger into her slick vagina and then another. Appearing entranced, Adam encircled his shaft and kept pace with the women. His entire body tensed as if he were about to pounce.

Maria picked up the pace, closed her eyelids and moaned something in Spanish.

"Don't make yourselves come," Adam snarled. "I want to do that."

"And we want you to do that." Maria scrambled to the edge of the bed. She reached for Adam's cock and drew him toward her lips. She turned and grinned at Sarah. "Come and join me. We must make sure our man is ready for us." Maria licked his cock from base to crown.

Not about to be left out this time, Sarah hurried to join in. She and Maria worked in tandem, traveling his full length, and when they reached the tip of his cock they greeted each other with a wet kiss. Their smiles radiated around his cock.

She beamed at Maria. Adam was theirs. She wasn't sure *he* knew that. But in this moment of desire, she and Maria were claiming Adam for themselves — a man to be loved and to be shared.

Maria took him in her mouth, made a show of sucking him and then backed off and offered his cock to her. Sarah didn't hesitate but took him deep. Back and forth they switched off until Adam's muscles strained toward release. He was close. Maria winked at her and they both left his cock to its own devices.

"Lie back down on your back, Sarah," Maria said, retaking the role of conductor. "Spread your pussy lips, dear. We don't want Adam to miss his target. Not after this long wait." Maria grabbed Adam's cock. "Come on, dude. We've got a pot of honey for you." She pouted at Adam. "Actually, two pots."

Adam couldn't conceal a smile. "I count six pots."

Kneeling, Maria groaned. "You've had two already. You're about to sample two more. Don't be greedy. The other two are for another day. Remember, I'm conductor."

"How could I forget?" he sighed. "Get on with it."

Sarah watched Adam scrunch forward as Maria, kneeling beside them, guided him between Sarah's wide-spread legs.

Maria grinned happily. "Sarah, let me reintroduce you to my favorite cock."

Sarah nodded as Maria inserted the head of Adam's cock into her pussy entrance. He shoved forward without finesse.

"Too long," he grunted. "Damn, you're hot. I denied myself too long."

"You denied me, too." Smiling, Sarah raked her fingernails along his back. His nostrils flared. She swallowed an expletive as he seated himself deeper still. Thankfully, her sheath quickly expanded to accommodate him. She wished she could read his mind. Would he try to pound her into submission?

He smiled as if he knew her thoughts. "No, I'm not going to play rough. Not tonight. I'm here to give and take pleasure, and that's all. Sometimes pain and pleasure are inextricably intertwined, but not tonight." Adam began an easy cadence.

So sweet. Sarah knew better than to put her

thoughts into words. He would be furious. Maria's fingers tapped a little tune on Sarah's clit. This wasn't going to be a marathon. Her orgasm swirled behind her pussy—just out of reach of Adam's cock. Maria stroked her clit, mimicking Adam's movements.

Sarah bit down hard on her lower lip, but there was no stopping the tide that unfurled from overtaking her loins and spreading upward and downward.

Vaguely, she heard Maria giving Adam instructions. "Don't come in her. I want you, too. We share you tonight—equally."

There was no waiting for Maria, or for Adam, even if she'd wanted to. Sarah couldn't even wait for herself. She wrapped her legs tight around his butt and lifted her pelvis, meeting him thrust for thrust. She dug her fingernails into his back. She squealed. The tide crested. She mewed. Her legs, like lead weights, dropped to the bed. Waves of loss swept through her when Adam pulled out.

Through a sated haze she watched him plow into Maria, who was bouncing beneath him like a rag doll and urging him on with epithets she understood without knowing the words. How could the man not have come while inside her? Clearly, he hadn't.

She marveled at Adam's stamina and Maria's abandon. "What an amazing sight," she murmured to no one in particular.

Maria twisted her head to grin at her. "You

were, too. If you can move your hand, can you fondle a nipple?" Maria's head lolled to the side.

Sarah managed to twirl a nipple between thumb and finger. She pressed a finger against the dark nipple. Quickly lifting her finger, she relished the sight of it springing back to life.

"Terrific," Maria gasped. "Look at our man. His chest is so puffed out I think he's ready to pop." Maria giggled. "Literally. Don't come in me, Adam." She raised her buttocks off the bed offering Adam a deeper angle. "Don't wait for me," she said through clenched teeth. "When you're ready, pull out and spray over both of us. We're sharing you tonight. That's how we want you. Don't we Pepper?"

"You bet." Sarah licked her lips and widened her thighs in anticipation. She didn't have long to wait.

"Ah...son of a bitch," Adam howled, sliding out of Maria. His hand worked rapidly over the length of his shaft. Within seconds, he spewed over Maria's pussy and then he turned and emptied the rest of himself onto Sarah.

"That's fantastic," Sarah breathed. "Hot. Sticky. Such incredible power."

"Holy shit," Maria screamed, "I'm coming."

Sarah's fascination with Adam's eruption had caused her to lose track of Maria, who she now could see was furiously fingering herself. Her legs flailed and then quieted.

Maria smiled faintly. She scraped fingers across

her belly and lifted them to Sarah's mouth.

Sarah eagerly licked Adam's come from Maria's fingers. Then she dipped her fingers in the whiteness he'd spent on her belly and offered them to Maria, who just as eagerly sucked them into her mouth.

"Lovely," Maria murmured. "Absolutely lovely."

"Aren't you forgetting something," Adam admonished, holding his softening cock with come still oozing out.

"Oh my." Maria scurried to clean him and Sarah followed. Both women giggled when their task was finished. The giggles overtook them and they flopped back on the bed, hugging each other.

Sarah felt a weight shift on the bed. Dumbfounded, she gawked at Adam as he picked his robe up off the floor.

"Sleep soundly," he muttered, and left as quietly as he'd entered.

She could hardly see through the tears. Maria kissed them away. "Don't cry, Pepper. What we just shared was splendid — precious, really."

"I know. God, do I know," she sobbed. "But Adam doesn't. He's not even spending the night with us."

"This was a huge first step. He wants to pleasure us and himself. But he's still entangled in emotions. We can't expect him to work that through quickly just because he enjoys making love with us."

"No. I suppose you're right." Sarah furrowed her brow. "He probably doesn't even think of it as lovemaking—just good old fashioned sex."

"Maybe his brain doesn't." Maria flicked her tongue, grazing Sarah's nose. "His body knows it was well loved. I trust at some point Adam will listen to his body. Damn, it was good to feel his cock stretching me again."

"Delicious." Sarah pushed her sadness aside to revel in the memory of her first real threesome. "And that was some white waterfall he spilled on us. It must have been a while since he'd come."

"You did look a bit awestruck by that." Maria tapped at Sarah's nipple. "That reminds me, we probably should do a little more cleaning up. I'm still sticky. You want a wash cloth?"

Sarah didn't miss the gleam in Maria's eyes. "No. Your tongue is more to my liking. Why don't you clean me while I clean you?"

"An excellent idea." Maria moved to cradle Sarah's loins.

Sarah shivered at the first sensation of Maria's tongue swirling around her belly button. It was a fantastic night, and it wasn't about to end anytime soon.

- o -

The next morning, Adam purposely made sure he arrived on the deck before the women. He'd had a great time with them last night, but he'd never tell them that. He'd nearly come watching the two of them playing with themselves. Then when they'd licked and sucked him, his toes had curled into the carpet trying to keep his balance. Sarah had nearly torpedoed Maria's plan by wrapping her legs around him, but he'd managed to hold off. Then when he had come—*Jesus.* He shook his head. He could still feel it. He thought he'd blown the head of his cock off. He'd considered himself an expert at prolonging his own pleasure for that of a woman—at least until last night.

He sipped his coffee. He needed his caffeine fix to kick in so he'd be ready for the morning's confrontation. What would the two women expect now that he'd reclaimed his bed? Well, at least for sex. He wasn't about to stay the night. That might send signals he had no intention of sending.

Maria stepped onto the deck first, followed closely by Sarah. They sat in what now had become their accustomed deck chairs—Maria next to him and Sarah across from them. Maria smiled brilliantly, displaying her straight white teeth. Sarah's welcome was more subdued. She looked like she wanted to grin but wasn't sure she should. She wore white shorts, the outline of her pussy faintly visible through the thin fabric. He breathed sharply. There was something to be said for slight cover-ups. Both women had looked sexy as hell last night with their nipples pebbling behind satin.

"I trust you two got some sleep last night?"

173

Sarah nodded but said nothing.

"We did," Maria said, "but you did leave us with a fair amount of clean up work."

"I'm sure you were creative about cleaning up." Maybe he should have stopped by the anteroom to watch, but he'd been so sated there hadn't seemed any purpose to that.

"You know we pride ourselves on our creativity." Maria flicked her tongue at him suggestively. "If you keep coming back, we may share more of it with you."

"Oh, I'll be coming back all right. I may have a creative spark to add here and there." He smirked at Maria. "You are nothing if not inventive sexually."

"I'm glad you enjoyed us," Sarah chimed in softly.

"I never doubted I would." He smiled when she gave him a puzzled look. "But there's much more to this than a night of enjoyable sex. Don't you think?"

Sarah frowned. "I don't know what to think any more."

"Good. That may be progress. So do you have more girls scheduled for pictures today?"

Relief registered on Sarah's face. Clearly, she thought her photo shoots were a safer topic than their shared sex life.

"Yes, Pam Holiday will be back for a second shoot. She's seeing me at ten and you at eleven. I gather she has some very specific financial questions to ask. Then I see a new girl at eleven."

"Specific questions will be a welcome change," Adam scoffed. "It's frightening how many of these women have never tried to balance their checkbooks. They just accept what the bank tells them. And how many have never given a moment's thought to investments. Sometimes I wonder what they have between their ears."

"Most men only want to know what they have between their legs," Maria huffed. "You're right, some know absolutely nothing about finances. But it might surprise you how many are studying the stock market sheets when they're waiting between takes. Some graduated college with honors."

"I've really been surprised by that," Sarah joined in. "The women don't seem to fit a single mold at all — other than maybe being beautiful and being willing to show off their bodies."

"Do advertising execs fit a single mode?" Maria queried.

Sarah shook her head without answering.

"How about financial planners?"

"You know they don't, Maria." Adam rose and drained his cup. "I think we get your point. No stereotypes. Too bad the rest of the world doesn't understand that. But anyway..." He turned his attention to Sarah. "I'll be in my office if you need me. Maybe Pam Holiday will surprise me."

"You do like surprises," Maria teased.

"Almost always," Adam said, disappearing into the kitchen.

"He seems chipper this morning," Sarah said, eyeing Maria curiously after Adam slid the patio door shut.

Maria gave a Cheshire cat grin. "A well fucked man is a happy man."

"Well said. Do you think that observation is universally true?"

"I hope so. Of course I *know* a well fucked woman is a happy woman."

"At least some of them."

"You seem skeptical this morning, Sarah. Is there something bothering you?"

Sarah shrugged her shoulders trying to shake the chill that threatened to make her shiver. "I'm not sure. Last night went too smoothly. It was too easy. I can't help but suspect Adam is up to something."

"Could be. Knowing Adam, he's quite capable of concocting his own surprises for us."

"But will we enjoy his surprises?"

Maria stretched and yawned. "Some more than others, I suppose. But you know he won't hurt you."

"I know," Sarah murmured, feeling suddenly cold, "but sometimes I forget."

Sarah maintained a steady hold on her camera as the new girl, Alicia James, gyrated through what was supposed to be a sexy dance routine.

The girl could hardly be out of her teens, and she was marketing her youthfulness by wearing a skimpy cheerleader outfit.

Trying to keep up with the girl's movements, Sarah wondered if Alicia had ever been a cheerleader. She moved well enough for a slightly plump young woman. How had she ever gotten into the industry? Why? There were so many questions she wanted to ask the women parading before her camera, but for the most part she respected their privacy and waited for them to impart information if they chose to.

"That's enough movement pictures for now," Sarah said, setting her camera on the table. "Why don't we try some still shots?"

"That's fine." Alicia blushed. "I was tiring a bit. Do you want me to take this sweater off?"

"Not yet. Why don't we use my desk as a prop? Lean against it and hike up your skirt so we can see those light blue panties. That's good. Slip your fingers in your panties. No, not that far. Tease. We want to tease a little."

"Okay. Sorry. Now can I take my sweater off?" Alicia looked pained as if Sarah was taking far too much time doing her job.

"Slowly. Lift it over your breasts and stop. Nice." She snapped a couple shots. "Go ahead. Tweak your nipples."

"Thanks." The girl smiled broadly.

"Go ahead and pull it over your head." Sarah continued clicking. "Fluff your hair some.

Excellent. That brings your breasts up quite nicely. Climb out of the skirt if you want. Slow. Stay slow. Pretend you're seducing me. That's right. No rush. Very good."

Sarah looked around at the other props and kept eyeing Alicia trying to come up with poses that would best show off her considerable assets. "How about standing at the end of the cot? Try putting one foot on it. Yes, that'll do."

"Now the panties?" Alicia smiled, tugging them downward, teasing the photographer.

Sarah gulped. The girl might be young, but she was good. "Yes, panties, please." She hoped that sounded professional enough.

Alicia gave her a knowing smile and wiggled her panties down her thighs while the camera clicked. "Here I am," she said, letting her hands rest at the top of her thighs, subtly framing her nether region.

"Hold that position. Excellent!" Sarah knelt, altering the angles of her shot. "Have you been doing this long? You're superb at posing."

Alicia shrugged. "I've been modeling since I was ten. Girls' clothes, you know. I did a few commercials as a teen, a little more modeling when I was in college. That's where I met Ben, who introduced me to some exotic dancers."

"And you decided to be a dancer?"

"More money than I could make waiting tables." Alicia volunteered a coy smile. "And I like guys and women admiring my body. That's a real turn on. I need to have some more graphic shots in my portfolio. Is that okay with you?"

"Of course. You can pose however you want. I'm just providing the opportunity for you to expand your portfolio without spending an arm and a leg."

"I do appreciate that," Alicia said, parting her pussy lips slightly. She grinned at the camera.

"You do the feigned innocent look particularly well."

"Thanks. I practice often in front of a mirror."

"Really?"

"Of course. Can I borrow the dildo there?"

"Certainly, it's clean." Sarah added film to her camera and returned to her subject who by then was wetting the dildo in her mouth. Clicking the shutter button rapidly, Sarah tried to stay focused on picture taking and not on her own physical responses. The damn girl was young enough to be her daughter.

"Do you like what you see, Sarah Atkinson?" Alicia brought the tip of the dildo to an elongated nipple.

"You're a very beautiful girl, Alicia."

"Not too fat?"

"You're hardly fat."

"Nor am I skinny. Did you know some viewers prefer their women with a bit more flesh?"

"I hadn't thought about it. But I'm sure some do." Sarah knelt to get a close up of the dildo entering Alicia's pussy. She chewed on her tongue, not wanting to make a sound and spoil the moment. Had Alicia gone into her own world and left her photographer behind?

Ecstasy flashed across the girls features. Her soft whimpers made Sarah's fingers shake.

"That was good," Alicia said, a couple moments later. "I hope you got my face as well as my pussy. I believe a woman's face tells as much about the moment of orgasm as any thing else, don't you, Sarah?

"Yes." She fought to control her stammer. "I do believe you're right. But don't try to seduce me, Alicia. Pretending is one thing to help you pose, but I'm off limits."

"Too bad." Alicia pouted and then grinned. "But at least pretending to seduce you is helping me a lot. I learned long ago to put myself in the middle of the fantasy I was trying to portray — whether that was a kid having a blast at the beach modeling swimwear, or a secretary in an adult movie seducing her boss."

"Do what you have to do to be real for the camera. Just be clear I'm off limits."

"You mean you're not affected by me?" Alicia flicked her tongue between her lips and lifted a breast to her mouth. She had no difficulty twirling her tongue around a nipple.

"I didn't say that." Sarah softened her tone. "What I'm saying is I'm in control of my body and you won't be having it."

"My loss, I'm sure. That's okay, Ms. Atkinson,

but it is a huge turn on watching you exercise all that control. I must be pretty good if you have to go to all that effort not to step over here and sample me." Alicia pouted. "Too bad. Maybe you get off by watching." Without further announcement, Alicia moved the dildo to her anus, smiled at the camera and pushed the object inward.

Sarah emitted a gasp she hoped wasn't audible and continued clicking the camera. Alicia was one hot chick. Sarah fought hard to remember Adam's admonition against her having other women.

She frowned. But he'd been talking about thirds. She shook her head and refocused the camera on Alicia's gyrating buttocks. Adam no doubt had intended to mean no other women than Maria—period. Anyway, Alicia was too young.

But damn, the young woman didn't lack experience. The dildo was in deep. Alicia smiled at the camera again and surfed her fingers across her clit. "Oh," she muttered. Her mouth formed a perfect inviting *O* that Sarah did not miss. Alicia delighted in playing the temptress. She had a future in the business.

At last, the girl pulled the dildo out. "That should do it, don't you think?"

Sarah nodded. Thankfully, she had on a long skirt and Alicia could not see the juices slithering down her inner thigh.

Alicia stuffed the cheerleader outfit into a duffle and put on the tank top and ripped shorts she'd shown up wearing. She looked like so many young women who cruised the local mall. "You don't think I'm depraved or weird do you?"

"Of course not. Why would you think that?"

"And you don't think I'm only good for sex?"

"No." Sarah frowned at the girl. "Is that why you tried so hard to seduce me? That I would only see you as a sex object?"

Alicia shrugged her shoulders. "Most do. Guys and girls."

"You are an attractive young woman, Alicia. I won't deny you are sexually tempting. But I like to think I can appreciate the feminine body without necessarily wanting to hump it."

"Guess that could be a problem, given your profession." Alicia smiled and then sobered. "My mom thinks I'm sick because I aspire to be the best woman in the adult industry."

"I'm sorry." Sarah tilted her head to the side. "Though I imagine many parents wouldn't understand."

"But you would."

"I don't know. I don't have children. How old is your mother?"

"Forty-five."

"Ah." Sarah chose her words carefully. "I hope if I were a mother I'd support my daughter in whatever line of work she chose—and that I'd encourage her to be the best she could be."

Tears filled Alicia's eyes. Without any sexual nuance, Sarah stepped forward and hugged the young woman, who in turn wept quietly. Alicia shook her head from side to side and backed away. "Thank you," she muttered. "You've been a big help. I hope I didn't offend you earlier."

"You didn't." Sarah felt herself blush. "You flattered me."

"You're pretty hot looking, yourself, and I bet you're a firecracker in bed. It would've been fun." Alicia hugged herself. "But I know you're off limits." She looked very thoughtful. "I wish my mother was so understanding."

"Alicia, do you think there are other young women like you in the industry trying to find ways to help their families and others understand why they do what they do?"

"Sure. Some of us talk about it a lot. Generally though, we just sit around and bitch about our fucked up families. Why do you ask?"

"Just curious. Maria told you about how Adam is willing to work with some of you on financial issues."

"Yes, I'm going to see him next week. One thing my parents did drum into me was that it's never too early to start saving. But I'm not very good at it."

"I'm sure Adam will have some helpful suggestions. Maybe you and I can talk some more when you come by to look at your photos."

"That would be neat. I'll bet you have some great photos." Alicia turned the doorknob and turned. "It wasn't all a tease, you know. You did make me hot."

"I know. Thanks for the compliment," Sarah said, "I think. I'll see you next week."

Chapter Eight

"Aren't you going to be late for your swim with Maria?" Adam arched an eyebrow at Sarah, who had at least rapped on the door before entering his office.

He hoped he didn't appear too envious. The women shared something he wanted to be part of. It was so much more than sex. Yet while their relationship intrigued him and drew him, it also scared the hell out of him. His ambivalence kept him awake at night.

Maybe two women was one too many. No, he could deal with two women. He was more than man enough to do that.

"I told her I needed to talk with you," Sarah said evenly, giving away nothing. "Is this an okay time?"

"Have a seat." Adam pointed at a chair opposite the desk while stepping around to sit in a chair opposite her.

Sarah sat and crossed one leg over the other at the knee.

Although concealing more of her than he liked, the long blue dress with black buttons down the front looked quite sexy on Sarah. He knew she usually wore long dresses or long skirts for her photography work. This one hardly made her unappealing—though she probably didn't do photo shoots with a half dozen buttons open down the front. That dress wasn't designed to be left unbuttoned nearly to the navel. Her breasts managed to remain tucked in, somehow. She'd obviously dressed to grab his attention. It hadn't occurred to him a woman could look so provocative in a full length dress. But then this damn woman would be sexy in a traditional nun's habit. "What's on your mind," he asked, figuring she knew what was on his.

"How did your meeting with Rachel go?" Sarah asked, pushing strands of hair from her face.

The slight bob of her breasts as she rearranged her hair made him smile. She was stalling.

"Fine. You were right. She did have some specific questions. We talked a lot about a balanced stock and bond portfolio. She'd done a fair amount of homework. I gave her some additional pointers. If she follows through, she should be fairly nicely set by the time she retires from the industry. Though I think she has aspirations for directing."

"That doesn't surprise me. Rachel is about as level headed in regards to business matters as anyone I've known. She has a head for marketing."

"She has a head for more than marketing." That made Sarah's cheeks flush—*good*.

"You should know. I didn't come here to talk about Rachel."

Adam shrugged. "I didn't think you did."

"I had an initial photo shoot with a young girl named Alicia." Sarah paused and frowned.

"So."

"Her story is quite gripping."

"Many are, I suppose. So what did she have to say that has you so edgy?"

"She can hardly be twenty. Her family has rejected her because of her being in adult films."

He flashed and eyebrow at her. "That surprises you?"

"Yes. No. I don't know." Sarah clasped her hands at her waist. "Alicia seems quite bright and quite determined to work her way to the top of the industry."

He shrugged. "So she has to accept the consequences."

"Including the loss of her family?"

"Apparently. So what does any of that have to do with you, with us?" He narrowed his eyes. "You're not going to try to save her from the jaws of the porno world."

Sarah scowled. "Of course not," she stammered, uncrossing her legs. "Alicia has to make her own choices. She has a beautiful body and some decent acting skills. I wouldn't be at all surprised if she doesn't achieve her goals of stardom. It's just that she's carrying a lot of baggage. She's struggling with acceptance, including self-acceptance, I think."

"So you're a therapist now?" He crossed his

legs. It was nice seeing Sarah out of control.

"No." Sarah exhaled through pursed lips. "I'm simply thinking that some of these girls, maybe also some of the older women who are reaching the end of their stage careers, could use a place to come and talk freely and confidentially about whatever concerns them. You have the business acumen, Maria has the connections and gut for what these women have to contend with inside and outside the industry, and I have marketing experience and a sympathetic ear."

"Ah, yes. The sympathetic ear. You want to turn us into Ma and Pa Kettle. What did Maria say to this half-baked scheme?"

"She's for it as long as we keep it informal and include no professionals. It would be a self-help support group."

"Sounds like a bitch session to me." He paused. There was an expectant hope in Sarah's eyes. Like Maria, she could plead her case well. "If you and Maria want to put something like that together, it's fine with me, as long as it doesn't become too time consuming. But count me out. I'm not playing nursemaid to a bunch of young girls who thought the ticket to fame was their pussies only to discover the rest of the world thinks they're some sort of freaky nymphos."

"Adam!" Sarah sat straighter. Her rigid jaw was that of a fierce defender; she really had become committed to her girls. "You don't think that. I know you don't."

"I didn't say I did. I'm just saying what others think isn't something that should be so important. The world would look down on my lifestyle, too. But I don't spend a minute worrying about that."

"You're also thirty-eight years old. You've had to make your way over some tough hurdles, too."

"That I have." He steepled his fingers. "I'm looking at one of the largest."

Sarah's eyes sparkled. She relaxed and gave a small smile—the first he'd seen since she entered his office. He knew immediately when she shifted from the role of defender to provocateur.

"I'm glad I'm near the top of one of your lists." She undid one more button on her dress.

Only her stiff nipples kept those delightful breasts from springing free. His gaze lifted to her mouth which had bowed into a seductive pout. Adam drew in a breath. "You must be getting quite warm?"

Ignoring his question, she said, "Now that we have our business settled, are you going to fuck me, or should I let you get back to work and meet Maria for our swim?"

Adam tensed; his already rigid cock strained for freedom. "Why don't you undo one more button, and we'll both find out."

Her eyes snapped with invitation and challenge. She moved a hand slowly to the button in question and undid it. Her fingers held the fabric over her breasts and then let it fall. Rosy nipples lengthened before his gaze. His arousal strained against his zipper.

"Beautiful," he mumbled, quickly covering the distance separating his chair from hers. He pulled her to her feet and dropped his mouth on a breast.

"Nice," she murmured, raking fingers through his hair. She massaged his neck, pressing him tight against her chest. "It's hot in here."

Chuckling, Adam swirled his tongue over the round orb, relishing the taste of Sarah's warm flesh. Meanwhile, her hands moved with urgency to his belt. He gave her room until his cock leapt into her hands. Her fingers encircled his width.

He groaned and brought his mouth to hers. She met his kiss with her own. It was a bruising kiss. Her hands continued stroking him until he had to back away. "You've become one hungry, sexy lady. Haven't you?"

Her eyelashes lowered and then lifted. "Maybe I always was, and you failed to notice." She parted her lips and her tongue darted out like that of a snake. "Think of what you could have been having since you were sixteen."

Roughly, Adam grabbed his temptress by the hand and half dragged her to the desk where, without urging, she bent over and braced herself on the wooden surface. He flipped the long dress over her back, baring her ass. He clutched a creamy butt cheek in each hand trying to stay focused.

She widened her stance. "If you're going to spank me again, could you be a little more vigorous? The last time I hardly got warm."

He growled something unintelligible. "I should spank you until you cry for mercy."

"But you won't," she responded sweetly. "If I spend much more time bent over your desk waiting for you to decide what to do next, I'll need to bring my own reading material. Reading contracts upside down is not my cup of tea."

Adam ran the head of his cock along the crease of her pussy. "Damn, you're already wet."

Sarah giggled. "What did you expect? I've been sopping ever since Alicia tried to seduce me. She is very good."

Adam chilled. "But apparently she didn't satisfy you."

"Of course not. She was way too young for me, but when she crammed my pink dildo in her ass, I creamed. She was tempting."

"Shit." Adam rammed into her pussy.

Sarah's knuckles whitened as she secured her perch on his desk.

"Tempting is one thing," he grunted. "Remember my warning. No other women."

"I didn't forget." Her voice rose. "But you could be a bit more forceful, Adam. Don't make me regret waiting for you instead of taking Alicia when I had the opportunity."

Her words flipped a switch in his brain. He lost track of everything but bringing the quivering flesh beneath him to a fevered pitch. He repeatedly drove in and out of her, ignoring her wails of delight. She hovered on the edge of an orgasm that she'd apparently been prolonging much of the afternoon.

But she'd have to wait a little longer. He pulled out of her and laughed when he saw her grimace.

"What are you doing, Adam? Don't leave me hanging like this," she hissed. "You bastard."

He grabbed her arm to keep her from fondling her clit. "You won't have to wait much longer. But you should learn to be more patient." Adam spread her ass cheeks, positioned his cock at the entrance to her anus and watched himself sink slowly in until meeting with resistance. He paused and dragged his fingers down her shoulders and back.

"Ah," she moaned, scrunching her shoulder blades. "So you want my ass at last."

"Don't try to pretend this is new for you. I saw you take Maria's strap-on with ease when the two of you were banging Rachel. Remember?"

"How could I forget?" she said, demurely. "It took you long enough, though. But if you're half that good this will be a most delightful afternoon. I'm ready. Fill my ass."

If he had planned on going slow, her words trumped his plans, if not his sanity. He thrust all the way into her ass.

"Oh yeah. So sweet," she cooed. "You fill me so nicely. Even more than that false cock of Maria's. It is hard to beat flesh. Hard flesh, that is."

"You're really pushing me, aren't you?"

"I hadn't noticed," she said, clenching her butt. "I thought you were fucking me in the ass — or did you forget? You're not that old, to forget what you're doing. Are you?"

"Jesus," he growled. He clutched her shoulders in both hands and pulled nearly all the way out before slamming back in. He repeated that simple action over and over.

Sarah arched her neck and wailed. "I'm coming," she screamed. "Come in my ass, Adam. Don't hold back. Don't pull out, please. Fuck me. Fill me."

Her ass sucked him deeper into its dark interior. Her body blurred before his eyes. Her interior pulled him by his roots and then his brain crashed. There was little thought and no feeling other than the pulsing of his cock. His balls emptied and ached. She wailed for more, but he didn't have any more.

Gulping air, he collapsed over her backside. Her neck burned his face. Where had they gone to? Would they ever return?"

The first sound penetrating his awareness was Sarah humming softly. He kissed her ear.

"Welcome back," she whispered.

"Been here all along," he groused.

"Right." She canted her head so she could see him. "For the record, that was much, much better than the strap-on."

"Thank God."

"I knew it would be. In my college years, I was

an aficionado of ass fucking. You just moved to the top of the A list."

"Glad I'm at the top of one of your lists."

"That was so good I wish you could fuck me again."

Adam chuckled against her neck. "You need patience—a lot of it. Hopefully, I can find enough strength to get off you." He caressed her neck with his tongue. "That was spectacular. I don't think I've met a woman who can do more with her ass than you can."

"Practice. Patience is important. But patience without practice equals zero."

"You're sure as hell not a zero, Sarah Atkinson."

Sarah wiggled her butt. "Neither are you, Adam Granger."

- o -

"So how did your meeting with Adam go?"

Sarah righted herself on the flotation tube she lay on next to Maria's. The sun warmed her aching muscles and the soft sounds of water soothed her frayed nerves. All of her senses were still jumbled from taking Adam in her rear. She'd surprised him with her eagerness, but he'd also surprised her by losing control. "So-so, and splendid!"

Maria laughed. "I don't have to guess which part was splendid. Guess I no longer have to hold his hand while he fucks you."

"Guess not. He managed quite well without any handholding." She batted her eyelashes. "My ass is still humming a thankful tune."

"Wow." Maria chewed her lower lip. "I didn't think it'd take him long to get around to that. He can get carried away buried in an ass."

Sarah felt herself blush. "I noticed. Maybe that's what was best about it. He couldn't hold back if he'd wanted to. He was all mine and I took everything he had."

"That's fine as long as it's not habit forming— that is, fucking him by yourself."

Sarah peeked at the strained look of her friend. "It won't be, and you know it."

"I trust that." Maria cupped her hands and started paddling her float. Sarah did the same to keep up with her. They stopped in the shady part of the pool. "We don't want to get you burned. That'd put you out of commission and that wouldn't be good at all—for any of us."

"Not at all."

"So I take it Adam wasn't too keen on your idea about a self-help group our girls."

She shook her head. "Expect he thinks it's too touchy feely."

"Adam," Maria snorted, "could use a little more touchy feely."

"So how do we decide who to invite?"

"Guess he didn't veto our moving forward with this project."

"He knew he couldn't stop us if we wanted to

go on without him. Unless he wanted to kick us out."

"And he's not ready for that."

"Hardly. He seemed quite satisfied with our unspecified arrangements this afternoon. So how do we begin? Do we set an age limit?"

"No, I don't think so. Women of all ages have issues, and younger women can learn from the older ones and vice versa."

"I've noticed." Sarah gave Maria a knowing look.

"There used to be a premium on young women in the industry. There still is, but as the industry moves more and more to creating films for couples and for women, the potential roles for older women are expanding. Actually, a number of women who were quite successful in their teens and twenties and then retired are coming back in their late thirties and early forties."

"Really. Forties. I'm thirty-eight."

"Not too late."

Sarah shook her head at Maria's crooked smile. "Won't happen. Don't even think about it."

"Just kidding. But my point is the audience for adult film is expanding to include older couples and women. So we shouldn't exclude anyone on the basis of age. Or on any other basis, as far as I'm concerned. Let's invite them all. We're only working with twenty or so girls. I expect only a handful will want to participate."

"Why such a small number?"

"Many of these women pride themselves on being private. Some will have no need for such a group; they've got their shit pretty together, at least for the moment. Others will deny they have issues. We may get a half-dozen takers. As word of mouth spreads, we may pick up a few more if the word is positive."

Sarah tried not to flinch under Maria's hard stare.

"But it's their group," Maria insisted. "We're only helping out. They determine what they want to talk about and if they want to talk at all."

"Of course. We only want to provide a safe place for them to talk about whatever. If they want to share their most glorious moments, that's just as important as talking about matters that continue to nag at them."

"Sounds like you've been in these kinds of groups before?"

Sarah nodded. "After my second divorce, I figured I needed to do something. I found a group that accepted me without applying lots of pressure. Over time, I dredged up some crap I wasn't even aware I was carting around. Yeah, it's different, but similar."

"Guess we're all women—facing acceptance, rejection, longing for fulfilling relationships, integrating family expectations, dealing with significant others—male or female, raising children and managing aging bodies."

Sarah reached over and squeezed Maria's

fingers. "I haven't notice you struggling much with an aging body."

"Why do you think I swim laps and go down to our gym?" Maria's eyes turned wistful. "Plus I do have a biological clock ticking. Sometimes it pounds in my ears."

"You mean children?"

"Uh huh. Having children is as ingrained in me as breathing. I won't be a complete woman without bearing children."

Sarah winced.

"I'm sorry," Maria said, quickly. "I forgot."

"It's okay. I've had to come to grips with not being able to have children. It still hurts now and then. So do you think you really want to be a mother? Or is it your family, your genetics talking?"

Maria closed her eyes and inhaled deeply. "I'm never certain, but my heart often trips over itself when I see a mother with a baby. I want one of my own. Can I separate my wants from my family and my genetics? I'm not sure."

"What about Adam? Does he want children?"

"We don't talk about that." Maria grew uncharacteristically quiet and Sarah didn't push her. "I mentioned it once and he backed away like he was running a race backwards. I don't know if he thinks children will trap him or if he's scared of them."

"If he remembers his own childhood, he should be scared. I don't think he was the easiest kid, but then he also had a rather dysfunctional family."

"Didn't we all?"

Sarah shrugged. "Probably. To a certain extent. So what are you going to do about Adam?"

"I wish I knew. It's hard to imagine life without him, though I would survive."

"I'm sure you would."

"But I don't want that. And I don't want to have to choose between him and a child." Maria scowled. "That doesn't seem fair."

"It wouldn't be. But getting dumped by two husbands wasn't exactly fair either."

Maria chuckled softly and raised an eyebrow. "Although it does sound like you made them pay a high price."

"Yes, I did, and I don't feel badly about that at all. They used me for what they wanted." Sarah grinned. "They didn't pay in advance, but they did pay on the way out."

"And now you're taking control of your life and your body."

"You better believe it."

"You're a very clever woman, Pepper. I've seen you work Adam. He thinks he's stretching you beyond your limits, but he's not stretching you at all."

Sarah felt her ass tingle. "A little bit, maybe. But I choose to follow his lead or not."

"You sound like many of the women I've worked with in the adult industry. Maybe your story is not so different. The context is radically different, but the story isn't."

"Maybe that's why I feel such a bond with some of these women." Sarah closed her eyes and relaxed her muscles. "We're all trying to move through life the best we can."

Sarah followed Maria paddling toward the end of the pool, climbed out, and settled on a chaise lounge next to Maria. The air cooled their nude bodies as they lay side by side watching clouds float slowly across the robin's-egg blue sky.

"This must be pretty close to heaven," Maria whispered, as if not to disturb the moment. She squeezed Sarah's fingers.

Sarah squeezed back. "I hope heaven is this good." She draped an arm lazily around Maria's shoulder as Maria moved to lick a breast. "Um," Sarah murmured, "that's exquisite. You don't have to stop, but I don't have much energy for this right now."

"That's okay. We'll just cuddle. Adam must've really screwed you good. Maybe I'll cuddle with your breast in my mouth, if you don't mind."

"Not at all. It'll be my pleasure."

"Mine, too," Maria said in hushed tones as she swallowed a nipple and much of Sarah's breast.

"Don't want to interrupt this little love feast," Adam announced, joining them on the patio.

Reluctantly, Sarah opened her eyes to see Adam staring at them. Were his flushed cheeks a sign he was angry with them, or wanted to join them?

Initially, Maria didn't give up her perch.

Perhaps having second thoughts, she lifted her head and glared at Adam. Suddenly chilled, Sarah covered her damp breast, which only moments earlier had been so warm in Maria's mouth.

"Sarah has a phone call from Chicago," he explained. "The guy says it's urgent."

Sarah sprang alert and reached for her wrapper. "I wonder what that could be about. Only a couple people know where I am and how to contact me."

- o -

Adam sat in a lounge chair across from Maria, who had also donned a wrapper. They'd hardly said a word since Sarah ran into the house. Since when had Maria become shy around him?

The sliding door onto the patio opened. Sarah's face was drained of color. Adam sprang to his feet and gathered Sarah in his arms before she collapsed. Her legs gave way. He carried her to a chair and set her down. "What happened? Sarah, talk to us. Who was that?"

"My assistant, Harry." Her eyes clouded. "My folks were killed." She gagged. "In a car accident. It happened this morning. Good God, I can't believe it. They're dead and I'm all alone."

"We're here, Sarah." Maria's voice quivered.

Sarah nodded at Maria. She opened her mouth, but no words came out.

He massaged her neck and Maria knelt beside her, clasping her hands. They let her cry and sob

201

for several minutes. He caught Maria's eye, seeking help. She shook her head.

She was right. There was no hurry. He couldn't even remember what he was supposed to be doing this afternoon. Nothing mattered but Sarah. He fought back his own tears. The Atkinsons were good people. They didn't deserve to die so young.

"It was a drunk," Sarah finally said, gulping in breaths.

"What?" Her words jolted him back to the present.

"It was a drunk driver who killed them."

"Shit." He recognized the signs of shock. Sarah's voice was flat, devoid of emotion, and her words evenly spaced.

"Harry—my assistant—will take care of the arrangements," she mumbled. "The funeral will be in Bumper. Probably on Thursday. It will be held at the community church they supported for so many years."

"They probably sent the church money ever since they moved to Florida." He had no idea why his comment was needed, but it did seem to cheer Sarah up a bit.

Nodding, she half smiled through tears. "You may be right. I never thought about them dying or where they'd want to be buried. Harry knew. They'd told him, but not me. Why would they do that?"

"They didn't want you to worry." He hugged her tight. "And you probably weren't too eager to talk about them dying. That was an issue for my mother, too."

"Every time I go back for a visit," Maria said, squeezing Sarah's fingers, "my mother sets me down to talk through the arrangements, the service, and especially the meal afterward. She wants everything to be just right, as if she were going to be the hostess. Thank goodness my brothers are there and can deal with it when the time comes."

"I didn't know you had brothers." Sarah frowned.

"You never asked. Three older and one younger. Four good reasons for living in California instead of Brooklyn."

"I see."

"Maybe. My brothers are good people." Maria grimaced. "They love me to death. Sorry. But they don't appreciate my lifestyle. Mama may not understand it, but she says I have to live my own life. I can do that out here. I can't do it living under my brothers' watchful eyes."

"When will you go to Bumper?" Adam asked, handing Sarah his handkerchief. "I'll make the reservations, if that'll help."

"Thanks," she said, wiping her nose and eyes. "It's hard to think straight. I imagine there will be a viewing Wednesday evening. I hate viewings, but that's the way it's done in Bumper. So I'll need to be there by Tuesday evening or Wednesday morning." Sarah took a deep breath. "Will you come with me, Adam?"

"Of course." He tensed. "If you want me there. As I said, your folks were good people."

"And you, Maria. Will you come, too?"

"Me?" Maria's hand flew to her open mouth. "You want me?"

Sarah bobbed her head.

"Won't I stand out a little in Bumper, Iowa?" Maria glanced down at the hands she still clutched. "Are you sure you want to deal with the stares and questions?"

"I don't care about any of that. I'd like you by my side, if you're willing to join me."

Maria gave Adam a wild-eyed look and then sighed and hugged Sarah. "Of course I'll join you."

Adam nodded at both women. He admired their determination, but did either of them have a clue of how much of an oddity Maria would be in Bumper?

- o -

Lying awake in the arms of Adam and Maria, Sarah wondered if it was wise inviting them to the funeral. They'd been so kind and gentle with her since the terrible call had come in. No one suggested making love. They'd settled for a big cuddle, and it was tremendously comforting. But did she have a right to invite them to a social event that might subject them to stares and ridicule?

It wasn't a matter of right. She needed them to carry her through what was going to be a very difficult time. Essentially, she'd become a loner over the years. She'd lost two sets of friends — one after each divorce. She hadn't wanted to depend on anyone after that. Of course there was Harry, but he was as gay as they came — which didn't make him any less of a friend. It simply meant their relationship was the only uncomplicated one she had.

What would her folks think of Adam and Maria? Sarah shuddered. They might accept Adam. But would they accept Maria? Would they accept both of them?

She had no way to know now. Tears slid down her cheeks. She hadn't been as close to her parents as they probably wanted, but she'd loved them, and they'd loved her.

Now they were dead, and she was alone.

She sniffled. It was difficult to feel totally alone with two sets of arms enfolding her.

Bumper, Iowa would have something to talk about for weeks. Usually, gossip lasted a few days. Sarah hugged Maria closer to her chest. The three of them might just break the Bumper gossip grapevine all-time record.

If so, so be it.

Chapter Nine

Wakes were social occasions Sarah had made a practice of avoiding, but she could hardly miss her parents' wake. So, dressed in black, she stood in the funeral home parlor accepting the condolences of nearly forgotten friends, acquaintances and strangers. Adam and Maria traded off standing by her, lending physical and emotional support.

The Atkinson funeral must be the event of the week. She knew her parents were well liked and had stayed in contact with many of the friends they'd made during the years they'd live in the little town. How many of these mourners would also be present tomorrow for the funeral? Probably most of them.

She welcomed a break in the flow of people and tugged discreetly at the waistline of her dress. Her panties were binding. She hadn't realized how quickly she'd become accustomed to doing without them. But it hadn't seemed right when she'd dressed this morning. She'd also noticed Maria slipping on a pair. Adam never commented.

Adam. She clutched his large hand. He'd been like a rock standing by her. As promised, he'd made plane reservations and found them a suite at a hotel in nearby Des Moines. She hadn't wanted to stay in Bumper. The half hour commute was no hassle, and being away from the intensity of the wake and funeral as well as prying eyes would be a relief.

She glanced up at the man beside her. He wore a dark tailor-made suit. If it weren't for the occasion, she'd more fully appreciate how sexy he looked. Maria also wore black. Away from the funeral home, they must look like three scarecrows.

"Uh oh," she mumbled, just loud enough for Adam to hear. "Here comes trouble. My ex-husband. The first one. The senator."

Daniel Sullivan rushed up and hugged her tight. "Sorry I'm late, dear. I would've been here sooner, but I got caught up at the office. I was so sorry to hear about the accident."

She backed away from her former husband and stared into his steely eyes trying to feel something. Anything would do. But she felt nothing. Nothing at all. "I'm pleased you could make it, Daniel," she managed to lie. "Oh, I'd like you to meet Adam Granger." Daniel barely nodded and did not offer his hand.

"I'll be on time tomorrow, dear," he continued, as if she'd said nothing. "You can count on my support. I'll be sitting right beside you."

Sarah scowled and shook her head furiously. "No. I don't want you beside me. You haven't been beside me for years. I hardly need you now." So she did feel something—anger. It felt good.

Daniel's face darkened. He glared at Adam,

grabbed her by the hand and nearly dragged her toward a corner that offered more privacy.

Not wanting to make a scene, she reluctantly followed him.

"I won't be far away," she heard Adam say.

"What are you doing, Sarah?" Daniel fumed, gripping her by the shoulders.

She ducked out of his grasp. "I don't understand, Daniel. What is your problem? This is a somber occasion. Can't you at least be polite?"

"Polite! You bring an ex-porn star and a porn mogul to your parents' funeral and you want polite?"

Sarah blanched. Her palms turned clammy. How could he know? Why had he bothered finding out? "What? How?"

"I keep track of what you're up to."

She hated the familiar smug sneer. "But why would you?"

"Even an ex-wife can damage a politician's career. Are you going to spend my money producing porn?"

Sarah felt herself light up like a Roman Candle. "Now why didn't I think of that? That would be perfect—except it's not your money. It's mine. Can't you get some political mileage from the fact that you dumped me?"

"Maybe." He tried his boyish smile on her. "And then maybe that was a mistake."

Sarah nodded. She saw a lusty glint in Daniel's eyes. "So when did you develop a sexual appetite?

I don't recall much of a libido when we were together. In any case, I'm not available. And where is your wife — the one who turned out to be a baby factory?"

"She's home. We don't sleep together anymore, Sarah." He reached for her again but she avoided his touch. "We had some good times, didn't we? We could again. I can make it happen. I can visit Chicago or meet you in Des Moines."

She shook her head in disbelief. "I don't blame your wife for avoiding you."

"You slut," Daniel huffed, jerking her arm. "So which one is your lover? The muscle bound creep, or the Mexican cantina girl?"

Sarah's open hand connected with Daniel's cheek before he could stop her. Stung, he backed away.

"Listen, asshole, I wouldn't go to bed with you if we were the last two persons on earth." Sarah paused for breath. "Picture this, lover boy — your ex-wife is sleeping with both of them, sometimes at the same time." His jaw visibly dropped. She'd finally shocked him. "Yes, imagine that, Daniel. Imagine all the ways a man and two women can make love and see if your dick will harden enough to jerk off. Now I have responsibilities. If you'll excuse me."

Sarah stalked away. Daniel lurched forward to stop her and bumped into Adam Granger.

"If I understood the lady correctly, you're going the wrong direction, Senator."

"Don't get in my way, punk," Sarah's ex growled.

"I *am* in your way, Senator." Adam placed his hand on the man's chest. "How much of a scene do you want to make? Looks to me like friends, neighbors—and that means voters—are already more than a little curious about why their senator is browbeating his ex-wife, and at her parent's funeral, of all things. You must be pretty bad off."

Daniel's shoulders slumped. "Okay. I'm going."

"There's no need for you to show up tomorrow."

"I wasn't planning on it." He glowered at Adam. "May you rot in hell."

"Probably. But if so, you'll be right down the hall. Bye. Have a nice life."

"What kind of lowlife was that?" Maria asked, joining Sarah at the reception line.

"That was Senator Daniel Sullivan. My first husband."

"Holy mother," Maria whispered. "*He* dumped *you?*"

"He may be regretting that at the moment. But it's only a fleeting moment." She flashed a smile. "But he won't soon forget me and my friends."

Maria's eyes widened. "You didn't? You told him about us."

Sarah nodded. "In his face. He'd snooped enough to know about the two of you and your backgrounds. Now he knows the three of us are lovers. He'll lie awake nights thinking about how we manage that."

"I'm not sure that's so good. Hope he doesn't know any voodoo. He looked like the devil incarnate when he roared out of here with Adam drilling holes in his back."

"Good." Sarah sighed. "Now if we can only get through the next twenty-four hours."

Exhausted yet somewhat relieved, Sarah stood in a corner in the church fellowship hall the following afternoon watching the crowd finally thin out. She'd made it through the funeral. She'd been touched by the female pastor's eulogy and the tributes to her parents. They'd been loved and respected by many.

She sipped her punch, took a deep breath and tried to stretch stiffening muscles. She'd been on her feet on a concrete floor for far too long.

"You look worn out."

Sarah looked up and nodded, acknowledging Emily Grafton, the pastor. The slightly built woman, probably in her late thirties, had been at the church for seven or eight years. Her folks had mentioned the church hiring a female pastor before they'd retired to Florida. "I am beat." She smiled softly. "I do want to thank you again for the beautiful service you did for my parents. They would be pleased and honored."

Emily's eyes twinkled. "Your folks were special people. I don't know if you realize how special."

"What do you mean?"

Emily shrugged. "Rumors have been flying around this town since before Daniel Sullivan made his memorable entrance and even more memorable exit last evening. They've been raging since then."

Sarah stiffened. Was she expected to defend herself to a pastor?

Emily wrapped her fingers around Sarah's arm. "It doesn't matter what people are saying. That's not my point. When I came on board here as this church's first woman pastor, there were those who weren't very happy. I was quite open with them about my sexual orientation. My partner teaches in the local school system. She's an excellent teacher and has been widely accepted by students and parents. We lost a few members here at the church when I took over the pulpit, but it could've been much worse. Your folks always stood by me. They were among my most vocal supporters."

Sarah shivered. She hoped her jaw hadn't dropped. A lesbian pastor? Goodness. And her parents? They *never* rocked the boat. Or did they? They must've. "Why didn't they ever tell me? I never knew."

"Maybe they thought you knew they were non-judgmental and that was enough. They weren't the kind of folks who wore their values on their sleeves. They just practiced them."

"I'll be. Thank you, Émily, for telling me. Even Adam said they were non-judgmental when we

213

were growing up as kids. Guess I never appreciated that fact."

"Sometimes children are the last to see their parents for who they really are. Probably the opposite is also true. Well, I know you're exhausted and I don't want to keep you. I just wanted to say thank you for your parents. And," Emily winked, "I am a pastor. Always remember, Sarah, God accepts each of us for who we are."

Emily hugged Sarah soundly and headed toward the stairs and her office.

In a daze, Sarah looked around for Adam and Maria. It was time to begin getting on with their lives. She had so much to think about, and Emily had certainly answered some basic questions about her parents and their capacity for being flexible and accepting of people unlike themselves.

Three nights later, Sarah stood in front of the floor-to-ceiling windows in her lakefront condo peering out at the familiar lights of buoys and piers and who knew what else moving slowly in the dark. Perhaps those were ships transporting ore to the steel mills of northern Indiana, or maybe they were pleasure boats with people seeking escape from the tugs and pulls of day-to-day routine.

She sighed. What a whirlwind the last week had been. The call from Harry. The confrontation with Daniel. The funeral. Pastor Emily's freeing words. Every conceivable emotion had been touched.

Adam had been so comforting and willing to do anything she needed—until the funeral was over, and then he'd fled. He'd become antsy and decided to fly back to California that same night. Maria had stayed behind and came along to Chicago to support her.

They'd spent the past two days moving in slow motion. The two of them had tidied up the condo, drunk lattes at her favorite bistro, and held hands walking the beaches of Lake Michigan. Maria hadn't been demanding at all. And they'd hardly mentioned Adam.

Although he'd been so helpful, the funeral must have taken Adam well out of his comfort zone. Maybe having a healthy relationship with him was impossible. At last, she'd concluded it wasn't *she* who was scaring Adam—it was Adam, himself. He wasn't ready to own his softer side.

Sarah nodded at Maria's reflection in the window as she came up behind her and began kneading tight neck muscles. She immediately softened under Maria's superb touch. "Thanks. You're so good for me. That helps a lot. It's a gorgeous night out there. I never tire of the sight of Lake Michigan at night."

"You're the gorgeous sight," Maria whispered, untying Sarah's robe and letting the folds fall where they might. One breast remained covered. The other was visible in their reflection, as were

215

her loins.

Sarah made no move to cover herself. She trusted Maria implicitly. She ached with a kind of wanting she'd rarely felt. It was time. She dropped her chin to her chest. Maria had become an integral part of her existence. Did Maria know that? What were they going to do about it?

Maria pulled back her hair and grazed her neck with soft lips.

The view in the window nearly took Sarah's breath away. Their image was surreal. But then the entire week — hell, the entire time since that night with Adam at the reunion had been surreal.

She laid a palm on top of Maria's hand that cupped her breast. How had she come to love this sweet, generous woman so much? She did. She wasn't ashamed to admit it, at least to herself. Had the conversation with Pastor Emily opened her to accepting herself? How could she expect Adam to accept himself if *she* couldn't accept who she was?

She'd dabbled with women while in college, but that was entirely different from what she and Maria shared. That was a social experiment as much as sexual — it was the thing to do to be avant-garde. She rested her head back against Maria's shoulder. This had nothing to do with doing the *in* thing. This was who she was. A mature bi-sexual woman. There — she'd named it. Her skin prickled in response.

"You're not alone, you know." Maria's voice soothed.

"I know." Sarah patted Maria's hand. "But I'm the end of my family line, and I'll have no children." She winced. "So this is it."

"I can't make the hurt go away. You have a huge hole of grief that will never entirely disappear. But I am here to remind you, you're not alone. You have me, and you have Adam." Maria nibbled on her ear. "If you want us."

"You think." Sarah shook her head. "Didn't you see the fear in Adam's eyes before he bailed for the airport? He was afraid I'd trapped him, that the death of my parents had somehow moved him into a level of commitment he didn't want."

Maria wrapped her arms around Sarah's mid-section and hugged her close. "You may be right. I believe it's a matter of readiness. Adam isn't ready yet." She paused and caught Sarah's eyes reflected in the window. "But I am."

Sarah beamed at her lover's image. "So am I. You are so lovely, Maria. Why did it take so long to find you?"

"Maybe that had something to do with readiness, too. For both of us."

There was silence. Sarah could hear her own heart pounding in her ears and feel Maria's thudding against her back. They were on the cusp of something huge. This was about much more than superior sex.

"We haven't made love for a week, Sarah. Would you like to come like this? We can retire to the bed later. I'd like to love you as you stand

217

here, if that's okay with you."

Sarah's toes curled in the thick carpet. She couldn't contain the waves of giddiness. "Yes, please," she whispered, nodding her pleasure. Their relationship might be moving toward a new level of commitment, but they weren't about to leave that superior sex behind. Thank God.

She inhaled watching Maria tug on her nipple while slipping a hand lower across her belly to the juncture of hips and tuft.

"Can you widen your stance for me?" Maria breathed. "I need to be in you."

"Yes," she whimpered. "I need you in me."

Sarah gasped and tilted her pelvis as Maria's finger searched for her entrance. She rose on her toes when Maria found it and entered, then she lowered her torso, impaling herself as Maria probed.

"Always so hot," Maria purred, rubbing her crotch across Sarah's ass.

Canting her head to greet Maria's lips, Sarah ground back against Maria's loins. She swore she could feel the love coursing between their bodies. "So good," she murmured. "Too long." There was no hurry.

Her breast was left alone as Maria lowered her other hand to cover her clit. Sarah grabbed her own nipple and pulled on it. Her breathing had turned ragged.

"I love the way your body responds to me." Maria studied their reflection in the window. "Our reflection is coming alive.

"Yes." Sarah shook her hair. Her hips began to undulate against Maria's finger. "But faster, please. Help me over. Love me."

Maria ground her pussy harder against Sarah's butt, working two fingers into her vagina while stroking her clit. "Come to me, Pepper. Come to me. I'll always love you."

Sarah's mouth slackened. Her juices flowed. "Jesus. It's been too long."

Maria held her up when she thought she might fall.

Gradually, feeling returned to Sarah's wobbly legs and she turned to kiss her lover thoroughly. "Thank you. Thank you for being you. Now, we should do you." She held out her hand and Maria took it. "I've never made love to a woman in my bed."

Maria's finger curled tighter around hers. "I'm glad you waited for me."

- o -

Gleefully, Maria watched Sarah's dark head work its way across her belly to her patch of ringlets. Sarah never paused. She licked the edges of Maria's pussy. She nibbled on the folds. She separated them and pushed her tongue inward.

Raising her head, Sarah grinned widely. "You taste so refreshing, Maria."

Maria arched her back when Sarah's tongue

reentered her, joined by a finger. She soared, waiting for her own orgasm to build. It was there, tucked away in the mists. Her eyes closed as she coaxed her response. Then she frowned, aware of the absence of the tongue and finger that had been so pleasurable. Her eyes sprang open and she smiled.

Sarah kissed her way back up Maria's body and covered her lips. She probed her mouth and her crotch rubbed across Maria's. Soon Sarah found the critical spot, rose on her hands and worked wonders on Maria's clit, drawing tiny concentric circles around it with her pussy. Sarah's eyes rounded and she gnawed on her bottom lip.

Maria arched against her and then Sarah settled. Breasts against breasts. Clit against pussy. Tongue against tongue. Sarah started sliding slowly and then faster, increasing the friction between their bodies. Maria wrapped her arms around her lover and clung on for the ride.

Sarah had definitely found the key to the mists—Maria felt a ball of flame building in her loins. It burned, it scorched. "Holy mother," she wailed, bucking under ivory flesh. Sarah did not lose her perch.

Maria tensed. "Here I come. Oh, so sweet. Don't stop."

"Me, too," Sarah moaned. "Don't worry about me stopping." Sarah tossed back her head, pressing her loins against Maria's as if afraid of losing her.

Maria flexed her hips to match Sarah's until exhaustion over took her, then Sarah calmed. Her ragged breathing echoed in Maria's ear. Maria held Sarah in place, not wanting to lose the contact of pussy against pussy.

There was no telling how long they remained like that, glued to each other. "Wow," Maria groaned at last. "That was inspired. You know our juices are co-mingling."

"I know." Sarah said, smiling. "I'm pleased."

Maria knew they were giggling like new found lovers. They rolled over and cuddled, unable to keep their hands still. Maria breathed in Sarah's scent. She never wanted another day to go by without breathing in that scent. But what about Sarah? Would she be willing to consider their future? Or was it too soon?

Eventually, they quieted. Maria closed her eyes. Moments later she opened them to see Sarah staring at her wide-eyed. "You can't sleep either."

Sarah shook her head. "I don't want to miss a minute with you."

Maria said a quick silent prayer before forging ahead. "So what are you going to do about us?" Maria asked, running a finger down Sarah's nose.

"What do you want me to do?"

"Love me?"

"I do." Narrowing her eyes, Sarah added, "What about Adam?"

Maria shook her head. "We'll deal with Adam later. Right now we're talking about us. I don't want to be separated from you. I'm not into a transcontinental relationship. I want to wake up with you in the mornings. Will you move to California, or do I have to come to Chicago? I will, you know."

Shock registered in Sarah's eyes. Maria's heart lurched. Had she pushed her too far, too quickly?

"You would do that? For me?" Sarah's voice was plaintive.

Maria grinned. *That* kind of shock she could handle. "Yes."

"No, you have a network of people there. I have so few friends here I'll hardly be missed at all. There's nothing keeping me in the Midwest."

"Then you'll move to California?"

Sarah exhaled slowly. Maria thought she could see her lover's brain spinning.

"It'll take some time," she said at last. Maria's heart started beating again. "Some of the accounts I'm working on will have to be transferred to other agencies. Some I'll be able to keep. It doesn't matter where I work, as long as I meet my deadlines."

Sarah moved to sit cross-legged beside Maria.

Maria smiled—Sarah's pussy was still puffy and partially open from their lovemaking. She'd never tire of the view, though she expected lovemaking was the farthest thing from Sarah's mind as she began arranging a mental to do list.

"That would probably take a month," Sarah said, her brow furrowing. "Of course, I'd sell this condo. It'll take time to find a suitable place in California."

"Why not Adam's place?"

"Maybe I shouldn't rush anything." Sarah hugged herself, obviously holding back tears. "What if Adam doesn't want me in his life?" Her features contorted. "What will you do then? What will happen to us?"

"I have a lot of confidence in Adam. I believe he'll figure things out so we can all be together." Maria lifted Sarah's chin and smiled wanly. "But, and I have given this a lot of thought, where you go, I go. I said I'd move to Chicago if that's what you wanted."

Could Sarah look any more serious? "Are you certain?" she asked. "Absolutely certain?"

Maria gave a slow nod. "Absolutely certain."

Sarah slanted a finger across Maria's lips and then brought it to her own. "Then it's done. We'll be together in California. And Adam remains a mystery. But that's hardly news."

Climbing off the bed, Sarah paced the bedroom floor, apparently talking to herself as much as to Maria. "I can't believe what I'm doing. Is it risky? Yes, but it's worth the risk. Would my parents approve? Pastor Emily implied they would. What will Adam do?" Sarah stopped and whirled on Maria. "Adam will have a fit."

"Maybe." Maria stretched her arms high above her head, feigning indifference. "He'll probably accuse me of stealing you from him."

"He was hardly in a hurry to put his brand on me, not that'd I'd let him."

"But now you're carrying my brand."

"Right here." Sarah smiled, placing a palm over her breast.

"Me too." Maria covered her heart with her hand.

"Does that make us a couple of cowgirls?" Sarah did a little jig. Her breasts bobbed nicely. "So, I'm actually moving west. Come, Maria. Let's take a shower."

Maria stood and gave Sarah a half smile. "Do we want to wash these co-mingled juices away?"

Sarah pulled on her hand, none too gently. "Not to worry — I have ideas for more co-mingling. I hope you're not planning on sleeping tonight."

Scrambling toward the bathroom, Maria laughed. "What a terrible waste of time that would be."

- o -

Four days later, Sarah sat next to Maria on a plane headed for California — her new home. She held her lover's hand tight in her lap while her brain swirled. She'd put the condo up for sale. The realtor thought it was fairly priced and would not stay on the market long. She'd taken initial steps to transfer some of her advertising accounts. Harry would continue to work for her as her

Chicago-based liaison. She and Maria had spent hours of hard labor packing her things. She was ready to move.

But where would she move? Her current plan was to leave things in storage until she had a clearer idea how Adam was going to react to this new commitment she and Maria had forged.

While she didn't harbor a glimmer of doubt about them, she was having doubts about Adam. Would he blow up? Would he run? Would he kick the two of them out, or would he give them time to find a place of their own? Would he feel betrayed by Maria, by her?

No matter how Adam reacted, she resolved to follow her heart with Maria. She squeezed Maria's fingers and drifted off to sleep.

- o -

Maria scrunched around in the passenger seat and returned her dozing partner's squeeze. Sleep had been rare over the last several days. They'd made time for loving in and around packing boxes, finding a secure storage company, and interviewing realtors, but there had been little time for sleep.

Closing her eyes, she cherished the warmth of Sarah's fingers intertwined with hers. She was warm-hearted and hot as hell in bed. Maria smiled. What else could she wish for?

Adam's dark eyes surfaced before her. Maria

sighed. *Adam*. Adam wasn't going to be easy. He'd claim she'd stolen Sarah away from him, but he'd had his chance to move first. He either didn't or couldn't. Now things would have to shake out however they were going to.

She wanted to share her life with Sarah *and* Adam, but she wasn't going to give up the love she shared with Sarah for fantastic sex with Adam. There was more than sex between the two of them. She knew that, but Adam shied away from naming it. He'd been running like hell ever since his old classmate had arrived on the scene.

No, if he wanted in, he'd have to open up to her *and* to Sarah. There was no turning back now. She'd committed herself to Sarah. She'd never done that with anyone before, and she didn't take commitments lightly. She grinned to herself. Maybe she was a good Catholic after all.

- o -

Adam stared blankly toward the ocean. The women would be back today. That was good and bad. He'd missed them. He missed their ongoing battle to include him in their budding companionship. He grimaced. They'd been away from him for over a week. Would they even remember he existed? Would they be ready to move out? Would he let them? Did he want them out of his life?

Why the hell hadn't he gone with them to

226

Chicago? That was the original plan, but he'd panicked.

The funeral and all its arrangements had made him feel like part of a family. He knew better than that, and just in case he'd forgotten, the confrontation with Daniel Sullivan had been an apt reminder. He didn't belong. Sarah Atkinson was out of his league. He didn't deserve to have a family.

But what about Maria? She had to have stood out even more than he did in Bumper. He was a known commodity, and she wasn't. Yet she seemed to roll with the punches, and she hadn't run out on the woman she loved.

He knew. He had eyes. His heart even told him. Maria was in love with Sarah in ways he'd never begun to tap. Not that Maria hadn't been willing to take their relationship to the next level — *he* was the one who'd thrown roadblocks up any time emotions became too heated.

Did Sarah know? How would she respond to Maria's overtures? Overtures of love, not sex. Adam raked his unruly hair roughly. He had no answer to that question. The Sarah Atkinson he thought he knew in high school would've run like hell. This Sarah Atkinson he could not fathom.

He'd have to prepare for whatever. Wasn't that his lot in life? He tried so hard to be in control, yet he had to prepare for whatever.

Adam lurched to his feet and grabbed another beer. With beer in hand, he sidled toward the bathroom. He hadn't seen a shower in days and he'd better get the kitchen cleaned up.

His women were coming home and he didn't have a damn clue what that might mean for him.

Chapter Ten

Adam sat in his favorite chair in his spacious living room feeling sorry for himself. Sarah and Maria had been back for nearly an hour. They hadn't even come looking for him.

He'd heard them come in and go upstairs. He hadn't followed. The first move would be left up to them. When he played chess he always preferred black so he could counter his opponent's scheme.

Then he'd heard them padding down the stairs. They went to the kitchen. Glasses and ice rattled. He fought the urge to get up and charge into the kitchen.

Shortly, somewhat to his surprise, he glanced toward the archway and saw his two impish women beaming at him.

"Want some?" Maria asked, her eyes sparkling.

He accepted the glass of lemonade she offered him. "Welcome back," he said evenly, lifting his glass in salute. He eyed the women cautiously. Their smiles belied a tension in the air. Neither woman took a seat.

"It's good to be back," Maria said.

"What about you, Sarah? Are you pleased to be back?"

Her smile was hesitant. "Yes. Yes, I am."

Fighting a slight annoyance at the women for wearing long dresses, Adam asked, "So how was your stay in Chicago?"

"Fantastic!" Maria said. She sobered. "We have news, Adam." Her tone had become hushed.

"So tell me." He braced himself for the inevitable.

"Sarah's put her condo on the market and is moving to California. Isn't that exciting?"

"Really." He eyed Sarah. "So where do you plan on living?"

"That depends," Sarah answered.

He gave her credit for keeping her gaze fixed on his. She didn't look to Maria for help. "On what?"

"On you." She shrugged. She glanced at Maria. "And us."

"Adam." Maria wet her lips. "Sarah and I are committed lovers. She's moving in with me. As long as I am here, she will be too."

Adam arched his eyebrows, struggling to control his fury. "Where does that leave me? Oh, I guess I should say I'm happy for the two of you. But I'm still curious, where does that leave me?"

"Don't be sarcastic. Wherever you want to be." Maria said, stiffly. "We prefer to have you as our partner, but we didn't know if you'd want that."

"Why not?" he said, rising to his feet. "What's different? I thought you were quite committed before we left for Iowa. So now you have a name for what you are. Isn't that nice?"

"So we can stay?" Sarah asked.

"Of course. Why not? But things haven't changed. You're still available to me when I want you — both of you. One at a time or together, when I so desire." He glanced at Maria, who nodded. He looked back at Sarah, who also nodded.

"Any way I want you," he said icily.

Both women nodded.

"There, you see?" He smirked. "Nothing has changed. Not really. I trust you are both commando?"

Both women raised their skirts. Adam nodded his approval. "Very nice." He pursed his lips, unable to contain his amusement. "So what will it be? I could have you both on all fours and alternate from pussy to pussy."

Neither woman blanched. They each awaited his instructions.

"No. That sounds like a randy, overly eager young stud." He stepped in front of Sarah and lifted her chin. She didn't blink. "I will have to give this some extra thought. After all, this is your homecoming. I never was able to take you to a homecoming dance." He chuckled. "I assume you blew the homecoming king more than once."

Her eyes widened and she nodded.

"Damn, how could I have been so wrong about you back then?" He tugged on a nipple through her dress. A spark of anger flashed across her eyes, but she made no sound. "No matter, you're here now. I'll have to think up something extra

231

special to make up for my loss.

"And you." He glared at Maria. "You will be my assistant, as usual. Now leave me. This will take some time."

- o -

Sarah and Maria scurried out of the living room and headed directly to their sanctuary—the pool. Quickly, they pulled off their dresses and dove in.

When they reached the far end, Sarah rolled on her back, as did Maria. "Adam is royally pissed."

"That's for sure," Maria agreed, cupping her hands in the water.

"So what do you think he has in store for me this evening?" She didn't try to explain the heat coursing through her body in anticipation, nor the icy chill edged with a trace of fear.

"I don't know, but he won't hurt you."

"How can you be so sure? He thinks I stole you from him."

"I know Adam." Maria shut her eyes. "He's wounded. He'll growl. He'll kick and scream. But he won't hurt the women he loves—and he does love us. He might hurt himself, but he won't hurt either one of us."

Sarah turned sharply to Maria. "You don't think he'll actually hurt himself."

Maria's eyes snapped open. She shook her head. "Not physically. But he could do a number on himself emotionally until all of this is

232

resolved."

Sarah inhaled and let her breath out slowly. "So we play along and wait."

"What choice do we have? It's play along or leave the game."

"I'll play," Sarah said quickly.

"I'm sure you will. You play so well." Maria stood in the waist deep water. "Come on, lover, give me a kiss."

Sarah stood and they joined hands. "But Adam?"

"If he's watching, it'll serve him right. He needs to be constantly reminded of what's he's missing." Maria winked. "Now shut up and kiss me."

Sarah giggled. "Yes, Mistress Maria." She moved into an easy embrace. Her lips played with Maria's, dabbling and tasting. She chewed on Maria's upper lip and then the lower one. Maria's tongue entered her mouth. She sucked it deep. She broke the kiss and rested her cheek on top of Maria's breast, gasping for air. "You are the best kisser I've ever been with. How can I get so aroused by a single kiss?"

"Because you love me, Pepper." Maria lifted her chin. "Now kiss me again," she said, lowering her head.

And she did. Their lips sealed like glue. Her hands entered the water to cup Maria's butt just as Maria's squeezed hers. The friction of pussy rubbing pussy beneath the surface and the soft probing kiss set her off. She smiled when Maria shuddered in her arms. They clung together for long moments letting sweetness wash over them.

"Damn," Maria said, "that was a pleasant surprise."

"Um. It sure was. Not all surprises have to be gift wrapped." She traced the outline of Maria's jaw with a finger pad. "I hope Adam enjoyed himself half as much as we did."

- o -

Adam slammed his fist into the wall. They couldn't even wait for him. They couldn't wait for tonight.

Why did that bother him? It was only sex. Oh, they wanted to call it something else. But he'd just witnessed two women humping each other in his pool. Looked like sex to him. So it must have been sex. He bet it smelled like it, too.

Perhaps it was good Maria had taken the edge off of Sarah. The woman would have to prolong her desire this evening in order to satisfy his. He smiled as Sarah climbed out of the shallow end of the pool. She stretched like a satisfied cat. She might need nine lives before he was done with her. She grabbed Maria by the hand and they raced to towels lying on the poolside chairs.

His lips curled up as he watched them toweling off. She didn't have any inkling her clinging to Maria almost assured her of getting way in over her head.

234

She thought she knew him. She didn't have a clue. Maybe after tonight's adventure she'd have a little better idea what kinds of passion lurked within him. Would she move out in the morning? Would she take Maria with her? Did he give a damn?

- o -

On her back with her hands extended over her head, her raised butt resting on a cushion and her legs splayed wide, Sarah eyed Adam with what she hoped was sufficient aloofness. He hadn't tied her to the bed, but he might as well have. He'd told her in no uncertain terms not to budge. If nothing else, his glare kept her riveted in place.

Thankfully, Maria knelt by her side with a reassuring smile. Yet even she had an edge about her that seemed different. Maria's flared nostrils and elongated nipples embodied sexual excitement. She must know what Adam intended.

But like her, Maria awaited Adam's next command. He was in charge of choreographing what was going to pass for lovemaking. Sarah wasn't in charge, and neither was Maria.

Adam could be mistaken for a Greek god kneeling between her legs. His chest and corded thighs glistened with a sheen of oil. His eyes bore into her as if capable of reading her mind. Her heart skipped several beats as she watched him squirt oil along the full length of his cock. He

235

worked both hands along the length of his shaft, spreading the oil thoroughly. She could hear the squeak of the oil against his hard flesh. Her mouth watered at the sight of the purplish crown peeking out of his fist.

"See something you want?" Adam asked. His grin made it clear he knew her response.

"Yes," she replied, trying to sound as meek as possible.

"Where?"

"Anywhere."

"How?"

"How?" She frowned at his fingers skimming his cock. "Not that way. Come in me," she pled. "Now."

Adam gave Maria a caustic smile. "Haven't you taught her better than this? She still thinks she can control the game." He glared back at her. "You don't get to decide this time. I will do what I want to you and with you. Right?"

Sarah smacked her lips, resisting looking at Maria for help. She girded herself for what was to come. She knew she'd brought this on herself. She'd teased him, taunted him, and mocked him. She'd wanted to crack his exterior. Now she wasn't so sure she wanted to peer into his interior world. She did her best not to outwardly tremble. "Yes. Do what you will." The strength of her voice surprised even her.

"Very well." His eyes snapped a warning before he nodded to Maria. "Put the blindfold on your lover."

Horrified, Sarah watched Maria pull a black blindfold from beneath a pillow.

"It'll be okay, Pepper," Maria whispered. Her lips parted into a half smile. "Believe me, this only makes sex more vivid."

Resigned, Sarah nodded and lifted her head for Maria to knot the blindfold. Her world went immediately dark. There were no edges where light seeped in. She had been thrown into a complete blackout.

"We'll give you a moment to adjust," Adam said.

Sarah was surprised by his soothing tone.

"Cutting off your visual cues will heighten others," he added. "Have you ever been blindfolded before?"

She shook her head. "Only in trust walks with youth groups."

Adam chuckled. "Having sex blindfolded does demand trust, but this is no trust walk. Before we are done with you, Sarah, you won't know who is doing what to you. You will be completely at our mercy, totally under our control. You won't be able to stop us or yourself. How does that feel?"

"Scary," she whimpered.

"Good. I'm glad I finally found something new for you to experience. I must admit you've surprised me. Now it's your turn to be surprised."

The mattress shifted beneath her. Too much time passed without anyone speaking. Sarah struggled to remain calm.

"You do look so vulnerable lying there spread eagled and blindfolded. It is so tempting to just give in and ravage you. You'd like that, wouldn't you?"

She nodded and wet her lips. Tensing, she prepared for the shock of his cock entering her swiftly.

"But that would be way too quick. Satisfying, but not satisfying enough."

Fingers tapped her swollen nipples. She jerked. His laughter filled her ears.

"That was just a test, and you failed miserably. Remember whatever you do, don't move unless I tell you to. I can still tie you down if necessary."

Sarah shook her head wildly. That was the last thing she wanted. She'd never liked feeling confined. And this was already too confining. "No, that won't be necessary."

Her nipples were unceremoniously twisted, sending bolts of pain to her brain. Her brow furrowed but she made no attempt to pull away.

"Better, much better," Adam praised her with only a trace of derision. "She may be ready. What do you think?"

"She's ready." Maria's squeaked. "Let's get on with it. I'm creaming already."

"That's unusual?" Adam laughed. "First, we're going to pour some oil on your beautiful skin and work it in thoroughly. A well oiled body helps prolong orgasms, don't you think?"

"I don't know," Sarah murmured. Initially, the oil chilled her, but four hands massaging the silky liquid into her flesh soon warmed her all over. She quickly lost track of which hands belonged to Adam and which to Maria. Then their hands blurred. It was as if they were everywhere at once.

Had others silently joined them? Was she involved in some sort of orgy? She swore fingers caressed her from ears to toes. No more time was spent on her breasts than on her knees. With one aching exception, every square inch of flesh was massaged without lingering. No touch seemed explicitly erotic, yet she'd never felt more sexually alive in her life.

Sarah ran the tip of her tongue along her lips. They'd become dry. Her flesh did a slow burn. What was in the oil? Or was her hypersensitivity simply the result of highly skilled fingers? She caught her breath as four sets of fingers moved slowly but deliberately up along the inside of her thighs. She couldn't determine whose fingers touched her labia first, but she nearly leapt off the bed when they did.

"Don't move," Adam hissed, breaking the silence. She hadn't even realized how quiet they'd been for the past several minutes until he spoke. Her complete concentration had been on twenty fingers. Oil saturated her pussy and fingers continuing kneading it into the engorged flesh. If this wasn't meant to excite, why was she so excited? Two hands traced a path of oil toward her anus.

Involuntarily, she clenched her buttocks. "Don't resist," Adam warned. "You have no choice in this. If we desire your ass, it's ours. Remember?"

She nodded and tried to calm her breathing. Two hands spread her butt cheeks while two hands spread oil over the crease of her butt. Two fingers rimmed her ass. She'd swear one was Adam's and one was Maria's. They were equal partners in this sweet torture. She lifted her butt off the bed wanting to scream for one of them to enter her, but she bit her tongue and remained quiet.

"You'll get what you want," Adam said, pressing her back down on the mattress. "Maybe more than you want, but not yet. There is much more to do to you before that. Touching is more intense without seeing, isn't it?"

"Very," she murmured, unsure of what they might've left out. What would happen next to prolong her agony—she shuddered—no, her pleasure?

She didn't have to wait long. "That tickles," Sarah gasped, keeping her arms locked in place. "What? Feathers?"

She blew at the feathers grazing her upper lip and giggled. Her giggles stopped as the feathers slid along her neck and then toward her cleavage.

"You're quick," Maria whispered next to her ear. "Feathers can be tantalizingly delightful. You'll see."

Sarah swallowed, tracking each tiny flick of each feather. They worked in tandem, one gliding along the rise of each breast. The tips of the feathers drew circles tracing the edges of her aureoles. Her nipples ached reaching out for the feathers that must be hovering over them. Then a feather tapped each nipple. She tensed, but applauded her determination not to grab the feathers, or her nipples, or her lovers.

Adam laughed aloud. "My original plan was to save you for one giant orgasm, but I have so much planned for us that doesn't seem reasonable even to me. So a change in plans is in order. We'll see how often we can make you come. But you can only come on command. I remain in control of your body. Understood?"

"Yes, I think so." The tap-tap-tapping of feathers against taut nipples continued until she could bear it no longer. "I'm ready. Please. Please Adam, let me come."

"Only if you don't curl up and turn away from me afterward. I want to see you come, Sarah. I want to see all of you. Agreed?"

"Yes, please."

"You may come."

The feathers continued rapping on her nipples as if they were priming a pump. She gasped, holding herself rigid, letting the small orgasm rush through her body and warm her from the inside out. "Nice. Thank you." She fought the urge to roll into a ball and nurse it to its completion.

Her pussy needed fondling, but no one touched her there and she wasn't about to ask. She knew better than to try and do it herself.

"Exquisite. You flush so nicely when you come. Don't you agree, Maria?"

"Yes." Maria sounded hoarse. "Pepper's extremely expressive when she's hot. And she's damn hot right now."

Sarah smiled to herself, regaining her composure. Maybe she was exciting them as much as they were exciting her. How long could they last before taking her the way she wanted? How long could she put up with this slow, delicious torture? Maybe forever.

The feathers slid lower across her belly. They rimmed her belly button several times and then moved lower. Each of them grazed her clit, which no doubt had come out to see what the hell was going on. She longed to see. Was she turning on her partners as much as they were turning her on?

The feathers didn't tarry at her pussy but glided all the way down to her toes. Involuntarily, she scrunched. Her feet had always been ticklish.

"Don't move," Adam chastised. "Roll over. Leave your arms stretched out over your head and pull your knees up into a tuck position."

Without too much difficulty, she complied with his command. The blindfold never shifted. When she opened her eyes all she could see was darkness. If anything, she felt even more vulnerable tucked in this pose, knowing full well it exposed her pussy and ass to close inspection.

"Excellent. What an erotic picture. Damn, your pussy and asshole are so ripe for plucking. Each is begging for attention. But I bet you know that."

Sarah tried to nod.

"Which one do you think we should play with first?" he asked, brushing a palm lightly over the curve of her buttocks.

She shook her head, refusing to answer. She just wanted them to touch her. One feather tip slid across her inner pussy folds and the other teased her anus. Her butt wiggled of its own accord. A hard slap was immediate. Her butt cheek reverberated from the sting. It felt like Maria's hand, not his.

"Well done, Maria. I love it when you get bitchy. Do you want to paddle her to orgasm?"

"No, that won't be necessary," Maria responded, her voice strained. "I think she's learned her lesson. She looks quite innocent and meek lying there waiting for our next move."

Adam chuckled. "Yes, she looks as meek as a novitiate. Hand me one of those."

Sarah held her breath. What now? "Oh my God," she mumbled into a pillow. She'd used candles often as a teenager. She'd wager her life savings that one pressed against her pussy and one her anus.

They entered her at the same instant. She grunted and bore back, but hopefully not enough for Adam or Maria to notice. If they were aware of her clenching, they didn't respond. Instead, they paused, allowing her anus to open, and then the candles moved deeper. Sarah tried to swallow. The pleasure was nearly unbearable—or was it pain?

"You're making me come again," she whispered urgently. "May I come?"

His response was immediate. "No, not until I say so."

"But I can't hold..." The second slap on her rear stung more than the first and it did serve to divert her orgasm, at least briefly.

"You will wait for your orders. I am master of your body. Understood?"

Sarah sighed. "Yes."

Warm lips soothed her butt cheek that still recoiled from the last slap. "Pain often leads to pleasure," Maria murmured.

"We are going to pick up the pace some, but don't you dare come until I tell you too."

She nodded as the candles began to twist and move slowly in and out. She clamped down on her inner muscles trying to hold back.

"Faster," he said to Maria. "She's building toward a much bigger one this time. Look at how her back is straining. She's working hard to please us by not coming, don't you think?"

The rapidly moving candles were driving her over the edge. She scrunched her shoulders. She so wanted to clamp down on the intruders.

"Remain open to us, girl," Maria chided. "Your

heat must be melting these candles."

"I'm going to count to five," Adam said, "after which you may come when ready."

When ready! Didn't he know she'd been ready five minutes ago?

"One...two...three...four...five." Both candles sank into her depths and spun around. She was gone over the top. Her body shook and she mewed softly. She so wanted to treasure this one—to go off by herself and embrace it and leisurely return to her lovers. But she retained enough awareness not to do that. He gave her more time to recover. She drew in deep breaths of air. Warily, she settled and waited further commands.

"How are you doing, Sarah?" Adam asked, a touch of warmth in his voice.

"Okay," she whispered.

"We aren't nearly finished. Are we?"

"No."

"You wouldn't want to be done yet, would you?"

"No."

"Why not?"

"You haven't fucked me."

"You do catch on quick. What say you, Maria? Is it time?"

"Oh yes," Maria chirped. "Our Pepper is well prepared."

"This a very tempting position," he said, pinching a butt cheek, "but I want you on your back. Roll over. Keep your legs spread wide."

Four hands helped her turn over onto her backside. Again, a cushion was slid under her rump, raising her lower torso off the mattress. Without saying another word, Adam fondled her pussy methodically. He pushed beyond her folds. She tried not to whimper when one finger entered her followed closely by a second.

He probed briefly before withdrawing his fingers. Sarah grimaced when he left her.

"Maria is right—no more preliminaries are needed. You're soaking the bed." He chuckled. "Maria is looking as hungry as you. With a little effort she could get her entire fist in you."

Sarah flinched, then widened her knees. She heard Maria's sharp intake of breath. She trusted Maria would only do what brought pleasure to them.

"But she'll have to try that another time," Adam interjected. "I don't have the patience to watch you two tonight. You may be wondering who's going to fuck you. Well, I'll tell you. There won't be any false cock this time—only the real thing."

She tried not to react when he used his cock to separate her labia. She wanted to flex her hips and entice him to enter, but she didn't. She balled her fingers into fists and waited. With a grunt he plunged into her. She started to lift her hips to meet him.

"Don't move," he warned. "I'm fucking you.

You're not fucking me."

"What do you want me to do?" Maria asked.

"Sit on her face, lean down and lick her clit. That should be a familiar position for you."

Wishing she could see, Sarah inhaled the familiar scent of cinnamon and nutmeg. She flicked her tongue out to caress her lover.

"Don't tongue her, Sarah," Adam cautioned. "Stay focused on what we're doing to you. Keep your arms stretched. Concentrate on your clit and your pussy—on the tongue licking and the cock fucking."

She tried to breathe as his cock slowly filled her, retreated, and filled her again. Maria's tongued flitted along her clit, keeping pace with Adam. She couldn't hold back a whimper.

"Are you concentrating?"

"Yes," she nearly screamed. "I can't stand much more without coming. Isn't anybody going to come with me?"

"Later. Maybe. If we choose to. Are you ready?"

"Yes, damn it."

"Good. Don't flex your legs or thighs. Just let it happen, Sarah. That's right. I feel you squeezing my cock. That's okay. You're coming. I feel your juices pouring over my cock."

Sarah collapsed into herself almost beyond feeling. It was as if someone had pulled her plug and she was draining onto the bed. She might've had wilder more ecstatic orgasms, but this one wasn't stopping, and she wasn't doing a damn thing to prolong it. Neither was Adam or Maria. It scared her more than a little. Was she losing her life energy? And Adam hadn't released yet. She held back a sob and breathed rapidly.

"Do you have enough energy left to kneel on the floor with your breasts and shoulders on the bed?"

"I think so." Without disturbing the blindfold, she eased her sore legs and thighs over the side of the bed. Adam stood behind her. Was he going to fuck her in the ass? That might be a relief for her poor tired pussy.

But no. She grunted as he rammed into her pussy. She bit down on her lower lip. Where was Maria?

"Slap my ass, Maria."

"What?" Maria sounded as shocked by his request as she was. Now, what the hell was he doing?

"Don't you think I've been a bad boy? Haven't I been harsh with your lover? Slap my ass."

Sarah heard the sound of flesh meeting flesh. It became a steady cadence. The sounds became louder with each strike. Soon Adam was pumping in an out of her with the same rhythm. His thighs would pummel her rear just as Maria's hand slapped his butt.

"That's enough, Maria. Now rub your wet pussy over my ass. That's right. You're soothing the pain. Fuck me while I fuck your lover. That's it. Grind my ass.

"Do you feel it, Sarah? We're both fucking you. Reach around and do her clit, Maria. I'll get her nipples."

There was no escape. Sarah didn't want to escape. "Fuck me," she screamed. "Yes, both of you. Fuck me. I'm coming. Can't I come, Adam?"

"Yes. Maria is already creaming over my ass. Come for us, Sarah."

His hips never stopped pounding until hot sperm lodged deep in her interior. She stretched her torso over the bed, spent. She'd survived. She'd survived his fury and his passion. If he had really been trying to punish her, he would've stayed with his initial plan of preventing her from climaxing. He hadn't possessed the heart to do that to her.

His fingers fumbled at her blindfold. Even the dim light blinded her momentarily. He reached around her neck from behind and settled his lips on the corner of hers. She opened for him. He might be reluctant to use words, but she wondered if he had any idea what his caresses were communicating.

Maria sat beside her on the bed. Her lips joined his. They each shared a corner of her mouth. If they didn't stop, she was going to come again.

Had they finally crossed the chasm of intimacy?

"You have one hell of a lot of spunk, lady," Adam said, roughly. "More than I gave you credit for."

The next sound she heard was Adam snoring softly on her back. He'd never pulled out of her pussy. They were half on the bed and half off. Oh well. It wasn't the easiest position for sleeping, but she was game if he was. She couldn't even think anymore, much less move.

A couple hours later, stiffness caught up with Sarah. She had to stretch out on the bed or she wouldn't be able to move in the morning. She might not be able to move now.

She turned to awaken Adam and only then realized he wasn't there. Maria lay on the bed sleeping, but Adam was nowhere to be seen.

She crawled onto the bed and snuggled against Maria.

"He did it again, didn't he," Maria said. "He fled when the emotions got hot."

"Looks like."

"But we've got him hooked. All we have to do is play him and reel him in."

Sarah hugged her lover. "If the play doesn't kill me first."

"You loved it; you know you did."

Sarah licked Maria's shoulder, savoring the slight salty taste. "It was pretty damn spectacular."

Chapter Eleven

Normalcy. Sarah puzzled over the latest pics of Alicia James spread across her work table. The young woman definitely had rising star power.

Maria had shown her several of the girl's erotic videos. She was very adept at her chosen profession. Sarah's mouth went dry as she recalled the images of Alicia intertwined with two other women in a meadow of colorful flowers. While it had taken several scenes before she became comfortable watching her young friend cavorting with naked men and women, she'd finally acknowledged that Alicia genuinely enjoyed her work. The air of innocence, enthusiasm and pure unabated enjoyment she projected could not be taught or coached. It was either there or it wasn't. Any viewer could be forgiven for believing Alicia wanted to step through the TV screen to share her body with him or her.

According to Maria, Alicia now needed a backer to advance farther up the career ladder. That might be a director who was willing to give her a starring role, or a financial backer who was willing to make sure she got that chance.

Sarah picked up a picture of Alicia posing leaning against her desk. She wore a man's white shirt knotted beneath her boobs. While her breasts were covered, there was no mistaking the outlines of large aroused nipples. With one hand on her left hip, Alicia used the other hand to hoist the checkered cheerleader skirt high enough on the other hip to barely show a hint of pussy. Her smile seemed natural, innocent, almost curious, as if she were willing to go further but unsure of the observer's desire. The result was indeed tantalizingly erotic.

Trying to ignore her own pebbling nipples, Sarah wondered if the girl would want to take acting lessons. Did she have the motivation and discipline for study? Would those lessons help her hone her innate acting skills, or would they harm them in some unexpected ways? Alicia James hardly needed lessons on how to perfect her sexual skills. Even Adam agreed Alicia had star potential.

Sarah hated being indecisive. She glanced back at the pictures, studying Alicia's doe-like eyes. They'd attracted her even more than her full breasts and undulating hips.

Sarah scrunched her shoulders, then got up and walked to the couch, where she sat and examined more of the photos displayed on the coffee table. Why was she agonizing so? Why was she even considering getting involved? She'd said nothing specifically to Maria or Adam about her thoughts, though they probably suspected what she was thinking about.

Was Alicia the daughter she never had? Sarah

hugged herself. If she was about to go out and find a daughter, why did it have to be a porn starlet? "Why not," she muttered aloud.

She hadn't dared breathe a word of her musings to the girl. There was no need to get her hopes up and then have them dashed by something not yet considered. It wasn't the money. She could easily afford bankrolling Alicia's career. If she did, though, she'd expect a percentage return on her investment. This was strictly a business deal she was evaluating.

Well, okay, not exactly. She *was* emotionally tied to Alicia. It wasn't sexual, but it was emotional—and that could be much more dangerous.

So was it normal for her to consider becoming a patron of the arts—of an adult film star? She'd supported the arts when she lived in Chicago. But no one, not even she, had questioned the propriety of that support.

Eyebrows would go up questioning her involvement with Alicia James. Many wouldn't think of the porn industry as an art form worthy of patronage. Detractors would question its entertainment, moral, or educational value. There would be those who'd naturally assume she and Alicia were lovers. Daniel would, if he ever found out. But did any of that matter?

She knew better. She'd come to know and respect a number of the women who'd approached her for help with their portfolios. Like her, they had goals, laughed and cried, and wanted happiness. Some were wives. Some were mothers. Some saw themselves contributing to causes larger than themselves—sexual freedom, women's rights, sexual education. She wasn't naïve. She was aware of the underbelly of the industry—of too many drugs, too much intimidation, of too little attention to the health of the performers. Plus there was always the issue of equitable pay. Those were issues that challenged many industries and professions, yet the pervading view held that participating in the erotic industry was not normal—and now that would include her, if she decided to underwrite Alicia's career.

Sarah laughed softly. There was very little about her current lifestyle that smacked of stereotypical mid-western normalcy. She'd been back in California for four weeks and something resembling a routine had set in.

Adam was turning into the kind of compassionate lover she'd always believed him to be. He could be quite demanding in bed, but then she'd discovered somewhat to her surprise that she could, too. The three of them played at finding innovative ways to express themselves sexually. She smiled. Adam remained much more expressive with his fingers, tongue and cock than with words.

Without establishing anything resembling a schedule, they had made time and space for each other. They were together as couples and as a threesome. Sometimes the third party watched, sometimes not. There were no rules and thankfully there seemed to be no need for rules on how to divvy themselves up.

They'd become comfortable as a sexual threesome, for which she was grateful. But they had not yet achieved an emotional equilibrium. She and Maria outdistanced Adam on that score.

He still hadn't spent an entire night with them. That emotional rampart proved more than he could apparently surmount.

Yet, she was surprisingly quite satisfied. She'd adjusted. She probably couldn't have stayed in a relationship with Adam without the presence of the effervescent Maria. Her Latin lover supplied her the emotional fervor and nurturing that Adam at least thus far seemed unable or unwilling to share.

Would Adam come around? She hoped so—she and Maria were counting on it. Right now they were giving him time, but there was Maria's biological clock. At some point they'd have to come to terms with it.

She placed Alicia's pictures back in the folder she'd established for her. There was nothing stopping her from trying her wings as an arts patron for the adult film world. She'd request a formal business meeting with Maria and Adam. That was the first step. She had to know if what she was considering had business merit.

Was she considering a pipedream? Sarah rose to her feet and filed the folder away. Alicia James. Would Alicia even want a patron? If so, would she accept Sarah Atkinson as that patron?

Sitting at Adam's round office table, Sarah chewed on her cheek waiting for Adam and Maria to respond to her idea. Maria had flashed a smile at him when she'd begun to set forth her business plan. Sarah had laid out the whys, the costs and the potential benefits as well a marketing scenario. Marketing was her forte. She'd made hundreds if not thousands of such presentations. So why was she so nervous?

Adam leaned back and scratched his ear. "This isn't a shock, of course. You've been asking a lot of leading questions the last several days. My gut says your plan is quite plausible. I would suggest upping your take from any film Alicia stars in. That'll be significant as she becomes more recognized by the industry and the public and therefore becomes more in demand."

"I appreciate the suggestion." Sarah nodded and smiled. She inhaled deeply. "So I'm not totally crazy. It's not like I need to make a lot of money from this venture, but I don't want Alicia to believe this arrangement is a gift or charity." She turned toward Maria. "What do you think?"

"I expect Alicia has found what she needs in you whether she was looking for it or not." Maria crossed her arms and tilted her head slightly. "But

I wonder if you are at all aware of the stigma you're setting yourself up for? Most people don't think fondly of folks involved with porn. Some of your friends will think you're certifiable no matter how highly they thought of you before. Are you ready to handle the negative fallout?" Maria settled back into her chair. "Of course, you could stay behind the scenes, so to speak. I could front for you."

"No." Sarah shook her head vigorously. "I appreciate what you're saying. But if this is right for me to do, then I don't want to hide. There aren't many people close to me I have to worry about anyway. And maybe even my folks would've approved."

Adam cleared his throat. "What about Daniel?"

"What about Daniel?" she snapped.

"He'll bust a gut if—let me correct that—*when* he finds out his ex-wife is a patron of the adult film world."

"Tough shit!"

"You go, girl." Maria piped, grinning broadly.

"Adam, I have several sizeable certificates of deposit signed over to me as part of our divorce settlement that still identify Daniel as the original owner. If I use those for this venture, would Daniel be at all implicated?"

Adam tried unsuccessfully to hide a grin. "Not legally. But the press would have a field day. You're not really thinking of doing that? He'd probably recover, but he'd have to do some fancy wheeling and dealing."

"That's what I figured. I'm planning to save those funds for a rainier day than this one. But if Daniel wants to give me any crap, the next funds slated for the arts are those with Daniel's signature appended. Not bad, huh?"

"I wouldn't want to cross you if you ever got ripping mad and me."

"Don't you forget that, bad boy of Bumper, Iowa." Sarah flashed him a quick smile. "I've told you before you should've taken me for a ride on your motorcycle. Think what might've happened if you had offered me a single ride." She hollowed her cheeks mimicking a sucking notion, in case he'd forgotten.

He shook his head at her and murmured, "My mistake. Clearly."

She stood and crossed her fingers. "Hopefully, Alicia won't balk at this idea."

"She'd be a fool if she did." Adam returned to his desk.

"Alicia James may be young," Maria added, following Sarah toward the door, "but she's no fool."

The next afternoon, Sarah rose from her work table to greet her visitor. "Come in, Alicia."

"Hi, Ms. Atkinson. Good to see you again." She matter-of-factly unzipped her top and her large full breasts sprang forth with nipples quickly pebbling.

"Whoa, Alicia," Sarah hurried to say. "Zip back up. This isn't about more pictures."

"Oh." Alicia looked confused but tucked her boobs back in.

Sarah breathed again, congratulating herself for resisting the urge to palm those amazing boobs and tease those attention seeking nipples. Why did the girl have to be so damn innocently provocative? How many adults had ever wanted to talk to Alicia with her clothes on? "Why don't we sit at the table? It's small, but it'll work."

"Okay." Alicia sat down, still with a puzzled look on her face. "So what's on your mind if not pictures, Ms. Atkinson?"

Where to begin? How to begin? Why did this girl throw her off kilter so easily? "First," Sarah said, steepling her fingers, "nothing that I have to say should be interpreted as having anything to do with us sexually."

"Okay." Alicia arched an eyebrow. "But what else is there?"

"We've gone over this before, Alicia. Yes, I find you quite attractive. No, I will not now or ever entertain the idea of going to bed with you. Is that clear enough?"

Alicia shrugged. "I'd like to be able to be that clear with some people."

"I'm sure you would. What I have to offer you is a business opportunity that Maria, Adam and I believe can benefit both you and me."

"Okay." Alicia winced and slouched farther

down in the chair. "You're taking a long time to get to the point, Ms. Atkinson."

"I'd like to financially support your career."

Alicia gawked. "You're kidding. In the adult film industry?"

Sarah nodded.

"Wow. How would you do that? You already aren't charging for my pics."

Sarah leaned back and chuckled. "I have much bigger aspirations than that. I watched three of your videos with Maria."

"You did! Wow!" Alicia sat up straighter. "What did you think? Did you like what you saw? Am I good, or what?" The blonde scowled. "And you still don't want to have sex with me?"

"Maria provided a helpful commentary. You are quite good, Alicia. We feel your goal to become an adult film superstar is reachable, if you have the proper sponsorship."

"How would you sponsor me?" Alicia had turned surprisingly serious.

"Marketing is my expertise. We'll package you in ways that play up your genuine innocence and your apparent willingness to try anything sexually."

"I try." Alicia's lips curved into a provocative bow. "I enjoy discovering new ways for getting off."

"Yes, I saw." She glanced away from Alicia's inquisitive stare and took a deep breath. Could her soon-to-be protégé ever be less saucy? "In addition to marketing to directors and potential producers, I am willing to fund up to three movies with my own money. They'd have to be the right kind of movies. We'd rely on Maria to help with script selection. For you to become a star in a few years, you have to do more dialogue—appeal to a wider audience, probably a couples' audience."

"Why couples?"

"It's your apparent innocence that's so appealing, on screen and off. You have a girl-next-door look that appeals to guys, but also to wives and girlfriends. They'll be able to identify with you, if we can find you the right roles. You don't have the look of a hardened sexpot."

Alicia stiffened. "I won't have to settle for wishy washy sex, will I?"

"Hardly," Sarah said chuckling. "We don't want to deprive you. You can be as hot as you want. You can do it all. Deep throat. Take it in the ass. Three-ways. Light S and M—nothing too heavy and dark. By the way, that part is Maria talking, more than me."

"I figured that," she said, nodding. "I trust Maria's judgment. I've seen some of her work. She could give me some pointers. Now wouldn't that be a three-way—the three of us."

Shaking her head, Sarah couldn't help but be impressed with the enthusiasm of youth. "In your dreams. It won't happen. But I trust Maria completely—I'm pleased you trust her. Hopefully, I'll also earn your trust in time."

Alicia remained silent.

"So you'd do much of what you currently are doing. We will simply aim for a slightly classier style and stage presence."

"Can I talk dirty?" Alicia pouted.

"Certainly. Words are a turn on, but trash talk is trash talk, whether in the bedroom or on the ball field. You can tell your partner what is happening for you and to fuck you harder or faster or whatever, but saying *your cock is like a battering ram cramming my cunt* is a bit over the top."

Alicia laughed, and this time, it reached her eyes. "You have done your homework. I didn't write that crap, Ms. Atkinson. That's what I was told to say."

"I know. I know. I just wanted to illustrate the difference in what we have in mind for you. Are you okay with this so far?"

"So why are you doing this?" Alicia responded, ducking her question. "It sounds like you're prepared to shell out a lot of money without any guarantee of return."

"Every investment has its risks." Sarah raised and lowered her shoulders. "I believe investing in your future is worth the risk. I do expect over time to make a nice profit on my investment. This is not a freebee."

"And you want some say in the roles I accept and so on?"

"Yes."

Alicia crossed her arms and narrowed her eyes

giving what Sarah expected was the classic petulant teenage glare. "But you won't get into my personal life?"

"I'll try not to, unless you put my investment at risk." She frowned, suddenly aware of her own oversight. "You don't do drugs, do you?"

Alicia's eyes snapped. "You should've asked that question earlier. But I don't. And I'm not an alcoholic. I try to go to church twice a month."

Sarah coughed. She wasn't sure she needed to know that.

"Going to church regularly was a promise I made to my grandmother on her death bed. Not that grandma would necessarily agree with the theology of the church I belong to."

Sarah scribbled on the notepad at her place. "No shoots on Sundays."

Alicia grinned. "I only go twice a month; I can usually shoot around that."

"Of course. There is one other thing, Alicia. I want you to take acting lessons. I'll pay for them."

"Really? You want me to go to a regular acting class."

"Yes. That doesn't bother you?"

"Not at all," she replied, pushing back a lock of blond hair from her forehead. "I know a number of girls who take drama classes; I've never been able to afford them, but I've listened to what my friends have to say."

"Good. I believe you have natural acting talent, but it can be improved. You are very skilled at expressing a vast array of emotion. That's apparent in the pictures we've done in the photo lab as well as in some of your erotic work. Classes should help you build on that talent."

"This sounds fantastic." Alicia broke into a wide grin. "Bigger than any dream I've allowed myself to dream. So what percentage of my take do you want?"

"Excellent question, Alicia. Adam would be proud of you. I'm not sure. I certainly don't want to rob you, but I do want a fair share. We can talk more with Adam and a lawyer or two he might recommend. I imagine arrangements will differ depending on whether I'm backing you to obtain a part in a film or whether I'm funding the film. You don't have to agree to anything until we work out the details. Right now, I'm trying to find out if this strange idea of mine has appeal to you to you and whether you even want to work with me."

"Like I said..." Alicia bobbed her head up and down.

Sarah smiled as the girl's breasts followed suit.

"It's beyond my wildest dreams. And I think I'd enjoy working with you."

"That was a non-sexual statement, correct?"

Alicia didn't miss a beat. "Absolutely."

"You're not going to try to get into my panties?"

Alicia's grin split her face. "You don't wear panties, Ms. Atkinson."

Sarah felt her cheeks burn. "How do you know

that?"

Alicia made a face that showed she questioned Sarah's brainpower. "I've worked with you for at least a couple hours—more than that, actually. You flutter all about while you work. Believe me. You don't wear panties."

"But," she protested, "I wear long dresses when I shoot."

Alicia shrugged her shoulders. "You're not nearly as straight-laced as you'd like us girls to believe. We know about your relationship with Maria and Adam."

"But..."

"We're not stupid, Sarah. You're getting laid almost as much as we are. Each time I've come in here you've looked like a well-fucked woman. I hope when I'm your age I can look the same way."

"My age aside," Sarah stammered, "I think maybe we're done for the day." She began gathering her items from the table.

"No, not quite," Alicia said. "Our panty dialogue got us a bit off track. Even though I'd love to, and you present such a lovely challenge, I won't try to get into your pussy."

"Good. Thank God for that small favor."

Alicia raised her hand to silence her. "I wasn't finished. I won't seduce you, and I'm not at all convinced I couldn't succeed if I really, really tried...but I won't, if you don't get too hung up on being my mother."

Sarah slumped back into her chair with the

wind knocked out of her. Had she been flushed out of her hole? She hadn't really wanted to admit even to herself that her motherly instincts might play a significant role in her desire to help Alicia. "You're a very smart girl," she muttered at last, nodding her agreement. "I think between the two of us we've named the pitfalls in our future business partnership. You won't be my lover and I won't be your mother. Though I would like for us to be friends as well as business associates."

"Business associates," Alicia replied, looking smug. "I never thought those words would be used to describe me. So can I hug you—not as lover or mother, but as friend and business associate?"

"I believe that's allowable, as long as your hands don't rove too much," Sarah consented, folding the girl into her arms for a discreet hug.

Two days later, Sarah happily accepted congratulations from her friends and lifted her glass in a toast. "To Alicia," she said, nodding at her new official protégé. "May she dream big and realize those dreams."

Sarah beamed at the others. "May this be a fun as well as a profitable venture. We're launched," she announced, after signing the final document.

Everyone applauded—Adam, Maria, Alicia and Alicia's friend, Amanda. The thin redhead had been introduced as Alicia's friend and lover. Clearly it was important to Alicia for Sarah to know she had a stable relationship outside the industry.

The two young women looked extremely happy with each other. How did they manage Alicia's chosen profession? *Don't even go there,* Sarah cautioned herself. They seemed to be doing fine, and Sarah wasn't her mother, though it had pleased her to learn Alicia was in a caring relationship.

"I've made a special treat to celebrate this occasion," Maria said, uncovering a cake. Nestled in its top layer sat a tasteful partially nude statuette resembling Alicia. "I have a friend who is a magician with clay," Maria explained.

"It's beautiful," Alicia screeched. "It's almost too good to eat. Oops." She flinched and ducked. "Wrong thing to say. I just signed a contract that pays me a lot of money to eat." She tucked her arm around Amanda. "But the best is free."

Sarah saw the sheen of elation on the two young women and suddenly felt old. Had she ever looked that carefree and happy? No matter. It was a good day, young or old. It was a day filled with promise and dreams.

She looked over at Adam, who scrutinized her closely. Now what was he thinking? Was he remembering when they were that young? Or was he plotting his next assault on her body?

Her skin tingled under his steady gaze. Her physical response clearly indicated she wasn't too old yet. She stuffed a piece of cake in her mouth and chewed thoroughly, amused that Adam's color darkened before he glanced away from her challenge. How soon could she send Alicia and her lover off on their own so she and her lovers could play?

Her antics must not have gone unnoticed. Alicia winked at her. "Thanks for all you're doing for me, Sarah. I'll do the best I can for you."

"I know you will."

"Come along, Amanda," Alicia said, grabbing her friend by the hand. "Let's leave before we have to witness an orgy too hot for our innocent young eyes. Bye," she said to everyone, "Enjoy yourselves." She arched an eyebrow at Sarah. "Don't do anything I wouldn't do."

- o -

"You're quite adept at eating, too, Sarah. Even though, unlike your business partner, you're not being paid to nibble pussy." Adam watched Sarah sliding her tongue along the outer folds of Maria's vulva. Lying on her back, Maria had her legs draped over Sarah's shoulders. "You look fantastic, actually. I always enjoy watching you munch on Maria — and vice versa, of course."

Peeking over Maria's abdomen, Sarah winked at him without dragging her lips away from the dark pussy. Silently, Maria clasped and unclasped her thighs, encouraging her lover's exploration.

Kneeling at Maria's side, Adam smiled

268

indulgently down at her. The reason she couldn't cry out her demands to Sarah as usual was because she'd stuffed her mouth with his cock. He brushed his fingers through her curly hair while her hands and mouth glided over his shaft, working their magic.

With hollowed cheeks, Maria peeked up at him, her eyes rounding in delight. She clearly loved this. He knew she loved how the three of them seemed so compatible, so in sync. Hell, *he* loved it. He looked at Sarah with her tongue and fingers slipping in and out of Maria's pussy. Thankfully, she loved it, too.

Why had it taken him so long to realize they each shared a voracious appetite for sex? Sarah was as eager and innovative as Maria. More than once they'd managed to push him beyond his comfort zone.

Maria arched her lean torso into Sarah, seeking her first orgasm of the evening. Adam withdrew from her mouth, allowing her to concentrate solely on her own needs. He shifted slightly down the bed on his knees until he could easily reach Maria's clit with one hand and stroke Sarah's backside with the other.

He saw Sarah's smile reach her eyes as he joined her in bringing Maria to a crescendo, but she didn't give up her purchase or slow her pace. Her finger and tongue had become a driving force the bouncing Maria could hardly keep up with. Stroking Maria's clit between two fingers, Adam kneaded Sarah's butt cheek. His cock banged freely against her shoulder.

"Jesus, guys. Whatever you do don't stop. I'm..." Maria's eyes rolled until he could see their whites. She slapped his fingers away from her clit. Sarah covered Maria's pussy with her mouth. He could see her throat muscles working, gulping repeatedly.

Maria slung an arm across her forehead. Her legs fell to the mattress. Her ragged breathing eventually steadied. "Sweet," Maria whispered. "So sweet. Let me catch my breath."

Sarah gave Maria's pussy one last kiss before rising to kneel beside Adam. She turned his chin and slanted her lips across his. He tasted and smelled Maria's familiar essence.

"I've got an idea of how to spend our time while we wait for Maria," Sarah said, running her fingernails up the inside of his thigh.

"Tell me," Adam replied. "No—better yet, show me."

"Lie on your back. I want you vibrating in my mouth."

"Ah. How do you plan to manage that?"

Sarah pulled a vibrator and some lube from under a pillow. On her knees beside him, she winked and made a show of spreading lube over the dark vibrator. "But that does mean this little gal has to slip in your ass. Are you up for that?"

Adam grabbed his weaving cock. "It appears so."

"Excellent. Raise up your knees. I need to see what I'm doing."

Sarah's soft hands massaged his butt cheeks. She rimmed his anus with lube and then slid a finger in while simultaneously licking the tip of his cock. Adam sighed, very pleased he wasn't blindfolded. He clutched her head between his hands. He watched his cock disappear slowly into her mouth and felt the vibrator replace her finger. His ass expanded, accepting the foreign object.

She took him all the way down her throat. He took in the vibrator as far as it would go. She raised her head. "How is that for you?"

"Perfect," he said, licking his lips. "You're perfect."

"I'm going to turn the vibrator on."

He nodded. "Do it."

He felt the rapid tingling before he heard the hum. She smiled at him and worked the vibrator slowly back and forth. "Looks like that's good for you."

He nodded. "Don't forget..." He peered at his cock.

"Him? No way would I forget him. I wanted to feel him vibrating in my mouth. Remember?"

Again, her mouth slithered down his cock. He felt it humming against the inside of her cheek. Slowly she worked her hand and mouth up and down his cock while rotating the vibrator in his ass.

Adam closed his eyes but immediately opened

them. He had to return her passion, her love. He reached out and massaged her buttocks.

"Um," she said around his cock, then twisted her body, giving him easier access.

He knew better than to disappoint. He easily worked two fingers inside her pussy. She began backing farther onto his fingers on her upstroke and pulled nearly out on her downstroke. Adam grinned. This was one inventive lady. She seldom missed an opportunity for improvisation. Maybe the three of them should teach a class on improv and sex.

Adam peered down as Sarah hollowed her cheeks, increasing her suction. She wasn't going to back off. He didn't want her to. His fingers in her pussy stilled as his climax began overtaking him. Was that where it began? In her pussy. Or was it his ass. Or her mouth. He couldn't tell. It didn't matter.

"Son of a bitch," Adam yelped. His body jerked of its own accord. Vaguely, he heard Maria cheering beside them. Sarah's movements blurred before his eyes. "You got me," he bellowed. "Take as much as you want."

His hips convulsed, driving his cock and pacing his spurts. Sarah never backed away. She sucked him until he was dry. She held him in her mouth until he went limp. He never knew when she removed the vibrator.

"Wow!" Maria said, stroking Sarah's neck. "That was beyond huge. Let him be, Sarah. He's done. Maybe for the night."

Sarah raised her head, grinned and wiped her mouth against the back of her hand, pleased with her efforts. "He may be, at that," she said, examining his flaccid cock. "I'm happy to be a woman." She arched an eyebrow at Maria. "Faster recovery time."

"Was that a request? You haven't come have, you?"

"Not enough."

"Is that possible?"

"Hope not. Did you have something in mind?"

"Uh, huh." Sarah tingled at the sparkle in Maria's eyes. "You gave me an idea for a variation on a theme."

Within moments, Sarah lay on her back with a very familiar pussy hovering over her mouth. The variation was occurring at the other end and Maria was giving her a play by play account of her plan.

"I'm going to tuck this pink vibrator in your ass for safekeeping."

Sarah arched her neck, prepared to accept the vibrator poised at her entrance. Maria pushed it in slowly and stopped, allowing her to adjust to the welcomed intrusion. Shortly Maria again tested Sarah's opening and eased the vibrator in to its hilt. "How's that?"

"Spectacular," Sarah gasped. "Turn it on. Oh, yeah. And people think they need a drug to get a buzz?"

"You're going to be ringing before I'm done with you." Maria pressed her lips into Sarah's wet slit. "You always smell so good. Now I'm going to turn this vibrator on and watch your pussy opening up for it."

Sarah smiled as the head of the second humming vibrator furrowed her folds.

"Wow! Is she opening!" Maria laughed. "Not to disappoint. Here you go, pussy. Is this what you want?"

Sarah reveled in the tingling sensations as the vibrator eased farther in. She knew when it bumped into the vibrator in her ass. She squeezed her legs and then widened them. She gulped. There was no escape from the steady vibrations. Her entire loins quivered. She tried to lift her head to lick Maria.

"Don't bother," Maria chided. "Enjoy your trip."

When Maria sipped her clit, she had a sudden rush stronger than most. She tried not to buck her hips, not wanting to dislodge anything or anyone. She lay still, letting the rush build. She threw her head about. Tears formed behind her closed eyelids. She wrapped her arms tightly around Maria's ass and held on as if her life depended on it for security. The rush might have started in her

274

loins, but it ended in her ears. They were indeed ringing.

Her hips began undulating. She began to break up. She crashed. "No more," she moaned. "Please."

Obligingly, Maria gently removed the vibrators before swinging back around to sip at Sarah's flow. Maria's mouth and tongue were gentle and soothing. Tears spilled down Sarah's cheeks. She felt so loved, so cared for.

She turned her head to peek at Adam through her wet eyelashes. His face was filled with adoration, pain and unspoken love. She didn't apologize for her tears. He took her into his arms and cradled her upper torso while Maria cradled her lower body.

She sobbed. Could life get any better?

Chapter Twelve

Drying nude on the chaise lounge after a swim, Maria studied her lover dozing on the lounge beside hers. Sarah was still recovering from their evening of lovemaking with Adam. Maria closed her eyes and let the memories wash over her.

She no longer questioned how Sarah had become so important to her so quickly. That had simply happened. She was like quality air. She was a fresh drink in an arid desert. She mattered a hell of a lot.

Maria smoothed the skin of her tight belly. Things were completely right with Sarah. But what was going on with Adam? She'd have to find out fairly soon. She hated not knowing where she stood with him. Was he jealous? He seemed satisfied enough with their current arrangement. Why shouldn't he be — he was fucking two women who demanded very little from him, other than his cock.

That was about to change. She stretched her arms above her head and lowered them, crossing them beneath her bosom. She wasn't going to settle for fantastic sex. She wanted commitment beyond swearing off other partners. Marriage wasn't what it was about, either. She wanted Adam to agree to father her child and to commit to being that child's father for the long haul. She smiled to herself. The child would have two mothers, but it would only need one father.

What would Adam say about her desire? He'd freak. That's what he'd do. Could she—could she and Sarah—keep him from running so far they wouldn't be able to find him?

"Why so depressed, Maria?" Sarah asked in hushed tones. Yawing, she added, "After last night, I'd think you'd still be spinning."

Maria turned to rest on an elbow. "I am. Last night was so wonderful I want more—more nights like that, and more for us and for Adam. I want us to own the fact that we're becoming a family. I want us to be a real family."

"I understand," Sarah said softly. "A child."

Maria nodded, trying not to cry. "Yes. Wouldn't you like to mother a child? Alicia is not going to fill that need entirely."

"I know. Alicia doesn't want me to mother her." Sarah grinned. "You're right. You'll be a fantastic mother. We'd be very nurturing mothers, I think. But what about Adam? I doubt he sees himself as father material."

"He'd make a great father. He'd stand by the child come whatever. We might have to fight him for time with the kid."

"You're probably right about that—once the child is a reality. But I'm not convinced he's going to easily accept the idea of having a child."

"Convincing him may be dicey, but I have to

try. I want this baby, Sarah, and I can't wait very much longer. I don't want to be rocking in my rocker at the old folks home before the kid graduates from college."

Sarah's laughter reverberated off the patio tiles. "You are a hoot, Maria. I can't imagine you rocking in a rocker—unless you're riding a cock, real or fake."

Maria batted her eyelashes. "Tuck that thought away for the future. We should try that. So," she hesitated. "I need to know where we stand, girl. If I push Adam too hard, too fast, he may flee like a madman. Are you staying with me, if he does?"

Leaning across the small space separating them, Sarah slanted an index finger across Maria's lips. "Hush. You know I will. I thought that was clear when we left Chicago."

"Some people change their minds."

"I'm not some people, Maria. I love you with all my heart and soul. And yes, I'm prepared to love Adam in the same way. But you return my love. Adam doesn't, or at least he hasn't acknowledged he does. So if he's adamant and boots us out, so be it. Maybe we can find you a surrogate."

Maria fought a sudden lump in her throat and heaved a sigh of relief. "Thank you for having patience with me. I needed to hear that. I love you so much I almost can't stand it." She wrapped her arms around her mid-section. "Surrogate? I wonder what Adam would think of that. He wouldn't have to be the actual father."

"Oh, now you're playing a nasty game, if you're seriously thinking of tempting him with the notion of taking on a surrogate to get pregnant. He'll be furious." Sarah sat up and pursed her lips thoughtfully. "Dangling the idea of a surrogate before him would be like playing with fire, but it might just pry him loose. He *is* too complacent with our current relationship. Your willingness to take on a surrogate without changing our relationship with Adam ought to either get him to commit or really send him over the top."

Maria could see her own fear reflected in Sarah's eyes. Did she really have the guts to push Adam that hard? If not, when would she ever have a child?

"Do you want me with you when you talk with him?"

She shook her head. "No. I don't want him to think we're ganging up on him. He probably thinks that too much already. He'll know we've talked. He'll know what the stakes are. The question is how to approach him."

"After making love?"

"Probably," she responded quietly. "He won't be as tense then."

"I'd be happy to plead for a night off. I'm not sure I'll be refueled by this evening anyway. But are you ready to take him on, or do you want to think longer on it?"

Maria pushed herself to a sitting position. "No, I'm ready. Putting it off is only going to make me more uptight, which won't help at all when I do confront him."

- o -

"Too bad Sarah can't join us this evening," Maria murmured. Curled on Adam's lap on the living room couch, Maria nibbled his chin and snuggled closer. She kissed his neck and rested her head on his shoulder. His arousal curved under her buttocks, announcing its desire. Her heart fluttered, and it wasn't only from anticipating the sex they'd have.

She'd planned the evening step by step, beginning with her wardrobe. She'd worn one of his favorite outfits—a buttoned white blouse knotted above the navel and a short black mini.

"It is." Adam kissed her and inhaled deeply. "You always smell so intoxicating." He hugged her tight. "Maybe we took Sarah too far last night?

"Hardly." Maria chuckled. "She's just tired. Do you still believe it's possible to take your teenage vision of love too far?"

Adam kissed her eyelids. She lowered them, accepting his tenderness. Maybe everything would be okay. Maybe he was coming around to their idea of a committed relationship.

"I've wondered about that," he said. "She does seem to be eager to try anything." His tongue traced the length of her nose. "But she still wants to take control too much."

"Isn't that part of what makes it exciting?" She leaned back against his arms. "Enough about Sarah. I guess you'll just have to make do with me. I hope that doesn't disappoint you too much." She gave him her best pout and was rewarded with an immediate grin.

"We'll make do. Sort of like old times. Did you have something special in mind?"

Maria shook her head. *Not until after lovemaking.*

Adam reached for her shirt knot. "You look more ready than ever, Maria. I can see your nipples begging to be uncovered. They look even darker behind white fabric. We don't want to disappoint them, do we?"

She shook her head and wet her lips. The knot easily gave way. He unfastened the first button and slipped a hand inside to fondle a breast. She tensed, then sighed.

"They are so eager." He peered into her eyes. "So does that mean you're wet below?"

She nodded.

"Thought so. But first things first, right?"

Again, she nodded.

He undid the last two buttons and freed her breasts. "Leave your blouse on," he said. "Let me play with these as they are."

"Be my guest." Her husky voice surprised even her.

Adam needed no additional encouragement. His lips brushed against an aching nipple. She arched back, thrusting the breast closer. He complied with her request by taking it into his mouth. He teased it and then pulled nearly all of it into his mouth. She gasped. He wasn't done. He came back for more. God, had he taken her entire breast? She clutched his neck and dragged her fingernails across his back.

"Good God, Adam, I'm coming. Don't move, please." She shuddered and fell against his chest. When she quieted, he slid off her breast and smiled. "You okay?" He tapped the nipple with his tongue.

"No more, please. It's very tender now. I'm sorry."

"That's okay. How about the other one?"

"You can say hi to it, but don't try to deep throat it. Once was spectacular. I'm not sure I can stand twice."

"No problem. Let me be sure it doesn't feel neglected." He laved the underside of the other breast. He lifted her easily off him and set her back on the couch. He knelt on the floor before her and spread her knees, opening her to him.

Was she his offering? Was he her supplicant? Maybe for the moment, but what about later? She tried not to think about that now.

His tongue found her belly button. He circled it repeatedly.

She glowed, filled with his adoration. Did he have any idea how loved he made her feel?

He didn't bother removing her skirt. He merely flipped it up over her waist and draped her legs over his shoulders. His tongue fluttered along one inner thigh and then the other. She clasped her hands around the back of his head, guiding him to her most sensitive spots.

"You're the eager one, tonight." He flicked his tongue along the edges of her pussy. She flexed her buttocks. "Where's your patience?"

She darted a finger in each of his ears.

"Goddamn woman," he complained. He complied by placing his tongue at the bottom of her slit and used it to part her labia as he worked his way upward.

"Yes, Adam. Eat me. Do it. I'm so open for you." He tapped her bud tenderly. She bucked and gasped. Two of his fingers plunged into her interior and he sipped her clit between his lips. He was driving her insane, and she loved it. "That's it, Adam. I'm coming for you."

He placed a hand under each of her butt cheeks, lifted her and tenderly drank from her. She quivered against his lips. When finished, he gingerly set her back down on the couch and looked up at her with a gleam in his eye. He licked his lips. "Succulent," he said. "Like that first taste of buttered lobster you once mentioned."

She grinned—it seemed so long ago that she'd described Sarah that way.

"You are both tasty morsels," he added.

"I'm glad," she said, holding her hands out to him. He pulled her to a sitting position and slanted his lips over hers. She tasted herself clinging to him. The kiss took whatever breath she still had. She lay back against the cushions and gave him a half-grin.

"You look so beautiful lying there open to me. Where do you want me? In your pussy or your ass?"

"You're asking?"

"Is that such a surprise?"

"It's not usual."

"Well, I'm asking. Pussy or ass?"

"That's a hard one." Maria leaned forward to encircle his shaft. "No, this is the hard one." She batted an eye at Adam. "I'd like you in both at once, but since that's not possible, I think my pussy."

"Since that's not possible," Adam placed the thick head of his penis at her entrance, "this will have to do."

She lifted her thighs and clutched them to her torso. Her private space expanded to accommodate him until he was fully seated. She clung to his ass with her heels and held on as if he were the holy grail.

"Damn, you're hotter than hot," he grunted, sinking deeper.

"And you're still expanding. I can feel you getting bigger and bigger," she murmured. "How is that possible?"

"I must like the heat."

"Adam?"

"Um."

"Maybe you better fuck me before I do you permanent damage. I wouldn't want to scald you."

"You are the playful minx tonight. I wouldn't want to disappoint you." He moved easily in and out of her.

She opened even more, welcoming his deeper penetration.

He stopped. Her eyes widened. "That was just a test drive," he said. "Put your arms around my neck."

He stood, lifting her, cradling her butt in his hands. He braced his legs and began easing her back and forth along his cock. Her nails dug into his back. She clung onto him, hoping he'd never stop. Gradually, he picked up speed. She was coming apart. Could he hold onto all the pieces?

"Oh wow, Adam! This is so good. So smooth. I'm suspended in air. Your cock is my focal point."

"Don't ever forget that." Adam's voice was strained. Was that the result of physical exertion or emotion?

"Never ever stop." She contracted her inner muscles tightly around him.

He grimaced. "We're going to be done sooner than you want if you do that."

"It's okay. I'm ready. Fill me with your seed, Adam." She bit down hard on his shoulder and clamped him in her vise. He churned into her, bouncing her around like a rag doll. She squeezed harder. Together they milked him of his substance. She had no trouble imaging his seed splashing against the walls of her vagina. Gradually, they ceased pounding each other. He held her comfortably in his arms. She couldn't hold back the tears. What a waste — all that sperm and nowhere to go.

Her eyes sprang wide. She could simply stop taking the pill. She hugged Adam tighter. She wasn't going to trap any man that way.

Too soon he lifted her off his cock and set her back down on the couch. Breathing raggedly, he plopped down beside her and draped an arm around her shoulders. Her skirt tumbled, hiding her well-loved pussy. Her breasts stood tall and free as reminders of the ecstasy they'd just shared.

How much more of himself would Adam share? This was her moment. She imagined Sarah lying in bed upstairs wondering and waiting to find out what Adam would do.

"Adam," she whispered, once his breathing had returned to normal.

"Yes."

"How do you feel it's going with the three of us — you, Sarah and me?" Her heart skipped several beats.

"Fine. Couldn't be much better, I imagine. We all seem quite compatible in bed and," he chuckled, "at least tolerable out of bed." He turned to face her. "Why, is there something wrong? Is Sarah unhappy? Or you?"

"No. Nothing's wrong. Not really."

"You don't sound convinced. What's up, babe? We've been together too long not to talk to one another."

Her throat went dry. "Unless the talk has to do with feelings."

Adam scowled. "That was below the belt." He crossed his arms. "So I'm the problem, then?"

Maria shrugged her shoulders. "I love you, Adam."

His eyebrows shot up.

"I know that's not a word you want to hear."

"You know I don't believe in it," he huffed. "Love is bullshit."

"And I love Sarah," Maria continued, ignoring his comment. "And she loves both of us."

"She said that!" The look of incredulity on his face crushed her. Didn't he have a clue about Sarah's feelings for him — or hers?

"She loves what we can become."

"And what's that?" he grunted.

"A family."

"What the hell!" Adam leapt to his feet and glowered at her. "Now what cockeyed fantasies are you foisting on her — and on me?"

"I want us to have a baby." She shrank from his darkening glare. "You know I do, Adam. It's just that you won't talk about it"

"I'm no father. Don't want to be. Couldn't be if I wanted to." His eyes grew large. "Sarah buys into this?"

Maria nodded, afraid to say anything that

might cause him to erupt.

"Figures. She couldn't have kids. But I thought Alicia would fill that need," he muttered.

Was he even talking to her anymore? He'd already fled emotionally into his own little safe world.

"Not me, Maria." His sneer made her stomach churn. "You knew that before even bringing it up. Was that why you were so hot for me tonight? And Sarah—I bet she's upstairs bringing herself off with a vibrator. Worn out! Bullshit! I doubt that woman could ever get enough sex."

Adam turned reddish purple. She'd never seen him this livid—ever. She clenched her teeth, steeling herself before speaking. "We want to be a family. We love you, Adam. Why can't you accept that?"

"Because you want me to say the same thing, and I can't." He shrugged and held himself rigid. "So that's that. Now what are you going to do?"

She hesitated to play her trump card, but what was there to lose? "We did speak of a surrogate."

"A surrogate?" His eyes narrowed. "You mean some other guy is going to fuck you to get you pregnant?"

The rage and disbelief in his voice brought tears to her eyes.

"And the resulting kid? You're expecting to raise the bastard in my house?"

"Bastard?" Maria leapt to her feet, her blood beyond the boiling point. She hadn't been this enraged in years and damn it, in the moment it felt good. "No child of mine will be a bastard. If you don't want us, so be it — that's your choice. We will start our family somewhere else. But Adam," she raised her fist in the air, "with or without you, Sarah and I will make a family. We would like you to be the father — not only the biological father, but the nurturing, loving father."

Adam stretched to his full height. "If that's what you're looking for, then you'd better start searching elsewhere. But there isn't going to be any fucking surrogate or offspring of a surrogate in my house."

Spinning on his foot, he stalked from the room.

Maria called out his name as his steps echoed down the hallway and the door to his office slammed shut.

- o -

Sarah blanched at the sight of her disheveled lover entering the bedroom. Maria didn't bother buttoning her shirt or taking off her skirt. She pulled down the sheet and clambered into Sarah's outstretched arms.

"I take it Adam wasn't too smitten with the idea of becoming a father," Sarah comforted, rubbing Maria's back.

Maria shook her tearstained face. "He won't even talk about it," she sobbed. "And he really blew up when I mentioned the possibility of a surrogate."

"That may be positive," she murmured. "I'm sure he despises the image that conjures up. So that means he still cares."

"But he said he wants me to search elsewhere for a father. He's willing for us to move out, if that's what we want."

"We'll see." She tried to soothe her lover with words. "Don't give up on Adam yet. He is pig-headed. His brain is as thick as a rock, but he does have a decent heart. Let's not do anything too quickly. Give him time to cool down and maybe we can play this out a little more."

Maria sobbed and nodded her head.

"Is there anything else I can do for you, Maria?"

"Just hold me."

"I will. You can count on that. I won't leave you." She kissed the top of Maria's brow. What would Adam do? It sounded like all the chips were on the table. Maybe she should go and talk with him. But she wasn't about to rush downstairs. She'd take her own advice and let him cool off. She hoped that was possible.

- o -

"A baby," Adam shouted to his office walls. What in the world had gotten into his women? He paced back and forth in front of his desk.

A baby. Him, a father! Even looking at him through rose colored lenses wouldn't lead anyone to believe he'd be a good father. Hell, he'd never had one himself. Maria and Sarah had gone beyond reason this time.

A surrogate! Son of a bitch! If he was going to be saddled with living with some damn kid, it sure wasn't going to be some other guy's kid.

Shit! Why did they have to go and wreck a good thing?

The three of them had shared some fantastic sex. He'd even begun to wonder if maybe he should sleep with the women. That might make things easier. They'd be there in the morning for him as well as at night. He was missing some fine loving by not waking with them. But now! What the hell!

They'd screwed things up royally, and he couldn't see a way out. The only thing he could do was show them the door.

Damn, he hated even thinking about having to replace them. He grabbed his keys and headed out of the office toward the entryway. Sometimes he did his best thinking while driving. He slammed the door behind him and pushed the remote button to the car.

He stopped short in his tracks. Why the hell was he leaving? It was supposed to be the women leaving. He shook his head and climbed into the car. How could he figure the women out if he couldn't even figure himself out?

Adam sped down Highway Five toward San

Diego. Not that he was headed there. He was headed nowhere. If the ocean was calm or if it raged, he didn't notice. It didn't matter.

His body raged on and surprisingly in rare moments it calmed, as if stopping to examine a newly found pearl.

He'd actually begun to believe their lives were settling into a workable pattern. There'd been plenty of sex to go around. None of them had compunctions about the other two going off at any time of the day or night to make love.

Love! Shit! When had sex become love? That thought was only a slip. Wasn't it?

He banged a fist against the steering wheel and slowed to the speed limit. What would life be like without them?

The solution had seemed so simple when he'd stormed out of the house. Kick the damn women out on their cute asses. There were hordes of women more than willing to fill their places—some with even cuter asses.

But could any other woman really take the place of Maria or Sarah?

Adam took the next exit, drove back over the overpass and headed north toward Pacific Palisades. Ragged breaths escaped his lips. He tried not to imagine what the women were doing now. Were they already packing their bags? They had to work it out. He knew that. But how?

He couldn't be a damn father. He didn't know the first thing about being a good father. But a surrogate! Over his very dead body!

He fumed and then his rage subsided some. Were they serious about a surrogate? Surely they knew he wouldn't stand for that.

Trapped! They'd laid their trap well. He smiled grimly. But he wasn't entirely netted. How many trout had that thought before succumbing to the skills of the fisherman?

But what if? He'd prided himself on advising clients to play the *what if* game with their investments. Could they weather a sharp downturn in the market? What if the housing market bubble burst? So what if—big *if*—he agreed to the women's scheme?

Which one would he marry? He had to marry one of them. Wouldn't it have to be Maria? No son of his would be a bastard.

Jesus. When had the hypothetical child become a son? His heart clinched.

Marriage. Fatherhood. He ground his teeth and shook his head. What was the alternative? Back to the meat market of a different woman every night? Life without Maria's laughter or Sarah's challenging smile?

Sex without feeling something deeper? God, he hated those feelings. Damn, had he already become addicted to them?

Running the back of his hand across his mouth, Adam knew he had a choice. Just like the women, he had a choice. Which one would make him the greater fool—booting the women out, or accepting their offer? They were certainly determined to go after the whole enchilada — commitment, marriage...a kid.

Was there an honorable way out that kept them together without taking such drastic steps?

Adam pulled into his Pacific Palisades driveway and took note of an unusually splendid sunrise. Many mornings, smog prevented seeing anything resembling the sun until noon.

He got out of the car and walked toward his house. He was calmer than when he'd left. His options were clearer. But his choice remained elusive.

Maybe the women had backed down by now. At least he could hope.

Chapter Thirteen

Haggard. Sarah had never seen Adam so haggard. He looked nearly as wrung out as Maria had. Sarah had been worried and wasn't surprised in the morning to see his car still missing from the driveway. She and Maria had been up for a couple hours before they heard his car pull in. Maria escaped to the deck before Adam entered the house.

Sarah grimaced. Now the lost was found. Adam's eyes drooped. His unkempt hair looked like his fingers had been raking it wildly. He sagged against the kitchen door jamb, seemingly lost in his own home. He probably hadn't slept at all since Maria's confrontation.

Sarah grabbed another cup and quickly filled it to the rim with coffee. "This may help a little," she said, handing him the cup.

He nodded, accepting her offering without speaking. She watched his Adam's apple rise and fall as he swallowed deeply. "Heavenly."

"You need a shower and some rest, Adam. Looks like you've had a rough night."

"You could say that. It's not every night a guy is served up an ultimatum by his women."

A jolt of hope shot through her. Had she heard correctly? So they were still *his women*. Maybe all was not yet lost. "An ultimatum might be a little strong — at least for the near future."

"But in the long run?" His glare hardened.

She shrugged. She wouldn't lie to him or string him along. "Maria wants a child. We want a child. We want to have your child."

His shoulders sagged. "So I heard."

She didn't flinch from his glower.

"You know I can't be a father, Sarah. You saw me as a kid, as a teenager. I wouldn't know the first thing about being a father."

"You have good instincts," she countered, brushing the back of her hand against his unshaven cheek. "So your mother had to be both mother and father. Get over it. You weren't the first kid not to have a father in his life, and you won't be the last. Most of those kids have gone on to be more than adequate fathers. So what's really holding you back?" A sudden awareness flooded her. "Are you afraid of failing as a father, Adam?"

He turned his back to her.

"Adam, I haven't been a parent so I can't speak from experience, but I've seen lots of families. It seems to me parents are always overcoming mistakes and celebrating their small and large successes." Sarah moved up behind him and kneaded his tight shoulder muscles. Neither of them spoke a word as she worked on his knots.

Some of the tension eased from his body. She didn't press him to say more about his feelings. He'd need time to weigh her words.

"Come on, Adam," she said softly, turning him to face her. "Let's get you in the shower and to bed."

He blinked, nodded and allowed her to lead him out of the kitchen.

The hot spray stimulated new life in Adam's muscles. He closed his eyes and let the steamy water pelt his back. Sarah stood in front of him soaping his chest and arms. The compassion in her eyes filled him in ways he couldn't describe but he wouldn't ignore — not any longer.

She seemed determined to cleanse him of the aches and pains — not just from the prior evening, but from a lifetime. The tears welling in her eyes threatened to turn him to mush. Her fingers teased his nipples. She lowered the soap bar between his legs.

He watched her drop to her knees and lovingly fondle his penis. She washed it thoroughly as it hardened. She kissed its crown and washed the sack containing the seeds that had all of a sudden become so precious.

Sarah lathered his legs and scrubbed his knees. "Turn around," she said.

The spray pounded against his chest. She directed her attention to the back of his legs and thighs. She lathered his buttocks and parted them. With due diligence, she soaped the crease of his butt and anus. She worked a soapy thumb into his ass just far enough to let him know she hadn't forgotten his pleasure.

She rose to her feet and scrubbed his back and shoulders. She soaped his hair with strong fingers and rinsed it. Apparently satisfied with her efforts, she turned him around and smiled. She reached around him and shut off the water. "Come with me," she whispered.

Making no effort to tend to her own wet hair, Sarah led him into their bedroom and began drying him with a large towel. His skin heated from her proximity as much as from the drying.

After she finished with his backside, she turned him around. "You are such a male specimen," she said, hoarsely. "I will never tire of looking at you." She ran the towel over his chest and dropped to her knees. "I could touch you for a hundred years, Adam. And that wouldn't be nearly enough."

She dried his cock with the towel and wet it again with her mouth. It leapt to the back of her throat. She held it there while she dried his balls and thighs. She swiped the towel at his legs, but didn't let go of his penis.

She tossed the towel aside and backed off his cock, increasing her suction as she went. He saw her cheeks hollowing. He inched his legs wider apart and she caressed his balls.

Adam moaned a mixture of pleasure and pain.

Sarah pulled off him and grinned as his shaft lurched about seeking her mouth. She flicked her tongue at its head. It stalled in mid movement. She formed her lips into a ring and settled back over him. Glacially, she worked her way down its length until she held him securely in her throat. She slipped a hand between his legs and found his anus. Her finger entered easily. He gasped. She alternated stroking his cock and then his ass.

"Jesus, woman," he mumbled, "you're going to be the death of me yet."

She pulled out of his ass and held his cock tight at its base. "Not that way. Lie down on the floor, Adam."

He did as she asked and watched Sarah straddle him. Facing him, she stuck her tongue out and backed her rear toward his erection. She levered up on her knees and grabbed his cock, bringing its head to her pussy folds. She used his penis to spread those folds. His felt his eyes go wide as she prepared to take him inside. Sarah grinned, obviously loving his response.

After positioning him at her entrance she pushed down, impaling his full, throbbing length in one movement.

"Holy shit," he cried out.

She didn't move. He backed away from the edge of his climax and closed his eyes.

"You okay?" she asked, through pursed lips.

With clenched teeth, he managed to nod.

"Good." She raised and lowered her body. "Don't close your eyes, please. I want you to watch me. I want to watch what I'm doing reflected through your eyes.

He nodded again and pried his eyes open. He

hoped his half-grin was enough to tell her he also enjoyed the view of himself disappearing in her only to reappear at her whim. She picked up her pace. His raised hips provided her with a fleshy cushion. She stopped. He stifled a curse.

Sarah shook her head slowly and smiled. "Don't try to rush me. You won't finish there, either. Trust me. I'll take care of you, I promise." She rose off his cock and repositioned it at a slightly different angle until it found her darker portal. She settled fractionally. "Yes," she murmured. "This is where I want you. Are you ready to wash my ass with your seed?"

Adam nodded. Sarah sank lower. Again he watched himself disappearing. She sighed and took him as far as he could reach. "Nice," she muttered. His hips jiggled against her bottom, expressing his need.

"You seem ready enough."

"And?" He used every ounce of energy to resist grabbing her by the hips and making her bring him off. She gave him a coquettish grin before swiftly gliding up and down his pole. She suddenly stopped. Again? He winced. Now what was she doing? She delighted in torturing him.

"Adam."

"Um."

"I hope you know I'm making love to you." Her eyes filled with an emotion he'd begun to recognize and treasure. "I'm not just having sex."

"I know," he whispered. "But can you get on

with it? Whatever you call it."

"Good. This is my gift to you. I give myself to you because I love you." She raised and lowered on his shaft again.

"And because I love Maria. Do you understand?"

"Yes. I think so. Please."

"One more thing, Adam."

"Um. What now!"

"I feel your love pulsating through your cock, quivering in your thighs. Someday you'll find the words. I trust that. But for now, this is enough. Don't close your eyes, please. They look like pools of love at the moment. I'm ready for you — are you ready for me?"

"Yes, damn it."

"Good." She pulled on her nipples and dropped one hand to her clit. "Here we go." She began slowly but soon hammered her body over his cock. She clenched her inner muscles.

"Son of a bitch," Adam screamed.

Laughing hysterically as she rose and fell, Sarah drained him of any substance he might have to give her. She eased forward to kiss his lips tenderly. His cock slipped from her ass.

Adam stared at her with awe and fright. She closed his eyelids with a finger. "Sleep, love. You deserve some rest. I'll get a washcloth and clean you. We'll work things out. Somehow."

His heartbeat settled. His body calmed. He didn't trust himself to raise his eyelids. "I don't want to lose you or Maria."

"You won't. I'm confident of that. We don't want to lose you, either."

Adam didn't even have the strength to nod. Darkness overcame awareness.

- o -

Freshly showered and feeling right with the world once again, Sarah stepped out onto the deck, where Maria stood near the railing staring glumly out at the Pacific. Probably Maria didn't even see the waves crashing against the rocks far below.

Wrapping an arm around Maria's waist, Sarah said, "Don't worry so much. I think Adam will come around."

Maria looked sharply at her.

"I really do. He says he doesn't want to lose us, and I believe him."

"Is he afraid of losing us, or of losing his grip on some hot sex?" Maria returned her gaze to the ocean.

"Don't get your back up so far you push him away." Sarah softened her tone. "I believe he loves us—both of us. He just hasn't discovered how to say the words yet."

"Will he ever?" Maria snapped.

"I believe he will. We need to give him some space and time."

"How much?"

"I don't know. But we've laid a lot on him all at once. Neither one of us has been very vocal about our love for him. He may have been thinking we were into this only for the sex, too. And then the idea of a baby and fatherhood..." Sarah folded her arms across her chest. "I'm surprised he wasn't gone longer than he was."

Maria gripped the railing and pulled herself up on her toes only to settle back down. "I suppose you're right. Maybe we were too quick."

"Not necessarily. He needs to know how we feel about him and our future together. But we can't expect he's immediately going to jump up and down and sing our praises. He has to have time to adjust. When he'd get in trouble at the high school, he'd usually storm out of the building, hop on his motorcycle and we wouldn't see him for days. I used to wonder where he went when he was upset and who was comforting him."

"From the flush on your cheeks, it looks like you comforted him quite fine this morning." Maria giggled. "Don't look at me that way. I'm not mad at you. I'm not even sure I'm mad at Adam." She turned sober again. "Maybe I should've used more finesse."

"Finesse isn't necessarily your strongest suit."

"No, I suppose not."

"So what do we do now?"

"We exercise patience. We continue showing him how much we love him. And I think we need to name that love. Let's take the guess work out of this relationship. We're either going to make it or we're not." Sarah scowled. "But if we don't make it, I don't want it to be because we didn't make it crystal clear what we wanted and why. Does that feel okay with you?"

"Sure. How come you're so into communication and openness all of a sudden?"

Sarah pulled Maria tighter to her hip. "Maybe because I've gone through two divorces already. I never was clear about expectations going into those relationships. This time is different. Each one us of will know what we each value and want, and each one of us can decide whether to move forward or drop out. The fact remains we each love each other. That should mean we can make this work."

Sarah brushed tears from Maria's eyes and hugged her. She kissed her eyelids, then her nose and then her lips.

Maria deepened the kiss with her tongue.

"We should consider some practical matters," Sarah said as they pulled apart.

"We sleep together," Maria declared, jutting her chin out. "We can screw any place with only a single partner, but we sleep together."

"I agree, but that wasn't exactly what I was thinking about. Will you marry Adam?"

"What?" Maria stepped away. "Of course not. That would leave you as a second class partner. No way."

"But Adam will want to marry one of us—probably you, because you'll have his baby. He won't want the child to be a bastard."

"The child won't be a bastard," Maria hissed. "The child will carry all of our names. He or she will be a Granger-Ramirez-Atkinson or whatever combination we mutually decide. I won't have marriage cluttering up our relationship, Sarah. Over time, I know it would. Think about it and you'll agree."

Sarah didn't like the momentary envy that had overtaken her. "I hate to say it, but you may be right. I wonder if Adam will agree."

"He'd better, or he's going to be short two pussies."

"Whoa—calm down. Maybe I'm seeing a problem that won't arise."

"No matter." Maria shook her head vigorously. "I won't marry him and leave you out."

"Okay." Sarah grabbed Maria's hand. "Maybe we've concentrated enough on practicalities. So what do you want to do now—go for a swim, go shopping or make love?"

"Very pleasant choices." Maria brushed a finger across her cheek. "I know you're thinking when do I ever turn down lovemaking, but you've been well loved this morning already, and I really do have to get some shopping done before a meeting after lunch. You can tag along, if you'd like."

She shook her head. "No, I'm behind on my photos. I can use the time to catch up some. I doubt we'll see Adam until maybe this evening, if then."

- o -

Two excruciating nights passed before Adam found his way to his bedroom. He grabbed the doorknob and hesitated. Was he really ready for this? If he went in, the women would expect more out of him than he'd been giving them. If he wanted out of the relationship, he couldn't tell them that in his bedroom.

Would they accept part of a loaf?

Quickly, he turned the doorknob and entered before he could change his mind again. Both women put aside the books they'd been reading when he approached the bed. He couldn't resist admiring their nude bodies. And they were *his*. Well, at least they were his to admire.

Sarah smiled brilliantly at him. Maria remained more subdued and cautious. That seemed so out of character for her, but then maybe the stakes were highest for her.

"Maybe I should've knocked."

"Of course not, Adam," Sarah responded. "This is your bedroom."

"So what's up?" Maria asked.

In that moment his cock peeked through the opening of his robe.

"Ah, I see what's up." Maria grinned at Sarah. "Looks like we've got a job to do, if we want to keep a roof over our heads."

"Don't be catty, Maria," Sarah chided. "That dude between Adam's legs has done a lot for us. I expect we can satisfy him without losing too much self-respect."

Adam shook his head. Sometimes the women spoke in a code he failed to comprehend. However, he had little doubt what Sarah was after as she clambered on hands and knees toward him. Maria soon joined her.

Rising on his toes, Adam closed his eyes and relished the feel of Sarah's lips spreading across the head of his cock. Soon a different set of lips laved his sack. He still had the presence of mind to chuckle at the wisdom of letting Maria handle his balls.

Sarah took him in deep and settled her mouth against his groin. She wiggled, teasing. He placed his hands on her head to steady her. She popped off of him and smiled. "Why don't we have you sit in the chair, Adam?"

"That'll work," he said, casting off his robe. He sat on the edge of the chair and spread his legs wide. This time it was Maria who took him in her mouth. She worked leisurely up and down his shaft. Sarah kissed his mouth, then offered an upturned breast for him to nibble on. He flicked his tongue at the extending nipple and caressed the underside of the ivory breast. Her skin was as smooth as silk.

"Nice," she murmured. "Very nice." She

brought his fingers to her mouth and wet them before lowering them to her mound. He smiled and let her take the lead as she pleasured herself with his fingers. She tucked two in her pussy before he wiggled them. "Glad you thought to join us," she whispered. "I've missed this."

"So have I," he said. "I've missed both of you."

"As it should be. Did you hear that, Maria," she said, placing a hand on the back of Maria's neck as she continued her bobbing motion. "He says he missed us."

Maria let him drop from her mouth. "It's about time."

He watched the corner of her mouth turn up into a reluctant smile.

She rose to kiss him. He could taste his own salt on her lips. Then she turned to kiss Sarah. "Perfect," she mumbled. "Nearly perfect." Maria shook her long dark hair and smiled at Sarah, who was still riding his fingers. "Looks like you're having all the fun, Pepper."

"Find a way to share. Looks like this hard guy is still quite available."

"That he is, but not for long." Maria turned and backed up to straddle his cock. He watched it disappear abruptly into her tight sheath. He drew in a deep breath.

He was being fucked by two beautiful women. One rode his cock and the other his hand. They slowed and leaned over to tease each other with their tongues. He watched their eyes sparkle as they played a game they were each quite experienced at. They held out their hands and interlaced fingers.

Without needing words, they coordinated their movements like two dancers. Playfully, Sarah rose up his fingers and Maria settled lower on his cock. They held their joined hands high over their heads and squealed. Lips locked against lips and they began riding him in unison. His toes curled. Flashes of red crisscrossed his brain. His nostrils flared to suck in more air heavy with the perspiration of sex.

Both women surfed their own waves, changing the angles slightly, but never letting up. They weren't stopping until he came.

Maria's pussy clamped around his cock as if she was determined never to give it back to him. He rose partially from the chair and then collapsed into its pillowing support. "Christ," he cried out. Her pussy sucked him at his root. He tossed his head. He peeked at Sarah—radiant Sarah, who was nursing her own orgasm, spilling her juices over his fingers. Then he heard Maria's strident cry, "I'm coming, you son of a bitch. You better come with."

His release was immediate and prolific. His hips churned, driving in and out of Maria. With each thrust, he spurted more come. He didn't realize he had that much to give. At last, her slick butt settled against him. He wrapped his arms around both women.

Maria canted her head, seeking his mouth. He joined hers and Sarah joined both of them. Each woman embraced a corner of his mouth as if they'd just now discovered nirvana. He wanted to cry. He, of all people. He wanted to cry because they'd found a way for all three of them to kiss at the same time. It felt profound. The symbolism wasn't even lost on such a thick headed guy as him.

They were a threesome, and damn it to hell, they would make it.

He broke the kiss only long enough to mumble in a ragged voice, "I love both of you. I really do."

Breaking into broad smiles, Sarah and Maria pecked at his mouth and converged again to share another three-way kiss. If one could imagine exchanging high fives through kissing, that was what they were doing.

He closed his eyes. But would they settle for part of a loaf?

Adam opened his mouth to speak. The cell phone in his robe pocket rang shrilly. He never went anywhere without his cell, but this wasn't the moment for an interruption. Yet it was the personal line that only two people had access to besides Maria.

"Get off," he said. "I'm sorry." Sarah's eyebrows said quite clearly what she thought of him for answering his phone with his cock still buried in Maria. But he had no choice. Not this time. "It's my emergency line," he muttered.

"It's okay, Sarah," Maria said, her voice rising. She rose off his lap. "This can't be good."

Sarah stood and crossed her arms.

Maria bit her lower lip, her concern matching his.

"Hello."

"When?"

"Where?"

"Which hospital?"

"Don't panic. I'm on my way."

He flipped the phone shut. He probably didn't look much better than the women did. "It's Johnny," he said, reaching for his robe. "He overdosed. On purpose. He's at General."

- o -

In horror, Sarah watched open mouthed as Adam dashed out of the room and headed for the guest room and his clothes.

A very frightened Maria gawked at Sarah.

"What is it?" Sarah asked.

"Johnny is the boy Adam mentors."

"Oh my God!"

"Hurry. We can't let him go there alone. What if Johnny..." Maria nearly choked. "What if he doesn't make it?"

Sarah tossed on one of her long dresses and ran fingers through her hair. She heard the door to the driveway slam. Adam was already in his car.

They'd follow him to the hospital. No way

could they let him shoulder this burden alone. He hadn't asked her or Maria to come along, but then he'd stood by her at her parents' funeral.

She grabbed her purse and raced down the hallway following Maria, who was already praying in Spanish.

Chapter Fourteen

Trying to ignore the hollow echoes their shoes made as they hurried through the hospital corridors to the emergency area, Sarah steeled herself for what might lie ahead. Clutching her hand tight, Maria had grown extremely quiet.

They rounded a corner and found themselves in the waiting room where Adam stood cradling a slender trembling blond woman in his arms. The woman's chest rose and fell rapidly. Sarah saw Adam's shoulders likewise rising and falling as he braced himself to calm the woman. As they neared, he turned his head and nodded in their direction. A trace of relief flickered across his features.

She and Maria approached quietly and waited. The woman stopped sobbing and Adam separated from her to introduce them.

"Grace, this is Maria Ramirez and Sarah Atkinson. They are companions of mine. I'm sure they came here to support me and your family. This is Grace Caldwell—Johnny's mother."

"How..." Sarah began.

"He's alive." Adam's eyes glazed with pain. "He's in a coma. The doc says his body is protecting itself from additional trauma. He believes Johnny will make it, but there are no guarantees. Not yet."

"There's much hope then," Maria said, her dark eyes rounding.

"Yes, there's much hope. And yes, Maria, your prayers are appreciated." He smiled at her and kissed her forehead. "I love you, you know."

Maria nodded and tears stained her cheeks.

Adam reached for Sarah and she moved into his outstretched arms, enfolding Maria as well.

"I love you, too," Adam mumbled into her hair.

Unable to find any words, Sarah squeezed him back.

He clung to both of them and they held him tight. "Thanks for coming down. If one of you could get us some coffee, I think Grace would appreciate some as well as me.

"I'll go," Sarah said.

She walked down the corridor and followed canteen signs. What had Grace Caldwell made of that little scene? Something had clearly loosened Adam up. Was it only the near death of his young friend? She shook her head, thinking back. No, when they'd been making love earlier, he was much more emotionally present than he'd ever been before. She remembered feeling he was about to share something important with them when the phone rang. She'd been so numbed when his face turned chalky she'd even forgotten he'd already said he loved them. But he hadn't shared his intentions. Now, that would be tabled until the situation with Johnny Caldwell became clear.

Sarah peeked at the wall clock. Seven hours had crept by since their arrival. The first six had dragged by in a haze of worry, shuffling people back and forth to sit by Johnny's bed, and simply waiting. Then the boy had awakened, to tears of relief.

Now she and Maria had sat by themselves another hour while Johnny's mother and Adam met with the doctor.

Finally, Adam appeared at the waiting room door.

Sarah's shoulders sagged. She thought she'd seen Adam haggard the morning after he'd sped away from Maria's demand for a baby. She shook her head. *This* was haggard. He could hardly place one foot in front of the other or lift his chin. The rush of adrenaline that had gotten him through the night was clearly gone.

He walked over and knelt by her and Maria. They each took one of his hands. "He'll make it, this time." His stark stare chilled her to the bone. "They'll keep him a while longer for observation, then he'll go to a secure rehab facility for at least thirty days, longer if necessary. They have to assess his suicide risk and help him begin putting his life back together again."

Sarah nodded and curled her fingers tighter around Adam's.

"I'll stay and transport him to rehab."

She gave him a questioning look.

He shrugged in response. "It's either me or the cops."

"Oh," she whispered. "I understand."

"Why don't you two go on home and get some sleep? You look as exhausted as I feel. I'll be home as soon as I can." He glanced at the clock. "Probably not until tonight. Don't wait dinner for me. I'll grab something somewhere. Okay?"

"Okay." Maria stood and hugged him. "We love you."

He nodded. "We'll be okay." His voice turned husky. "After this, nothing looks too scary."

Sarah huddled close to Maria on the living room couch. They'd been there since after dinner, waiting for Adam to return. They'd said very little. Maria seemed as frightened as she was. Neither had voiced concern about Adam's well being, but clearly they weren't going to bed without him.

What was taking him so long? Didn't he know they'd worry about him? Surely he hadn't taken off on them again. His parting words had been so reassuring.

"Eleven-fifteen," Sarah finally said. "I wish he'd at least call and let us know everything is okay."

Maria's mouth contorted. "I don't think he's still with Johnny at this hour. He's probably trying to figure out what to do with us."

"You think?"

"Uh, huh. I'm afraid this thing with Johnny

could turn him off entirely about the idea of having a child."

"Maybe." Sarah squared her shoulders. "As you've said, Adam is a complex man. I'm not predicting what he's apt to do."

"And I thought he was coming around." Maria blinked back tears. "I did hear him right, didn't I? In the last twenty-four hours he's said he loves us twice."

Sarah grinned. "I believe so, but I wasn't counting. Maybe..." She hushed at the sound of a car pulling into the driveway. Maria's fingernails dug into her palm.

Sarah heard Adam close the door softly behind him. His steps were audible as he made his way to the living room. When he stood in archway, the gravity of the last twenty-four hours clung to him like a heavy mantle.

He collapsed into his overstuffed chair. "That was something," he began. "Johnny is settled in at the rehab facility. Some good people there. They had him laughing a little before I left. It'll still be a long haul for him, but he's in good hands, and he has a mother who cares and will stand by him."

"And a mentor who's not about to give up on him," Maria said, her eyes shining through tears.

"You got that right. I need a shower pretty bad. You two look fresh and soft. I feel like I've been wallowing in the sewer."

"What you need is a long soak in the tub." Sarah stood. "I'll go start the water."

"No!" The single word was a command.

She immediately sat back down.

"I'm sorry. I didn't mean to be short, but I've got some things to say. Some things both of you need to hear. And I need to do this before a bath."

"Okay. It's your show." She couldn't regulate her racing heartbeat. Here was her future. In the space of a few short minutes, she'd know.

Adam offered them a half-smile and lifted his palms as a gesture of surrender. "So which of you do I marry?"

"What?" Maria squeaked.

"Which of you do I marry? I don't particularly want to do prison time as a bigamist."

Sarah watched Maria sputtering beside her, trying to get the words out.

"No one," Maria finally said. "You're not going to marry either one of us. The one not married would feel left out. It won't work that way. We don't need to be married to have a committed relationship."

Adam sprang to his feet and glowered. "I see you've worked out the details." He turned away briefly, then spun around to face them. "My child will not be a bastard." His voice rose. "And forget the damn notion of a surrogate. Never! Not as long as I'm alive!"

Sarah smirked. "Now that's the Adam I've known and loved all my life."

"The baby will have all three last names: Granger-Ramirez-Atkinson," Maria insisted

320

calmly.

Adam's brow furrowed, then his face lit up. "Can we do that?"

"Why not?" Sarah asked. "Maria would be listed as the mother and you as the father, but we can name the child whatever we choose."

"And that's okay with you?" he asked, staring at her.

"Yes."

"And you, Maria?"

"Yes."

"Well, I'll be damned. Why won't that work? Oh, there'll be plenty of problems down the road, but the kid will have three parents to fall back on instead of two or one." A long pause ensued before his face broke into a broad smile. "Let's do it, ladies. Let's make a baby."

Maria was in Adam's arms before Sarah could stand up. He extended his arms wide to include her.

"Were you ready to do this" Sarah asked, "before the phone call from the hospital?"

"No." He brushed his chin through their hair and over their foreheads. His stubble scratched, but she didn't mind a bit. "No, I had some half baked idea if I finally told you I loved you, that would be enough.

"Sitting there in the emergency room— watching the two of you, feeling my blood curdle and then melt—seeing how Grace rode the emotional roller coaster of a parent with such aplomb—it hit me. This is what I want. It's what I need. Thankfully, I love two women who want the same thing."

Adam bent his head and kissed each of them. He placed a hand on the back of their necks, guiding them into a kiss.

Maria's lips had never felt softer or hotter. Sarah wanted this to last forever.

"Now about that bath," he said when she and Maria separated. "I sure could use one. While I'm in the tub you two can get ready for bed. I'll be joining you."

Looking up, Sarah caught the glitter in his eyes and felt tears start to pool in her own.

Adam held her gaze. "I won't leave you tonight, or ever again. So you'd best be getting used to sleeping with a third in the bed."

Sarah took Maria's hand and walked with her towards the door. As they reached it, she glanced over her shoulder at Adam, then gave Maria a wink. Simultaneously, they both flipped up their skirts over their bare butts and called out, "Yes, Master."

The End

About the Author

Adriana Kraft is the pen name for a husband/wife team writing sizzling romantic suspense and erotic romance. The award-winning pair has published over thirty novels and novellas to outstanding reviews. Long and Short Reviews: *"scorching hot...refreshing...something to read when you want straight up hotness."* Romance Junkies: *"filled with warmth, blazing hot sex, well-developed characters...not for the faint of heart."* Romantic pairings include straight m/f, lesbian, bisexual, ménage and polyamory, in both contemporary and paranormal settings.

We hope you enjoyed *The Reunion,* and we love hearing from readers! You can find all our links at our website:

http://adrianakraft.com

Adriana Kraft

When It's Time to Heat Things Up

BOOK LIST

SERIES

RIDERS UP Romantic Suspense novels
Book One *Cassie's Hope*
Book Two *Heat Wave*
Book Three *Detour Ahead*
Book Four *Willow Smoke* (forthcoming, January, 2015)

SWINGING GAMES Erotic Romance novellas
Book One *Anticipation*
Book Two *Hook-Ups*
Book Three *A Tempting Taste*
Book Four *Complexities*
Book Five *The Adventure Continue*
Book Six *Who's the Coach?*
Book Seven *Dare to Adventure*
Book Eight *Pushing the Limits*
Book Nine *Too Close for Comfort*
Book Ten *Triple Play*
Book Eleven *Summer's End*
Book Twelve *Foursomes and More…*

COLORS OF THE NIGHT Erotic Romance novels
Book One *Colors of the Night*
Book Two *Aria Returns*

PURGATORY POINT Erotic Romance novels
Book One *The Mistress of Purgatory Point*
Book Two *Return to Purgatory Point*

THE DIARY Erotic Romance novels
Book One *The Diary*
Book Two *Writing Skin*

STAND ALONE NOVELS AND NOVELLAS

The Heist Romantic Suspense novel
The Unmasking Romantic Suspense novel
Cherry Tune-Up Erotic Romance novella
The Reunion Erotic Romance novel
Atlantis Woman Found Erotic Romance novella
The Best Man Erotic Romance novel
Santa's Boss Erotic Romance novella
Through the Mirror Erotic Romance novella
Sheila's Prenups Erotic Romance novella
Full Circle Erotic Romance novella

SHORT STORIES IN ANTHOLOGIES
Accidental Contact, in *Sapphic Planet*
A Taste of Ginger in *The Cougar Book*

www.ingramcontent.com/pod-product-compliance
Lightning Source LLC
Chambersburg PA
CBHW071054250626
47159CB00002B/466